Wakefield Press

The Body

T0359555

The Body
an anthology

edited by
Henry Ashley-Brown
Chelsea Avard
Amy T Matthews
Stephanie Thomson

Wakefield
Press

Wakefield Press
1 The Parade West
Kent Town
South Australia 5067
www.wakefieldpress.com.au

First published 2004

Cover designed by Gerald Matthews
Designed and typeset by Clinton Ellicott, Wakefield Press
Printed and bound by Hyde Park Press

National Library of Australia
Cataloguing-in-publication entry

The body: an anthology.

ISBN 1 86254 654 1.

1. Poetry, Australian – 21st century.   2. Anthologies.
I. Ashley-Brown, Henry.

A821.4

*This anthology is dedicated to Tom Shapcott –
poet, teacher, mentor, friend.*

Contents

Introduction

T o m   S h a p c o t t

Professor of Creative Writing, University of Adelaide

A body of work. A body of words.
The carnal body (of course) with its parts,
Separate or together, the chafe
As well as the charm. Welcome
To The Body Anthology.
Here you might find the unexpected
In the expected, like a razor blade
In the pocket of the everyday, or
A lyric pulse in the neck of the *Grand Guignol*.
Be prepared for strippers stripped
And their customers dissected,
For blindness as a way of sight,
And the unaccountable itch within
That dreams of metamorphosis.
I would have this book tell more
Than an essay how this hubbub of minds
Has created its own energy in this book-sized space
And its own achievements. The new authors
Themselves have been sometimes startled
At the burgeoning growth in their work
After such a short time in the kitchen
Of creativity. The polish is gleaming already
But so is the substance.
The body is food, so prepare for the feast
But those at the feast may be dissected
In their own appetites. The body
Is play, movement, action: you might tap your toes
To the mortal element of music

Or you might join the dance
Given an opportunity like this.
Or, like the tired nurse, be bound
In the endless repetition of such basic facts
As birth. The body arrives, the body goes
And only the human body smiles.
How's that for a wake-up call?
Don't hide it. The parts of the body that matter
Are the parts an author hangs on to
To twist the story out of the expected place
Into its right place, however odd that is.
The parts of the book that matter
Are the insights that click into place
Telling us we ought not to be machines.
Here we have those other bodies,
Our metaphors. Life as a grape?
You take your pick. Life as a landscape?
We do not own the terrain but it
Claims us anyway. The body is always
A thing journeying. Come aboard.

Des Price

Leanne Amodeo

'Des Price,' Dad said.

He had been sitting so quietly at the kitchen table that we were all a little surprised he had actually even spoken.

Des Price?

Dad repeated the same two words. Slower this time and with more thought, 'Des Price.'

I looked across at my sister and then turned to my mother. Nothing.

Even slower this time, 'D-e-s P-r-i-c-e.' Dad's gaze had become a frown and his eyes were focused on something that only he could see. I put down my knife and fork. So did Mum and Melissa. We turned our heads. And waited.

'I grew up with Des Price,' Dad let us know. No one knew where this was going.

'He was a rough bastard.'

Mum raised her eyebrows.

'Rough as guts ... tatts everywhere.' Dad brushed his left arm, then his right, 'Covered in 'em.'

This could be interesting.

Dad continued, 'Was always gettin' into fights. All you had to do was look at 'im the wrong way and he'd beat ya to a pulp. A real rough bastard.' Dad shook his head, 'Played dirty too.'

Mum's eyebrows were still raised.

'If there was anything missin', you knew where to find it!' Dad laughed. 'Not that anyone was stupid enough to ask for it back, though!' He shook his head and his tone was serious again. 'Had a different woman each night. A real lad. Smoked like a train. Drank a lot too. The whole family did. Father was an alcoholic. Used to

3

beat up the mother. Rough as guts. People were scared o' the lot of 'em.' Dad shook his head, 'Rough as guts . . .'

Mum sipped from her glass and Melissa scratched her head. We were all confused. Exactly where this was going, we still had no idea. I looked down at my plate and contemplated picking up my fork. Just then Dad let out a deep breath. We turned to look at him. One hand was cupped under each breast. Now I was frowning.

'He comes into the factory the other day. Lookin' for work. Haven't seen him for years.' The toothpick in Dad's mouth shifted from one side to the other. His words were reflective, deliberate and slow, 'I took one look at him and I says . . .' Dad paused, took another deep breath and began again, '"Des . . . what 'ave you done to yourself!"' Dad's hands were still cupped and he sat up straight in his chair. His gaze was focused on something that only he could see. 'He had tits!'

He had . . . huh?

Melissa was the first to react. She burst out laughing and couldn't stop. Mum was quiet (I think from the shock) and I was a little unsure as to what to do with this information.

'He had breasts,' I ventured tentatively.

Dad nodded seriously. 'He had tits.' My father finally removed his hands from his own chest and raised them towards the ceiling. 'What on God's own earth could make a man do such a thing? Perfectly good bloke! Nothing wrong with 'im! Rough as guts! And he goes and does a stupid thing like that!'

'Well, Dad . . .'

'What the bloody hell's a man thinkin'?' The ceiling still offered no answer, 'What's he thinkin'?'

'You know . . .' I tried again.

Dad looked down at the table. His frown returned.

'I says, "Des, what happened to ya?" And he goes to me, "Frank, I just wasn't happy before. Inside myself. I just felt like something was wrong. Like I wasn't a complete person. Something was missing. I was living a lie, Frank."'

'Apparently it's a common . . .'

Dad didn't wait for me to finish. 'He's standin' there and he's

4

got his bloody eyebrows plucked and bloody lipstick on and ...'
Dad frowned and raised his hand to his own head, 'and he's got,
bloody – what are those bloody things?'

'Hair clips?' Mum offered.

'Bloody hairclips! And I looks at him and I go, "But Des, why?
Why, mate, why?" And he says to me,' Dad paused, placed both
hands on the table and emphasised each word, '"Frank, I'm happy
now. I'm finally happy, because I know that this is the person I
was meant to be all along."' Dad shook his head and let out a deep
breath, '"I've finally found myself."' Poor Dad. None of us knew
what to say to console him. Melissa had stopped laughing at least.
Mum took another sip from her glass (what more could she do?)
and I rested my hands in my lap. We all sat in silence. Until I
looked sideways at my father.

'What was he wearing?' I asked.

Dad looked up at me. It was the first time he'd made eye contact
during the whole meal. And then he looked away, slowly shaking
his head: 'I don't bloody know ... slacks, I guess, and a blouse,
I guess ...'

'What colour was it?'

'Aaah ... purple, a purplish ...' Dad shook his head.

'Like a dark purple or more lavender?' I offered.

'I'd say more ... lavender.' Dad looked back at me once he
realised what he'd said. 'What?'

'Was he wearing heels?' Melissa joined in.

'I don't bloody know!'

'How 'bout his hair? Wouldn't he be receding?' I asked.

'I DON'T bloody know!'

It was a valid question.

'The hormone tablets would have taken care of that,' Melissa
let me know.

I looked across at my sister and nodded, 'Yeah, you're right.'

Dad was horrified. 'The man's had a bloody sex change! Bloody
ruined himself! And all you can think about is what kind of shoes
he was wearing?'

Melissa and I looked at each other and then looked at our

father. Poor Dad. He really wasn't coping. And it wasn't that we wanted to make it worse for him. We were just curious, that's all.

Melissa finally asked what we had both been wondering, 'So, did he . . .' she began. Dad looked down at the table, closed his eyes and nodded his head.

'Bloody had it cut off,' he whispered.

'Oooo,' Melissa grimaced.

'That's gotta hurt,' I added.

Dad looked up. 'You're damn right it would bloody hurt.'

We all sat in silence. Until I looked sideways at my father.

'It wouldn't be as complicated as the other way 'round, though.'

Dad turned to face me.

'You know,' I continued, 'the other way 'round. It's harder to add than it is to subtract.'

Dad's face was blank. He turned to Mum, 'What the hell's she talkin' about?'

Mum looked worried. 'I don't know.'

'All her bloody university bullshit,' Dad mumbled under his breath.

'She means,' Melissa explained, 'that if he was a girl and she decided to be a boy then it would have been much harder to give her a penis than it would have been to give him the chop. So lucky for him, he is what he was.'

I nodded. Dad's face grew blanker. He opened his mouth to say something but decided against it. Instead he reached for his glass of water and took a sip.

I looked across at my father. 'What's he changed his name to?'

Dad put the glass down and let out a deep breath '. . . Kelly.'

'Kelly?'

He nodded his head, 'Kelly.'

I looked at my sister. 'I was expecting something a little more exotic.'

Melissa raised her eyebrows, 'Lola maybe?'

'Mmm, or Laetitia. Tamsin, even.'

'Dominique!' she yelled.

'Yes! Dominique!' We both laughed. And then stopped.

Dad wasn't smiling. 'So now I gotta call him Kelly.'

I was surprised. 'You're calling him Kelly?'

'No bloody way!'

'But Dad . . .'

'No! His name's Des.'

'But Dad, his name's not Des anymore.'

'Look, it's the way I bloody know 'im and it's the way I'll bloody call 'im!' Dad's fist hit the table.

I leaned back in my chair and looked across at my sister. She crossed her arms, looked down and slowly shook her head. *This was gonna be tough.* I leaned forward in my chair and rested my elbows on the table. My fingers were pressed together.

'It's a question of identity Dad.' A pause for dramatic effect, 'Des was always female in gender. Even though he was in a male's body, he always identified as female,' I looked from one face to the next, 'So you can see his conflict.'

My brother walked into the room.

'Calling him Kelly says that we accept his decision to reconcile this conflict.' *Simple.*

My father looked at me. 'So you're tellin' me he's a bloody poofter.'

'I'm home,' Paul let us know.

'No!' I said.

Dad was puzzled, 'So what are ya tellin' me, then?'

Now I was even more puzzled than Dad. 'That you need to call him Kelly, Dad.'

'Who's Kelly?' Paul asked innocently.

We all looked up at my brother.

'Kelly used to be a guy called Des but now he's a girl and he came into the factory looking for work the other day,' I answered.

Paul sat down.

'I don't know.' Dad sighed. 'In my day a man was a man. There was no question about it.' He shook his head and looked to the ceiling. 'Maybe it's television.'

The four of us looked at each other.

'It gives people crazy ideas.' He frowned, 'You got men dressing as women and bloody God knows what goin' on.' Dad's hands were on his hips and he looked down at the table, '*Tootsie!* Now there's a film I'll never forget.'

Mum looked concerned, 'I think that's a little different, Frank.'

A smile began to creep across Paul's face. 'Not Des Price? Not that bloke that used to come in a while back. No way!' My brother burst out laughing, 'He's a chick?' Paul raised his eyebrows at Dad. 'No way!'

Dad nodded.

'Woo hoo! What a bloody ugly mutha he'd be!' Paul slapped his leg. 'Ha! Can't believe it!'

'Yep,' Dad said seriously, 'you better believe it.'

Paul shook his head, 'No way.'

Way, I thought.

Then his tone became serious, 'So you gonna give 'im work?'

We all turned our attention to Dad. He caught our stares and looked from one face to the next. His eyes were wide and it took a while for him to respond.

'I can't give 'im a job!'

Our expressions went from expectant to disapproving in record-breaking time.

'He'll scare the bloody customers away!'

'But what about equal opportunity?' I reminded my father.

'Equal opportunity my arse! They won't buy from him, love! They'll see him comin' and run a mile! I'm havin' enough trouble with my drivers as it is!'

We still weren't convinced.

'Look. I like the man . . .'

Woman.

'. . . and there's nothin' I won't do for an old mate. But in this circumstance, I just can't afford the risk.'

I looked across at my brother and sister.

'Listen,' Dad continued, 'that day he comes in, I had to go pick up some parts for one of the trucks. I says to him, "Des, come along for a ride." I have no problem with that! He's sittin' there next to me with his bloody hands folded and with his bloody nail polish on. I have no problem with that! But I tells 'im. Tells 'im the truth. Tells 'im why I can't give 'im a job . . .'

We were waiting.

'. . . and he was fine with that. He understood.'

Mmmm.

'We gets back to the factory and I says to 'im, "Whatever you like Des! Help yourself to whatever you like."' Dad paused, 'and all he takes is a crate of Fruity Kola.'

'Fruity Kola?' Melissa, Paul and I looked at each other.

'Fruity Kola,' Dad said. 'Of all the drinks he could have chosen. But he reckons it's his favourite. Likes the fruity flavour he reckons. Always has.'

Mum smiled. 'Well there you go.'

Dad looked to the ceiling, 'Come to think of it . . .' and this time there was an answer to be found, 'that's what he took when he last popped in.' Dad nodded his head, 'Yeah! A dozen Fruity Kola! 'Cept back then we was still callin' it Kola Beer. Same bloody drink though. Same bloody drink.'

Mum smiled again and repeated her last four words, 'Well there you go.'

Feet are feet are feet are feet

Stefan Laszczuk

It was like a big fleshy hoof. Like half of her left foot had all melted together so that she only had the one normal big toe and a thick stump of flesh sitting alongside it. I was happy to see that it looked particularly hideous. I figured it would give me a chance with her. When I first noticed her leaning awkwardly, trying to jam her poor thong strap in between the two swollen mounds of flesh at the end of her foot, I decided to go over and introduce myself. I quickly walked over and told her that I was Bob and offered to let her lean on me.

She said thanks and introduced herself as Julie and then she asked me what I did for a living. I gave my usual answer that I was in between jobs. I was pretty casual about it. I used a tone of voice that made it sound like I was in between designing Opera Houses. The truth? I was a permanently unemployed bum who was in between jobs rather like the earth is in between the sun and the moon. Light years away from my last job and a miracle away from my next one. Stuck in a Centrelink orbit.

Usually when I tell a woman that I'm in between jobs there's an immediate awkward pause while she weighs up whether or not I'm worth talking to. At this point I usually look down and watch her feet shift awkwardly or tap slowly as she thinks. Then I watch them quietly twist around as she decides to go, then I listen for that God-awful lie: 'I'm just going to get another drink, I'll be back in a minute.' This time though, as I looked down at those pounds of flesh and waited for that twist of her feet and that paltry excuse, I saw nothing and I heard nothing. She stayed right where she was. My instincts had served me well. I was in with a chance.

I was at my mate's engagement party. Reg and I had been having a sort of an unspoken race to see who could get married first. Our close mates had all done the deed and we were the last two cabs off the rank. Today put Reg clearly in the lead. Both me and him knew this. That's why he had that sly smile on his face two weeks before when he personally dropped around to give me his engagement party invitation.

I'll never forget that day. I just couldn't believe his cheek.

'Reg,' I said, 'you could've just sent that to me. You didn't need to drop it around by hand.' Up until that point, Reg and I had never spoken about the fact that we were the last two to get married out of our group. As blokes, we were pretty immature. Not so immature though that we wanted to turn the act of getting married into a competition. At least we wouldn't admit to it. Or so I thought.

'I wanted to drop this around by hand,' Reg replied, smiling smugly. 'I just wanted to see the look on your face when you realised that you'll be the only single guy left.'

If I'd known that's what he wanted I'd have answered the door with my eyes shut and my fingers stuck in my ears. But I hadn't been forewarned. Reg got to see that look on my face, which I'm guessing was one of surprise, anguish, envy and dread. And feigned unflappability. Then he turned and clicked his heels and said over his shoulder, 'Seeya at my engagement party, pal.'

I shut the door. Immediately I tore up the invitation. I wasn't going to go to his stupid party. Then I went to sit on the toilet. I didn't need to do any business. I just always like to be in the smallest room in the house when I feel depressed and helpless. I sat there for a while, thinking about my life. About my good mates. Three of them had wives. We often went camping together. Each camping trip, me and Reg went along as a kind of fourth 'couple'. As the token couple of boozy scallywag jokers who just hadn't met the right girls yet. With eight of us in all, we only had to take two cars on long driving trips. We only needed to pack four tents. We had four people cooking and four people cleaning up. It was the perfect setup. But it would all go to shit if Reg got married before me. It would mean that he would take his new wife along and I would have to stay home. There's no way we could organise an extra tent, an extra car – hell, even an extra washing up roster – just so one other person could join the traditional eight.

Even if we did, it would still go to shit. I sat on that toilet imagining just what it would be like. Campfire burning. Crickets chirping. Knives and forks clinking. Hot food going down a treat. And then after dinner everyone saying the food tasted really nice but does anybody remember how it used to taste when only four people cooked it instead of five. And then somebody joking that too many cooks spoil the broth and perhaps Bob should have stayed out of the kitchen and then everyone laughing politely but then looking at me supportively when their laughter subsides and me smiling as if I'm thankful I'm still welcome but then suddenly realising that everybody else here but me is holding someone else's hand and so me getting up quietly and going off to sleep in the flimsy damp extra tent that Trevor had begrudgingly packed especially for the last single guy.

'NOOOOOOOOOO!' I yelled and jumped up off the toilet. I couldn't let this happen. I had to go to the party. I couldn't let Reg get in even tighter with our already married mates and squeeze me out of the fold even more. At any rate, I couldn't give Reg the satisfaction of me not turning up. I looked out my toilet window to see my neighbour, Mrs Roberts, looking back at me with a stunned look on her face. I tried to look as if everything was normal and flushed the loo, even though I hadn't done anything. I just wanted to mess with her mind. Let her spend her day wondering why that strange young man from next door was screaming 'NOOOOOOOOOO!' at the top of his lungs before he flushed.

I had a plan. I would beat Reg to getting married. After all, it didn't matter who got engaged first, it was the final deed that counted. And then we'd see who'd squeeze *who* out. The most perfect aspect of my plan was, I decided, that I would meet my future bride at Reg's engagement party. Or should I say, Reg and Agnoushka's engagement party. Agnoushka, who Reg had only met three weeks after Trev and Lynette got married, had barely said a word to me. I didn't even know if she could speak English.

What can I say? The beer was warm. The company was crap. The speeches were boring. It was a typical Reg show. I had half a mind to ask this Agnoushka if she was some kind of mail order bride but I wasn't drunk enough.

Instead I got just drunk enough to get the confidence to mingle. And mingle I did. I was, by all accounts, not a bad mingler. In fact I had it pretty well down pat. My only problem with mingling was when I got past introducing who I 'was' and started explaining what I 'did', which was nothing, except for the occasional session where I'd sit on the bog and conjure up stupid plans to upstage my friends. You could almost watch people's attention dissipate into thin air as I spat out the words 'I don't really have a job right now but I'm working on it.'

It's a sad rule in our society – much more often than not you are what you do and if you don't do anything, then I'm afraid you don't amount to very much at all. However, that night, I happened to have another sad rule of society working in my favour: that other sad rule which states that if a person looks in any way different, or slightly aesthetically awkward in any way at all, they should be shunned. At least I think that's how it goes.

And so it was with this girl and her foot. A foot that was so absolutely hideous that it was actually interesting. Had it been severed and placed on display in a museum I would have stopped to gape at it. I would probably have even uttered a curious 'Oooohh' and wondered whether it was of man or animal origin. Had the foot been served to me in some expensive restaurant, surrounded by truffles and baby squid, I would have assumed it was the rarest delicacy on the list and would have tucked in accordingly.

However, this foot was not in a museum case or on a plate. It was attached to the girl I was standing with. And it was a foot that for once wasn't twisting around and preparing to leave. It was a foot that was staying right where it was.

'Unemployment is a hard space to be in,' she said. 'I hope you find some work. You look very employable.' She smiled.

'Thank you,' I said, genuinely surprised and touched to hear her words of support. But then my heart sank when she spoke again.

'I'm just going to get a drink now.'

Oh no, I thought.

But she went on. 'Would you like me to bring you another Coopers Sparkling Ale? I noticed that you drink it. It's my favourite beer.' She was still smiling. I could have jumped ten metres in the air with glee.

'Yes thank you,' I said. 'I'll wait right here.'

She went off to the bar and I began to whistle to myself, wishing I'd called her by her name . . . but I couldn't quite remember what it was. Jenny maybe. Or Jodie. Something with a J. I'm terrible with names. I decided I would ask her when she got back. She wouldn't care about my memory, I reasoned. She didn't even care that I didn't have a job. When she got back though, I was so caught up in the fact that she had actually come back that I didn't remember to ask her name again. We just started talking about what she did, which was bush revegetation. She was telling me how she'd stumbled on top of a hopper-ant nest the day before and had been repeatedly stung on the foot.

'I guess you must have noticed how swollen my foot is,' she said.

I chuckled with relief. So *that* was it. 'Why, that thing is huge! In fact, to be honest – no offence – it's one of the most disgusting things I've ever seen,' I laughed. 'They must have got you quite a few hundred times there. You can't even see where all your toes separate. Does it hurt if I touch it?' I gently went to nudge her humungous fleshy hoof with my own sandal-clad foot.

She took a step back. 'No, not that one,' she said quietly. 'That's my clubfoot. I was born with it. I meant the swelling on my other foot.' She lifted her other foot up and sure enough one side was covered in red swollen lumps.

'Oh,' I said. And I must have stood there in silence for a whole minute before I said, 'I'm sorry.'

'Don't be,' she said. 'I'm happy with who I am. Feet are feet are feet are feet.'

'You know what?' I said. 'You're right. And so you should be happy. You're a wonderful, beautiful person.' And then for some reason I said, 'Any man that ended up with you would be a very lucky man indeed.' It was straight out of left field but she seemed to like it.

She laughed. 'And what exactly do you mean by that? What makes you think I'm even looking for a man?'

'Well I was kind of hoping you were,' I said. And then I just blurted it out like an excited schoolboy, 'Can I kiss you?' She closed her eyes and smiled but she didn't back away and so I took the plunge. I kissed her hard on the lips and was amazed and exhilarated to find she was kissing me back. I had forgotten all about her foot and I was just genuinely, ecstatically happy that she was happy to kiss me. Then we stopped and laughed because in the heat of the moment we'd both spilt our beers.

'Perhaps another drink?' she said.

'Yes please,' I said. As she moved away I resolved to ask her name when she got back. I also resolved that if I got drunk enough by the end of the night, I would ask her to marry me. It wasn't just about the race with Reg anymore, although that probably had some effect on my state of mind, as did the copious amounts of beer I'd been drinking. But there was definitely something in that kiss, I reckoned. I didn't know what it was about this girl but I thought there was a future there for us.

'Where have you been hiding, Bob?' It was Trevor.

'Um . . . I've just been hanging out,' I said. 'Not doing much at all really.'

'You'd better get used to that,' said Reg, popping out of nowhere. 'Game of darts Trev?'

'Hang on,' I said. 'Why had I better get used to it?'

Reg looked at Trev and looked back at me. 'Well you know,' he said. 'Now that I'm getting married.'

'Yes?' I said.

'Well, you know,' he said.

'Know what?' I said.

'Yeah, Reg,' said Trev. 'Know what?'

There was a bit of a silence, then Reg blurted it out like he'd just stepped inside the safety of his front door after bottling up a fart on a first date.

15

'Well we're not going to want to take three cars. And, I mean, we'd need to pack an extra tent. And it's just plain stupid to have to change the cooking roster.'

'What on earth are you talking about Reg?' said Trevor. 'Of course Bob will still be welcome. Janey's got a spare tent and we can probably all squeeze into the two cars.' Had my drunken brain heard what Trevor had actually said, the conversation would have probably ended right there with Reg looking like a bit of a dick. But I failed to compute the fact that Trev had stuck up for me. My paranoia and my fear of being left out had taken over.

'Oh fuck you Reg,' I said. 'You're not married yet. I might still beat you to it, you know. And then we'll see who's staying at home.'

'Oh yeah,' said Reg. 'Who's gonna marry you, Centrelink Boy?'

'I don't know. Maybe this girl I met tonight,' I said.

'Who's that then?' said Trev. 'Nearly everyone's taken here already.'

'I can't remember her name,' I said. 'She told me but I can't remember.'

'Shit. Big fucking future there,' sneered Reg.

'Shut up Reg,' I said.

'Is it Terri?' said Trev.

I shook my head.

'Naomi?'

'Nup.'

He went through the list. 'Helen? Gertie? Zoe? Kate? Sarah? Julie? Ber –'

'Julie,' I said. 'That's her name, Julie. Maybe I'll ask Julie to marry me.'

Reg snorted a muffled laugh. 'You're going to ask Julie to marry you? Julie Carter?'

'Why not?' I said.

'Now come on Reg,' said Trevor. 'She's a nice girl.'

Reg laughed out loud. 'So you're going to marry Hoof Girl. Where are you going to have your honeymoon? Club Foot? For God's sake man.'

I was becoming defensive and the hairs on the back of my neck were starting to bristle but I remained calm. 'I happen to think she's a beautiful person,' I said. Reg was laughing louder now and the louder he laughed, the madder I became.

'Do you mean to say . . .' he paused to get his breath, 'Do you mean to say you want to hook up with the girl who has a left foot like a baby's arse? I mean are you really aware of how absolutely grotesque that thing is?'

'Yes!' I shouted. 'I am aware that it looks like a baby's arse.' I felt Trev's hand on my arm.

'Mate,' he said. 'Leave it out'. I shook him off. I wasn't finished by a long shot. I stared at Reg.

'I am aware of her foot!' I shouted. 'I am aware that it is abnormal, defective and would probably prevent her from getting a passport in some countries. I am aware that if our kids ever go hungry we can lop it off and we'll have enough meat for a month!'

I may have been aware of these things but I was unaware of how loud I was shouting and that the party music and conversation had died down because people were suddenly trying to hear what the commotion was about, so I continued.

'I mean for pity's sake. It's the ugliest, most hideous thing a cruel God could create! If my child was born with a foot like that I'd probably shoot it. If it wasn't so terribly frightening I'd laugh. But the thing is –'

But I never got to say what the thing was. Because suddenly my face was drenched in what tasted like Coopers Sparkling Ale.

'The thing is: you are a disgusting pig. I can't believe I actually liked you, Bob. I can't believe that, for some ridiculous reason, I was even feeling like you could be the man I marry but now I never want to see you again!'

It was Julie.

'Julie,' I said. And then I said, 'I remembered your name.'

'Oh yeah?' she said. 'Well here's something else to remember.'

I would now ask sincerely that anybody who is reading this take a minute's silence in respect of the pain I endured at this point. I'm serious. Please put this story down and walk over to the nearest clock. Then please watch a whole minute tick around without uttering a word. If the phone rings ignore it. If your neighbour gives you a hoy, don't hoy back. Just stand there and show some respect for the pain I suffered that night. When you've thought about it for a whole minute, you may come back and read on. And perhaps when you do, you will understand why you just spent sixty seconds of your life thinking about my pain. The pain I endured when that woman raised her very aptly named clubfoot, slowly lifted it back and then swung it like a demolition ball into my testicles. I felt like I'd been kicked by an angry bull wearing steel-caps. The pain was so bad that it was barely there at all for a few seconds.

It was almost like breaking the speed of sound and light all at once. Only I think I broke the pain barrier. My life flashed between my thighs. I sunk to my knees, emitting a wheezy gasp as tears streamed from my eyes. Apparently I was in so much visible pain that even Reg stopped laughing. I stayed there on the ground until I could walk and when I could walk, I walked around the edge of the crowd and got out of there as fast as I could, which was about the speed of a blind tortoise on valium.

Two weeks later I heard from someone else that my mates had all gone off camping again. I figured this time I hadn't been invited. That bastard Reg, I thought. He got me in the end. I hope he has a good time, that fucking bastard. Then suddenly the phone rang. It was Reg, of all people.

'Reggie boy,' I said. 'How the hell are you, old chap?'

'I'm alright,' he said. 'Sorry about the party. I didn't mean to drop you in it like that. I was just having a bit of fun, that's all. How are the boys?'

'They're fine,' I lied, gingerly feeling my nuts. I was still having difficulty walking at normal speed. 'I thought you would have been off camping by now.'

'Nah, I wasn't invited,' he said. 'They took Julie and her new boyfriend instead.'

'New boyfriend?' I said. 'Who?'

'Stevo,' he said. 'Apparently he mopped up after your mess.'

'That shallow opportunistic prick,' I said.

'And I've got some other bad news. My wedding's off. Agnoushka couldn't get a Visa.'

Oh. Hilarious. I just knew that Agnoushka was one of those Russian mail order brides. I couldn't help myself. I burst out laughing.

'Sucked in Reggie! I knew she was a Russian mail order bride. I knew it. I knew it all along, Reggie boy. Oh you are a smart bastard, aren't you though? Nice try mate. Well I guess we're all even now, aren't we? Eh?' I took the phone and held it out in front of my face and bellowed down the line, 'YOU TOTAL LOSER!' Then I put the receiver back to my ear and settled back in the armchair laughing to myself. 'Don't you worry Reggie boy, she had a fat arse anyway and some of the guys reckon she had a terrible BO problem,' I chuckled and then I started wondering why Reg was being so quiet. Ah, that was it. His petty little mind was ticking over at a million miles an hour trying to think of a comeback.

'Bob,' he said.

'Yes Reggie,' I smiled, waiting for one of his famous witty retorts.

'The wedding's only off for a few months. It's being postponed. We were going to pay for it with Agnoushka's Visa card that she was applying for but it all fell through. So now we're going to save up for it instead.' His voice was curt. There was a pause.

'She's not a mail order bride, is she?' I said.

'I met her at a Jimmy Barnes concert,' he replied.

'Can I still come to the wedding?' I said. I think the phone cut off then.

Moishe the Nose

Amy T Matthews

'Moishe the Nose! *Shalom Alaychem!*'

'*Alaychem Shalom*, Pani Królikowska.'

Moishe smiled. He had always had a soft spot for Halina Benicki (now Królikowska). He remembered her wedding day: she had been a spring bride ... and so beautiful.

Her sure hands picked through the beets in his cart. 'Small today, Moishe the Nose,' she remarked.

'Any larger and they would take an age to cook! And they are sweet!' He picked up a larger beet and sniffed it dramatically, rolling his eyes in mock ecstasy. 'Sweet enough to make you weep!'

'I'm not a woman prone to weeping.' Her words were stern but her lips twitched as she turned and reached for her basket. It was only then Moishe noticed the girl behind her. His heart skipped. She was an angel. Her face was round and young and pink, with eyes the delicate blue of ice on the river. Her nose was small and straight and pert, perfect from brow to tip.

'Moishe!'

He jumped, realising Pani Królikowska had been speaking to him.

'Fine,' he said, taking the coins she offered absently. She frowned, expecting to haggle, disgruntled at winning the argument so effortlessly.

'Come Ewelina,' she snapped, leading her daughter to Hillel's stall of geese. *Ewelina Królikowska. Who would have thought? Who would have known?*

'Pretty girl, no?'

Moishe blushed as he turned to find Pella the Matchmaker watching him.

'A child,' he answered with a shrug, his Adam's apple bobbing wildly in his dry throat.

'Last year she was a child,' Pella the Matchmaker corrected, '*this* year she is a woman.'

'Beets for you today, Pani?'

'They look small.'

'They are bigger than ever. And sweet!'

'You have taken no wife, Moishe the Nose.' Her eyes were fixed on him, narrowed and calculating.

'They would make the sweetest borscht you ever tasted.'

'There are many marriageable girls this year.'

'Oh?' He kept his eyes on the beets.

'Zofja Golombiewski, the tailor's daughter?'

Zofja the Horse.

'Olga Ambrosiak, the rabbi's daughter?'

Olga the Sour.

'Danuta Mohsbock, Karol the Hero's sister?'

Danuta the Lip.

Moishe rubbed his nose. 'Ewelina Królikowska?' he asked tentatively. *Ewelina the Angel.*

'Maybe . . .' Pella the Matchmaker nodded with a sly smile. Moishe's cheeks burned.

'How much for the beets, Moishe the Nose?'

'A gift from me, Pani, a gift from me.'

'You are generous.'

'*Baruch Hashem.*'

He did not want to wake up. He dreamed of her. The *chuppah* snapped in the wind. Moishe's sidelocks danced against his cheeks. His palms were sweating. She stood beside him, dressed in white, the veil swirling about her like a cloud. Her hair was the colour of ripe wheat, as he'd known it would be, as her mother's had been. He willed her to look up at him. *Ewelina.* She looked. Shock registered in the ice blue eyes. Her perfect pink lips parted as she gasped:

'*Moishe the Nose!*'

He woke, his heart pounding.

Shabbat dawned clear and cold. As always, the walk into the *shtetl* was a long one.

'It seems we just get home after the evening service and it's time to leave again,' Moishe's father sighed, his breath frosting in the air before him. The uneven tread of their steps was hollow on the black ice. Now and then his father's crutch would break through the crust with a crack.

'What would you think if I took a wife?' Moishe asked abruptly.

'You are a man. You should take a wife.'

They walked in silence. From the corner of his eye Moishe watched his father's shortened limb swing. The bottom of his pants leg flapped like laundry out to dry.

'I have spoken to the Matchmaker.'

His father did not reply. Moishe cleared his throat.

'She suggested Zofja Golombiewski . . .'

'A good match.'

With Zofja the Horse?!

'Or Ewelina Królikowska.'

'Króliksowska? I thought they only had boys and babies?'

'She is a woman,' Moishe said defensively.

He could not turn and look at the gallery. He listened to the davening and imagined her eyes on him. His neck burned. Afterwards, outside, he looked for her.

'Moishe the Nose!' the Matchmaker called and his heart stopped.

'*Shabbat shalom*,' she huffed as she trotted over to him. Her nose was as red as a beet in the January air.

'*Shabbat shalom*,' he replied, swallowing hard.

'I have good news!' she declared. He found it hard to draw breath.

'The parents of Danuta Mohsbok wish to invite you to share their *Shabbat* meal.' She reached out and squeezed his arm. She was beaming, as though offering him an incredible gift. His saliva turned sour.

'I should tell them yes?'

He nodded dumbly.

'So excited he cannot speak!' she twittered to his father.

The Mohsboks lived on the square, opposite where he set up his cart every Wednesday. Pani Mohsbok fluttered nervously, nudging Danuta to serve Moishe. She did so dourly, turned vaguely sideways to hide the scar of her harelip. Across the table from him sat Karol the Hero. His face was long and expressive, with a generous mouth that always smiled. Danuta sat beside him, a muted reflection of her brother. Both had ruddy dark skin, wet black eyes and wild black hair. They made Moishe nervous. He found himself unable to speak. No one found this odd in a suitor.

Pan Mohsbok raised his glass. 'We are blessed . . .'

'*Baruch Hashem!*'

'We have food, shelter, friends,' he raised his glass to Moishe and his father, 'and today we have been blessed with wonderful news . . .' Pan and Pani Mohsbok looked to their son.

'I am to marry,' Karol the Hero announced with a wide grin. His black eyes danced.

'And perhaps soon . . . Danuta too . . .' Pan Mohsbek hinted broadly, winking at his daughter. Danuta blushed miserably.

'Who is the fortunate lady?' Moishe's father asked. But Moishe already knew. Karol the Hero would never marry Zofja the Horse. He saw Karol's grin and his long, straight nose and he despaired.

Moishe stood before the glass. It was a remarkable nose. It jutted straight out from his brows before taking a sharp bend south. Almost doubled over. His whole life he had been Moishe the Nose. Because of *this*. He pushed at it. The end flexed. He tilted his head back. Black hair bristled in the caverns.

'*This* is what you give me?' he muttered skywards. 'Karol the Hero you give a righteous nose and an angel to wife and me you give *this*?'

So it wasn't the trials of Job. Did that mean he didn't suffer? Oh, he suffered. When he was twelve, dreading his coming manhood, dreading honking his prayers before the entire *shtetl*, he had tried to fix it. He had taken his mother's green headscarf (God rest her) and tied it around his face, until his nose almost touched his lips, until it was flattened and reduced. Then he went to bed and prayed. It wasn't much of a miracle to ask for, surely, just a nose like Aharon Królikowska's, a nose like Karol the Hero's? He woke up every morning and removed the headscarf, only to have his nose spring proudly back to attention.

It was time to take matters into his own hands.

Many days later he was back in the square with his cart of beets. His throat was still thick with metallic mucous. The bandages made it hard to breathe. But they would never call him Moishe the Nose again.

'*Shalom Alaychem*, Moishe the Fool!'

Of Bodies Changed I Sing

Gwen Walton

Hermes looked along the range and thought he knew what it would feel like to be the only flea on the rump of a very large dog. A dog with a curly coat of dark grey-green. Perhaps not a dog but a creature, a monster of some sort which had flopped its body down here on the plain and simply gone to sleep. Perched on a flat stone a few yards above the entrance to his hillside cave, he scanned the vast plains to the east of the mountain. He liked to think of it as a mountain although, as the Professor said, it was only a pimple compared with the Alps. One of a range of pimples that seemed to have erupted out of the rough skin of the plain that spread out below him.

Being only halfway up this particular pimple he could not see as far as the River Murray. Even if he were to climb to the top he would see nothing but an even greater expanse of dreary mallee. The River must be fifty miles away and beyond that God only knew how many hundreds of miles of endless plain before the Great Dividing Range and the already booming town of Sydney. But Hermes had no intention of scaling the mountain, for it seemed to get steeper and rockier as it went up and he could, as yet, see no good reason for expending that amount of energy. Not that he had been short of energy when he had climbed Helvellen with the brightest of the Upper Sixth last summer holidays but that was another story.

Sensing a small change in the vast still landscape he instinctively turned his head to the left and squinted across the valley into the shadows on the opposite hill face.

'The Professor!' he muttered and shook his head slowly, the way people did at the mere sight of Menge. 'Back already!'

The sun setting behind the ranges had thrown them into deep shadow, making Professor Menge a dark goblin as he plunged recklessly down the steep slope across the valley, now visible in the clearings, now disappearing into thickets of bush. Menge's method of locomotion was unique. In spite of the gloom there was no mistaking the hurtling body with its dwarfish shape and its remarkable resemblance to Punch. The flat black hat ought to have blown off long ago but somehow had not. The baggy greatcoat ballooned behind him and perhaps slowed his body's dangerous flight. Even without the swing of the pair of geological hammers in his hands, there was no mistaking that wild flying shape.

Both feet together – *jump!* Hands holding the hammers – *back!* Feet landing – hands – and hammers – *up!* By all the laws of physics Menge should have fallen flat on his face each time but he was as sure-footed as a goat and as graceful as a kangaroo. Perhaps it had something to do with the length of his arms compared to the shortness of his legs. Or was it the weight of his great head and broad chest relative to his spindle-shanks? No, that should have had the opposite effect. It was simply that Menge knew he would not fall. He knew that his God would not let him fall, in spite of all the demons waiting to trip him up.

The old man disappeared into the thick vegetation at the bottom of the gully but Hermes, in his mind's eye, could see him crossing the creek at the stepping-stones above the rock pool. With the torrential rain that had fallen in the past two days the creek would be swollen and even the stepping-stones would be well under water. Hermes stirred himself, clambered down and began breaking branches across his knee to build up the fire smouldering in the ring of stones just outside the cave. The Professor would arrive with wet feet and almost certainly with a colossal appetite.

He went into the cave to see what food he could find; a remnant of salt beef, enough of yesterday's damper for one but not for two. He busied himself with flour and salt, mutton fat and water. Water! He had better boil some. The old chap would want hot tea.

He had only just hung his billycan from the iron tripod over the fire when Menge came up from the gully, only slightly out of breath.

'*Gott* bless you, my boy! You have the billy on.' Menge's long white hair and his beard were fluffed out by the wind.

'Only just, Professor. It will take a few minutes. Come and sit down. Take off your wet boots before you catch cold.'

'Acch! Wet feet do not cause colds.' Menge had laid down his hammers and was removing the pack from his back. 'It is the demons who cause colds and other such afflictions.'

Hermes had no intention of getting into that argument again. 'Sit down, Professor. You must be tired.'

'Tired? I am not tired. Only twenty miles I have walked today. But it is good to arrive here at my halfway house and find the fire going and a friendly face to greet me. What have we to eat tonight?'

'A little beef and some damper. I'm sorry, I did not expect you so soon.'

'You've had no success hunting? Your feet still troubling you?'

'My blisters are healed thank you. To tell the truth the prospect of hunger drove me out with the gun yesterday but I simply could not pull the trigger.'

Menge, who had now seated himself on the only stool, cocked his head and waited.

'It was a wallaby. Standing there on its hind legs, looking at me with such an expression, so gentle, so forgiving. How do you shoot an animal that stands up on two legs and looks you in the eye? It would be like shooting a child.'

Menge nodded slowly. 'I have never been able to do it myself,' he admitted.

'Yet you expected me to live that way. You said if I came up here to live in your cave I would be able to hunt for my meat.' Hermes knew he sounded petulant.

'I know. But I underestimated you, dear boy. You are more tender-hearted than I thought.'

At that moment Hermes found his tender feelings slipping away from him but he sugared a large mug of tea generously and passed it to the Professor, slopping a little of the hot liquid onto the outstretched hand.

'So how am I to live? What shall I find to eat so far from town? There isn't a shop within miles. And you know I have no money.'

'It was unfortunate that you were robbed.' Menge sugared his tea again and sipped it. 'And even more unfortunate that the bank will not honour your draft without confirmation from England. But you know I have lived for months with absolutely no money at all. Not a penny in my pocket.'

'How did you manage that?'

'The Lord always provided.'

'Ha!' Hermes knew what that meant. In the short time he had spent in Adelaide looking for work he had learned that Menge was renowned for arriving to visit his friends just at meal-time, whether in town or out in the bush. 'I do not intend to become a beggar.'

'You have found no gold yet?'

'Not a skerrick. You said these hills were awash with gold. Not to mention precious stones.'

'Which they are. It is simply a matter of knowing where to look. I shall stay a few days and teach you. Have you tried panning in the creek?'

'Once.'

'Once will not do. It is a game of patience. And knowledge. Never fear, when I have taught you to read the rocks you will find treasure beyond your wildest dreams.' He tapped his large head, knocking his hat askew. So it was not stuck on with wattle gum, as some people said.

Tap, tap, on that great skull, again. 'Old Menge has it all in here. Believe me. By an expert I was taught, the cleverest mineralogist in all Europe. I have travelled the mountains of Switzerland, of Germany, of Siberia. Even Iceland. Everywhere the same minerals occur in the same sort of rocks. There are families of rocks. This one is the cousin of that one, the grandfather of another. I know them as one knows one's children.'

'It is a wonder you are not a wealthy man,' Hermes said sourly.

'I am not wealthy,' Menge said, spreading his empty hands,

'because whenever I find something of value I give it away. When I have money I spend it on gifts for my friends in New Silesia. I do not need money.'

'Except for food.'

'Food? When food runs out I chew on wattle gum.'

'Well, thank you for the tip, I may be forced to try it.'

'You worry too much,' Menge soothed. 'Have faith. After supper we shall work out a plan.'

But over supper Hermes seemed to sink into deeper and deeper gloom. When Menge tried to jolly him out of it, he answered in grunts and withdrew into himself and in the end made no replies at all. Finally, in exasperation, the old man broke the silence.

'It is plain that a demon is troubling you. Let me help you.'

'I do not believe in demons,' Hermes snapped.

'The voice of a demon if ever I heard one! Fortunately for you, demons are my specialty. I do not wish to boast but I have a great power. I can cast out demons. They flee before me.'

'I told you, Menge, I do not have a demon and I do not need your services.'

'Tut, tut, boy. You may think you can fool me but let me tell you I have eyes to see and ears to hear. I knew from the moment I first met you that your soul was in grave danger. Why else do you think I brought you here?'

'To mind your cave, I suppose. To feed you the last of my food whenever you choose to drop by.' He had temporarily forgotten that it was the Professor who had paid for their supplies.

Menge was shaking his head sorrowfully. 'Look at me, boy,' he said softly. It was the softness, the mildness of his reply that made Hermes look him in the eye. It was the last thing he remembered doing, until he awoke next morning in the bed he supposed Menge would have reclaimed, since it was the only one in the cave. Not a grand bed but serviceable enough. A mattress filled with dried grass, laid over some sacking stretched on two sapling poles, the whole thing supported by four short, forked sticks driven into the earthen floor.

He was still fully clothed but someone had removed his boots and covered him with a blanket. He opened his eyes a fraction and saw that a second blanket lay nearby, on the hard earthen floor of the cave where Menge must have recently climbed out of it. He thought that when he had got his wits together he would suggest that they build a second sacking-and-sapling bed in the cave, so Menge could not make him feel guilty by sleeping on the ground. Turning his head surreptitiously he saw that the Professor was busy coaxing the fire into life. He closed his eyes again and feigned sleep. There was the rattle of handle against bucket. Menge was going to the creek for water.

When he heard the rich baritone voice against the chorus of magpies he knew Menge must be in a good mood. The Professor was renowned for his early morning renditions of the hymns of Luther but this one sounded particularly joyful. Hermes sat up and pulled on his boots, trying to recall the events of the last evening but could get no further than Menge saying, 'Look at me, boy ...' The hymn ended and Menge reappeared. Hermes stepped out of the cave into the bite of the morning air.

'Ah, awake are we? And how are we today?'

'Well enough,' Hermes said civilly, in spite of himself.

'Good. The tea will be a while, so we may as well do the next thing while we wait.'

'And what is that?'

'I want you to climb to the top of this hill.' Menge was pointing upwards, to the craggy peak. 'And then come down very rapidly. As rapidly as you can.'

Hermes blinked at him. He could see no good reason for this mad caper but he was mildly surprised to find that he could muster no good argument for not complying.

'You must take my hammers,' Menge said, pushing one into each of his hands, 'so you can come down the way I do. Remember now, feet together – *jump* – arms back at the same instant – feet land – arms up. Very fast. It must be fast.'

'Fast,' Hermes repeated, without question.

'Yes. Just remember that. Off you go.'

Obediently he scrambled up the rocky slope, using the hammers as alpenstocks, slipping and slithering and having to climb up again, barking his knuckles on sharp jutting stones, scraping his shins through the cloth of his trousers, puffing and grunting but with no thought of turning back.

At the top he vaguely observed the view across the plain and wondered whether it was a bend of the Murray that glittered in the distance. Probably just a mirage. He was tempted to linger but Menge's voice still rang in his ears and knowing he must obey it, he positioned himself for the descent. Fast, it had to be, which meant Menge-style, in kangaroo leaps. He hefted the hammers until they felt balanced, prepared himself for flight and launched himself into the air.

His first leap was not a success. His arms failed to time themselves with his feet and his face went forward into the spines of a grasstree, which fortunately cushioned his fall onto the rock behind it. He got up, shook himself and tried again.

This time he got it right. It was surprisingly simple once he got the hang of it. Feet forward, arms back. Feet landing, arms up. The speed of it was exhilarating. Almost like flying. Down, down the mountainside he went, dodging bushes and rocks, then small trees and thickets of scrub. Down, down. He was level with the cave, he was past the cave, heading towards the creek. He felt his skin glowing, his muscles unleashing their power. He heard Menge shout but could not stop. Did not want to stop. Why would a man want to stop flying?

He felt the wings on his heels. Teleria. Ye gods!

Near the creek the bush grew thicker. There was only one way through; the path Menge had worn through the vegetation to the edge of the rockpool, where it was possible to fill a bucket with water. Amazed at his own skill, Hermes navigated the path and stopped suddenly, just in time, at the edge of the pool. Leaning forward he rested his hands on his bent knees and drew in great gulps of air.

He was never sure which he felt first. The sole of Menge's boot connecting with his backside, or the sting of the icy water as it closed over his head. Luckily the pool was only shoulder-deep.

He found the rock bottom quickly and got his head out. Through a sparkle of water he saw the vague outline of Menge on the bank and heard himself bellowing in rage. He saw Menge pick up a long, forked stick and lean out towards him. Ha! he thought, the old fool is going to rescue me now he has had his little joke . . .

But Menge was not bent on rescue. He was applying the fork of the stick to the back of Hermes' neck, pushing him under. The old devil must be mad. So he does mean to drown me. I'll see about that . . .

He got his head out of the water and tried to shout 'Help!' As though there was anyone near enough to hear. All that came from his throat was a rusty croak. Menge was approaching again. This time he was hooking one prong of the forked stick in Hermes' collar and drawing him towards the bank.

'Here boy, give me your hand!' Hermes reached for Menge's clawing fingers, grabbed his bony wrist and was tempted to pull his rescuer into the water. Just in time he thought better of it. It might not pay to provoke the devil himself. He stumbled onto the bank, coughing and shuddering and shaking himself like a wet dog.

'I shall catch my death . . .'

'Nonsense. But get back to the fire and dry yourself.'

Magnanimous in victory, Menge was away up the slope ahead of his victim and by the time Hermes reached the fire he was pushing a towel into his hands. 'Where are your dry clothes, boy? Let me get them for you.'

Hermes scrubbed his wet head with the towel and pointed to his battered portmanteau in the back of the cave, where strange drawings adorned the wall. He wanted to ask about those pictures but at that moment he was too preoccupied with cold fingers that refused to undo buttons. Menge swiftly took over and dragged his wet garments from him.

'Here is another towel. Let me dry your back, boy. Your buttocks are quite blue.'

'I can dry my own buttocks, thank you.' Hermes snatched the dry towel.

'Yes, yes, of course. I'll make the tea. Ah, the porridge is ready. You'll feel better after a hot meal. Sit here. Have the stool. There, is that better?'

Hermes gave him what he hoped was a nasty look. 'Why?' he demanded.

'Why? My dear boy, it was the only way. I had to rid you of your demon.'

'Last night.' Hermes blew on his tea to cool it. 'Last night . . . what did you do to me?'

'I merely put you to sleep.'

'You mesmerised me?'

Menge nodded. 'It is another of my many talents,' he said with a modest smile. 'My name, Menge, means *many* in German. So I have *menge* talents. *Menge* talents!'

Hermes refused to laugh. 'You mesmerised me. You had no right to do that without my consent.'

'Would you have given it?'

'No.'

'There you are, you see. I was forced into it. It was the only course available.'

Vague impressions of the previous evening were beginning to form in Hermes' mind. 'And what was that mumbo-jumbo you said over me?'

'I was casting out your demon. In Hebrew.'

'I would rather you had done it in English. What did you say?'

'There is no exact equivalent in English. A mongrel of a language, English. Now Hebrew! A sacred, most beautiful language. Everyone should learn it because it is the language spoken in heaven.'

'Oh, yes?' Hermes was attacking his porridge. It was improving his temper but he was not finished yet. 'Just why did you send me up the mountain?'

'The *hill*. I told you, it is only a hill. I had to do it quickly while you were still under.'

'But why?'

'In case I had not been completely successful last night. Only by sending you up could I get you to come down fast enough. Demons can only travel at a certain speed. Unless you exceed their pace they will catch you again.'

Hermes was pleased with his self-control. By maintaining his equanimity he would draw out the old fool and find out what was really going on in that great dome of a head.

'And my plunge in the pool? Why did you do that?'

'I had to bring you round quickly, Narcissus. Before you fell in love with yourself. You see,' he added sheepishly, 'I was actually more successful than I expected. You thought you were flying . . .'

'I had wings on my heels,' Hermes reflected dreamily.

'Goodness knows what you might have done. I had to stop you.'

'Once I can understand. But twice! Why did you push me under again?'

'Ah.' Menge's small deep-set eyes twinkled darkly. 'When you came up the first time there was a rude little demon sitting on your shoulders, yelling obscenities at me. At *me*! He had to be got rid of.'

'You have taken great liberties, Professor, but I see you meant well.' Hermes was surprised by the mildness of his voice. He no longer felt angry. 'But seeing you have given me a place to live and the possibility of finding gold, I suppose I cannot by too uppity about it.'

'That is better. You are calling me Professor again. And your demon is gone.'

'If it existed!'

Menge was suddenly serious. 'Think of what troubled you when you first arrived. What had troubled you for a long time, in England, on the ship coming out, all the time you were in Adelaide.'

'You need not think I will tell you.'

'You do not need to tell me. Just ask yourself, does this thing still trouble you? Visualise it, hold it in your mind and see whether it has any power over you. Well?'

Hermes closed his eyes and thought. Then he opened them and gazed unseeing into the distance, over the treetops and across the plain.

'Well?' Menge asked again.

'It is gone,' Hermes admitted. 'But that is not to say it will not return.'

'It will not return.' Menge said it with such conviction and such kindness that there was no arguing with him. 'But if you are worried there is something I can give you, just in case. You will not need it . . . but just in case.'

'And what is that?' He supposed he had better humour the old fool.

Menge fished in his specimen bag and brought out a sparkling piece of crystal. Hermes gaped.

'No, it is not a diamond. It is common crystal. But this is no ordinary specimen. See the perfection of its shape? I found it in a dry creek-bed. My black friends say such stones will give a man courage to overcome the darkest of spirits, by which they mean demons. You must carry it in your pocket at all times and if you feel your demon returning, whatever sort of demon it might be, you must clasp it in your hand and let its powers flow through you.'

Hermes' tolerance was becoming strained but he remembered his manners. After all, he was Menge's guest, so to speak. So he reached out and took the crystal. He felt its cool smoothness and shivered.

'It is quite beautiful,' he said, turning it over and over in his hands. 'But I am not sure I can take it. It may be valuable.'

'Valuable! Of course it is valuable. Did I not tell you of its powers? But you must have it. I insist. Of course you must never try to sell it. It cannot be sold, only given away. And then only in special circumstances.'

'Such as? There is no need to look secretive. I must know if I am to have custody of this valuable object.'

'It can only be given to someone whose need is greater than your own.'

'Professor, I appreciate your generosity but I refuse to believe my need is greater than yours.'

Menge shook his head sadly. 'You must believe me, my friend.'

He tapped his skull again. 'I know. I have it in here. You are one of those who tend to let the body rule the mind.'

'The trouble is,' Hermes said, reluctantly pocketing the crystal, 'the body always thinks it knows best.'

Mirage

Lesley Williams

Journeying beyond Birdsville, heading out along the dotted line edging two States, Queensland and South Australia, destination Innamincka and the Coongie Lakes.

A plume of wake-dust streams high and wide, dry brush strokes linking movement to delight and the indelible nature of water.

The track ahead rises and curves, a shoulder of stone clad in a wavering mantle of air. The pediments of distant hills are cut to cliffs of glass. Close by the road sleek, Brahmin-brown cattle graze; dark hides smoothed over tanned earth-skin. Out here the land is red, and gold with grasses hillocking over wide plains that stretch to a glaze-shimmered sea. Out here, eyes and mind are challenged into a squint of contention over what is real.

Turning south, slow-driving, the colour and shape of the land changes. Red to bleached, leached white, with overtones of pink and gold in hills and mesas washed in palest green. Road edges sprout stones with sand-etched faces, dyed in stripes and blocks of water-colour wash. The track winds down to meet scrubby waterlines crossing, meandering, on through the land.

To Cooper Creek, wide, muddy wet, edged in a fringing shawl of Coolibah trees and voiced by the calls of wild birds. The Dig Tree beckons, pondering the riddle of Burke and Wills, dying in the midst of plenty. Not so long ago, same place, another world. If only they had known the future. Would they have waited? Would travelling in a four wheel drive have slowed the changing stories of the land? Cooper Creek will etch its way down country, west to south-west, to Innamincka and on to meet Lake Eyre.

Cullyamurra Waterhole, a bit further down the track, a living, meeting, trading place, stretching back through time. Tall gum trees edge and shade the water. The hot day fills with scuffled dust and the scent of eucalyptus. Baby corellas sit together in their holes in high branches, watch quietly, and wait. Far along a track above the waterhole, in a tumble of rock, black and smooth-worn, carved symbols, old, faded, almost obliterated; markers, signs, ancestors. Pelicans and other birds sweep in and out along the deep brown stretch of water.

The Coongie Lakes, beyond Innamincka, hide behind a fringe of sand hills. The sandy track lifts up and over. A curved stretch of water reaches out, a wide blue greeting. A narrow peninsula fringed with melaleuca becomes a campsite. Swags are unrolled, sheltered beneath the trees, facing water that captures colour as the sun loses its balance and begins to descend.

Three days on the bumpy stone-wracked, dusty track. Desire becomes absolute. Shoes are off and feet begin to paddle. The lake floor sinks, soft and silty; feet splodge, toes are chased by shrimpy, nibbling creatures in water so cold that numbness sets in, in seconds. An odd sensation, nibbled numbness.

On the other side of the spit of sand the lake is so wide that the sand hills on the farther shore are a narrow strip, pink and bright in the lowering light and the lake surface seems to curve. The bottom here is sandy, firm and shrimpless. Feet begin to wade, back and forth, slowly gathering in the cold along the edge of this tiny cove, at the edge of this eagle-winged body of water perched in the Cooper Creek flood plain – spread out between deserts of gibber, stone and sand.

Back and forth, back and forth, like an anchorite waiting for God. Gradually wading deeper, deeper, back and forth, eyes on the horizon, concentrating on a slow deepening of red-gold along the far shore. The fading day fans out slowly, gilding water and sky.

Waist deep. Cold enters the body's warmest places. The trees along the shoreline, papery-barked, piny leaves, whispering-green, begin to hide in the shadows of this long afternoon. Slowly, slowly, lowering, beneath the surface, lowering; arms reach out in frog-stretch, legs push out in frog-kick, slowly, slowly, back and forth.

Body as cold as the lake, cold as though bones have reached out to night, still and deep, through a long, long dream of time.

Limbs glow beneath the rough nap of the towel, heart beats steady and strong. The whole surface of the lake turns sunset-pink, its far line of sand hills becomes a band of gold.

Night falls. No fire (no fires allowed) to keep the sky at bay. Light from stars pierces the dark shine of water. From across the lake a trumpet begins to croon. Disbelieving, delighted applause. Encore as lullaby, hands become pillow, dreams drift out to meet the rising moon.

Reflections as words, fine-spun as water, transitory, as dreaming, as any mirage.

Walbia Gu Burru

Dylan Coleman

My mother's skin smells like rain-drenched mallee scrub earth breaking drought. I cling to the bough of her leg, arms tightly wrapped, face nuzzled into her thigh. She is strong and grounded. Her roots run deep into this land, golden with its skin of dry waving wheat beckoning harvest in a good year. And her fringes of wild mallee as defiant in the knowledge of being as they have always been, will always be; knowledge that no harvest can reap because it belongs to something more, something far beyond skin deep. Her layers of sandstorms wash over my mind in thundering resonance and her memories fall upon me like rain touching dry lips.

White cotton dresses billowed under a gust of wind as a *whirly whirly* dissipated into the crowd like the crack of a whip. Rocks shuffled beneath the feet of those who gathered in front of the old sandstone church. Then in stillness, a multitude of eyes bored into a young woman standing alone. A figure of solitude, baby held close to her breast. Crows shrieked from a eucalypt tree whose leaves hushed the shaded whisperings.

'Just look at 'er will ya! She's got no shame ... filthy *booba, indie?*' spat Maggie, a bulky woman in her mid-forties.

'I reckon. Fancy bringing ya bastard kid to church like that ... she wanna be careful the good Lord don't strike her dead on the spot,' replied Lucy, face screwed up, furiously scratching at bedbug bites on her thin spotted ankle.

'I 'eard her father gave her a floggin' last week when she come 'ome. Look there, she still got that black eye. But *Goojarb,*' jeered Lucy.

'Just look at that *minya gooling*, it's as white as white and blondest hair,' added Maggie. 'Shame job.'

'Yeah, no hidin' what she's been up to on Farmer William's farm *indie*? We thought she was milkin' them cows, but she been *ungerdie* way there, sniffing around,' Lucy scoffed.

'*Indie*, Farmer William's cows wasn't the only thing she was milkin',' Maggie snorted.

The women shrieked, thrusting hands over their mouths to stifle uncontrollable laughter.

'Oh, don't, please don't,' pleaded Lucy, 'you'll get me in trouble with Pastor in a minute.'

Maggie straightened her skirt, which had begun to ride up her bulky frame, then sniffed in an air of superiority, 'Anyways, I reckon she ain't nothin' but a *biggy biggy knunchu*, sloppin' from old farmer William's trough. And that bastard kid is nothin' but William's *minya* piglet . . . and always will be, just sloppin' in his trough.' Maggie spat at Ada, 'You ain't nothin' but *walbia gu burru*,' then bent down and scooped up two small sharp stones throwing them in her direction. One stung Ada's leg and the other bounced off her baby's head. The baby began to cry.

Ada shuffled back and stooping her shoulders inward, held her baby's head then sank into her battered, bruised body, taking her child with her. She imagined herself invisible. In the distance on the smudged horizon, dust settled and fused with patchy golden stubble and the scattered remains of green mallee scrub. The open sky blazed in brilliant blue.

Light spilled into the church through the door. In the shadows, Pastor stood in anticipation. With Bible in hand he squinted at the framed scene before him. Through the glare he could see a collage of fabric blotches; dabbles of white, grey, brown, black and blue, on the canvas of dark skin. In preparation for his sermon, he painted finishing touches in his mind. Through the power of God he was there to create, to eradicate sin and to shape decency. He took a breath, straightened the small of his back and marched towards the light. Standing at the threshold he gazed upon what he thought was a perfect image before him, then winced at a blemish.

'Quiet please, it's time for worship, file inside one by one,' called Pastor.

Ada lingered as the crowd spilled onto the wooden pews. Pastor cast a stern eye and waited for her.

'Hurry up,' he called, then added, with white knuckles on his fingers showing as he clutched at his Bible, 'You can stand at the back.'

As she passed through the church door Ada looked down, her seething anger masked by shame. She held her child close and could feel their bonded strength flicker and grow.

As the congregation settled, Pastor cleared his throat and began his sermon.

'I will begin by reading from the Book of Matthew, Chapter 13: the parable of the sower and the seed. Jesus likened the word of God unto a seed that is sown, like the wheat seeds that we have sown here in our paddocks and that others have sown throughout our district.'

Pastor's words faded in and out of Ada's hearing. She heard crows chorusing. The crows were perched on the branch of a tree. The branch's leaves swept the roof of the church. She thought the leaves sounded as if they hushed the cries of the crows. *Shhh, Shhh, Shhh.* Or maybe the sound of the brushing leaves soothed the church building, this 'House of God', with the burden of sins that it harboured; the burden of her sin, the sin of the father, the sin into which the child was born. She thought of her child's father and how he had recently spent time in jail for breaking white man's law by consorting with her. Why was it so wrong for a black woman to be with a white man when in the eyes of God, all are equal? And how strange it seemed that God would punish an innocent child. With her back against the rock wall, she wondered if her *gooling* would grow invisible too.

The sermon continued: 'Jesus said if this seed is sown in stony places, it is like hearing the word of God with joy but without the roots that go down into the ground. Any trouble that comes into your life you will become offended and will be easily uprooted.'

Ada's thoughts wandered back to her childhood. She saw herself standing on the edge of a paddock on the Mission, looking into a growing expansive nothingness of black soil. Her father's and uncles' faces straining wet and dust-stained from labour. She could see them axing, uprooting, then severing and burning the mallee scrub. Digging white stones from the earth and piling them into neat pinnacles at regular intervals in the scorched paddocks; stones that skinned knuckles. Rocky country that the stretched, grasping fingers of the mallee roots defied, not at all like the wheat crop country. And at night as Ada and her family slept, huddled close in their tiny house, the last resistant stumps would burn in the distance, just beyond their dreams; flicker on the perimeter, their hazy smoke rising to the heavens.

Pastor gestured with his hands. 'If the seed is sown among thorns it is like someone who hears the word of God but he careth for things of the world and the deceitfulness of riches chokes the word and he becometh unfruitful.'

He then paused and cast a stern eye over his congregation, as if to measure the weight of their guilt. Ada's feet and her back began to feel the strain. Tears welled in her eyes. An overwhelming feeling pierced her soul and began to spill into her conscious mind. She thought of her father and uncles working on the neighbouring farm. During reaping season they would gather the wheat into hessian bags, weaving them closed with large sharp needles, then plunge grasping hooks into the bails, hurl them onto a cart and later stack them into the barn one on top of the other. Ada knew she must protect her baby at all costs. She would protect her from the cruelty she had felt at the hands of others. She was determined to provide a better life for her child than the one she had lived.

'But when the word of God is received into good ground, he that heareth the word and understandeth it will also bear fruit and bring forth a good harvest,' echoed the words of Pastor.

Ada remembered her family gathering the yams and bush-tucker that were once prolific in the now bare paddocks. She wondered about the bush medicine plant and the eucalypt trees, with their leaves used for 'smoking', healing and for purifying the spirit. These were important things, things that her grandmother had taught her, things that were the birthright of her child and would give her a good strong grounding. Now all the good ground was gone.

'Jesus also spoke about the kingdom of heaven, likening it to a man who soweth good seed in his field. But while the man slept his enemy came and sowed weeds among the wheat and went his way. But when wheat grew, so too did the weeds.'

Staring at the wooden cross on the brick wall above the altar, Ada remembered the first time he laid eyes on her, piercing green eyes of hunger. At the time she knew it wouldn't be long before she was pulled under. Her father and brothers were gainfully employed on his farm; their wages fed her big, often starving, family who lived on the Mission. What else could she do when stripped bare but sink under the surface? Wiping her brow of sweat she thought about the moment she would disappear, rhythmically squeezing the soft teats, milk squirting rich and thick into the bucket between her legs. She was scared.

'So the servants of the householder came and said unto him, "Sir did you not sow good seed in the field? How come there are weeds?" And he replied, "An enemy hath done this."' Pastor paused for a moment, wringing his hands, a stern expression spreading across his face.

Maggie, who was seated near the back row on the women's side of the church, turned and sharply glared at Ada. Ada stared back, defiant. Maggie conceded, shrugged, screwed up her face then turned away. It was Maggie who had wanted the job on the farm but Ada's family were good workers. *Tjilpi* Williams had asked Ada's father if there were women in the family who could help with domestic work and tending the cows. Her father had suggested his eldest, Ada, a hard worker. Ada wondered how Maggie would have felt if she stood in her shoes now. They were painfully tight and pinched her heels. In hindsight Ada would have gratefully swapped her place with Maggie but what was she to know then? She had never known a man before and she had not known that such men have their own way.

Pastor's sermon continued: 'The servants said unto the householder, "Should we go and gather up the weeds?" But he said,

"No, because in gathering the weeds you might also root up the wheat with them. Let both grow together until the harvest. In the time of harvest I will say to the reapers, Gather up the weeds, and also uproot the wheat with them. Then gather together first the weeds and bind them in bundles to burn them but gather the wheat into my barn."'

There, in that barn, in a haze of scorching wheat dust, his lust spilled over her. She later thought it was not at all like milking cows, more like a horse drawn plough, cutting through her layers. Soon afterwards he left and she rolled over and cried into the hay, choking and coughing on the dust before disappearing back to the mallee scrub in her mind. All crops need rain to grow, she thought. And grow she did, like the *Walga* with its thorny stem and smooth inner skin that splits to release its ripe fruit. And beneath its tasty flesh, at its core, dozens of little black seeds are nurtured. Ada held her child close.

'Jesus said unto his disciples, "He that soweth the good seed is the Son of Man. The field is the world, the good seed are the children of the kingdom but the weeds are the children of the Wicked One. The enemy that soweth them is the Devil, the harvest is the end of the world and the reapers are the angels."'

Ada would not concede. Neither she nor her child were evil. When she gazed on her daughter's pale innocent face she thought it resembled an angel. Although she felt ambivalent about *Tjilpi* William's actions, she now had her child to consider. No suitor on the Mission would want her: she was *walbia gu burru*. She had to feed her child and after all, *Tjilpi* Williams had kept her family from starving. She would do what she had to, to keep her child.

'Therefore, as the weeds are gathered and burned in the fire, so shall it be at the end of the world. The Son of Man shall send forth his angels and they shall gather out of his kingdom all things that offend and those who do iniquity he shall cast into the furnace of fire; there shall be wailing and gnashing of teeth. Then shall the righteous be sent forth to the Kingdom of Heaven. Who hath ears to hear, let him hear.'

Ada's ears burned as she heard these words. She was sure she had already been to hell. As her stomach had grown so too had the abuse from the others on the Mission. She remembered her body aching, black and blue with bruising. Shame was a harsh punisher; sometimes she felt it at the end of her father's whip. Close to the birth she was shipped by steamboat to the city, over five hundred nautical miles away. Her terror matched the endless ocean as she leaned over the boat, looking into the lunging waves, endlessly vomiting.

On more than one occasion she thought to throw herself in, just to end her misery. But the spirit of her child cried within her and she could not forsake it. She feared the birth. She feared losing her child. When she arrived she ran away from the Home. The authorities brought her back. She was so homesick she couldn't eat, so they sent her home on the ship again. As she climbed off the jinker from an exhausting journey, her stomach swollen with her child still growing within, she was met by jeers and stone-throwing.

She wondered about the scriptures of forgiveness that weren't preached that day. Was she meant to endlessly suffer? Pastor had seen how people on the Mission treated her. He had even seen the stone throwing, not only at herself but at her new born daughter. He had seen the bruising from her father's shameful beating, yet he chose to cast a blind eye. And what of the scripture 'an eye for an eye', she thought? Could she do the same in return?

If God deemed her and her child evil and wished them to burn like weeds, then burn she would, on rocky and thorny ground alike, because she knew her own worth. She was like a rare black pearl. And what of the scripture that told of the pearl of great price? The man who found this pearl sold everything he owned to have it. How special it must have been. She wondered if God overlooked such treasures.

The congregation began to sing. 'The Old Rugged Cross' thundered through the church and echoed across the patchy golden paddocks; its whispers touched the branches of trees on the distant horizon, their roots earth-bound and silent.

Ada stood that day at the back of the church, aching but defiantly strong. She imagined her feet like roots of the mallee tree sinking into the ground beneath her and clinging like clenched fists to the heavy rocks below. She would not be uprooted, cut down, hewn from existence. She would drive her roots deep into her country and touch the smoldering glow of her ancestors to keep her strong, content in the knowing that her daughter would have a bough on which to cling until she grew strong roots of her own.

The hymn thundered on. Ada held her head high and began to walk out of the church. She stood for a moment in the doorway, turned, was seen as a silhouette in glowing light, then left in dignified silence.

Glossary
Biggy biggy knunchu – pig.
Booba – dog.
Gooling – baby.
Goojarb – serve your self right.
Indie – isn't that so?/yes, it is.
Minya – small.
Tjilpi – old man.
Ungerdie – sexually hungry.
Walga – wild bush tomato.
Walbia gu burru – white man's meat.
Whirly whirly – a gust of spiraling wind.

(The Aboriginal words used here are the author's phonetic approximation of words used on the west coast of South Australia.)

grape

Doug Green

emerald flesh bred royal
sun fatted into quivering curvature
borne in milk soft cradle
to thin patrician lips
luminescent belly
cast from seminal code
rooted to the earth
by tortured strands
lime-eyed spy
into broken night
sower of dream seed
and trawler of the unborn
you steal gold
from the dying sun
and huddle bunched
under dawn's cool whip
you are pastel horror
on a warm summer's day

The Beginnings

Anna Solding

The woman's scream is ancient. It is the scream of her mother and grandmother and others before them. It is agony, triumph, misery and ecstasy. She clenches her fists and pushes one last time.

Hilda catches the slippery creature covered in white vernix, sticks a finger in his mouth to make sure the airways are clear, then gently lowers him onto his mother's bare chest and spreads a sheet on top of them both to keep them warm. The father is by their side with tears in his eyes forgetting to photograph it all, forgetting that there was ever a life before this moment. She turns her back to give them some privacy.

The whimpering of the newborn, then a sudden sucking as he finds the nipple. There is no hurry to cut the cord. Hilda stays in the room just in case but her thoughts wander as she looks out the window. Everything went well. It was a great team effort. The woman is young and fit, her partner supportive. Hilda secretly wishes this was always the case. All the way through the gas had made the woman laugh like a kookaburra, which had made the others laugh too.

Outside the silver autumn dusk brings forth the first star like a gift. The shadow of a leaf falls to the ground. Dew shimmers on the lawn and she wonders if she'll ever have children. She knows what it takes but she's not sure that she has it. Putting the smile back in her cheeks, she turns around to the new parents.

'Now who'd like to cut the cord?'

The girl's mouth trembles with each contraction. Finally this baby is ready to come out. The girl, no more than fifteen according to her journals, has been here for a fortnight. Alone. No one has come to visit her, no boyfriend, no family. She doesn't want them to contact anyone.

Hilda takes her pulse and checks her blood pressure. The girl has had strong Braxton Hicks contractions for over a week and seems relieved that it is finally happening. There is no fear in her eyes.

'Would you like a drink?' Hilda tries her mildest voice but the girl still jumps as if she never expected Hilda to address her.

'Yes,' she hesitates, then adds, 'thank you'.

Hilda goes to the kitchen to fetch a glass of iced water. When she returns the girl is shuffling around the room tenderly stroking her belly as she sings 'Twinkle twinkle little star.' She stops, as if caught doing something she shouldn't, when she hears Hilda putting the glass on the bedside table.

'That was beautiful. You can really sing.'

Hilda isn't sure why she tries so hard but there is something about this girl that makes her want to hug her and never let her go. She needs someone, someone who isn't Hilda, but instead she will soon be the one needed. How is she going to cope with a baby?

'Are you in pain?'

The girl shakes her head while still stroking her belly lovingly. Then the contraction sets in and doubles her over. Hilda tries to reach the bucket but she isn't fast enough so vomit sprays across the girl's front and creates pools at her feet. Hilda wipes her forehead with a damp cloth and gently helps her change her hospital gown and socks before mopping the floor.

The girl's big blue eyes are cloudy. There is a force within her that she obviously didn't know existed.

Suddenly it becomes important to check how dilated she is. It would be easier on the bed but the girl is already leaning heavily on the back of a chair whimpering through the next contraction. Hilda holds her shoulders and waits for it to subside.

It'll be a quick labour. She has seen it happen before. The girl will have to push soon; she has no desire to go back to bed now. Hilda spreads sheets and pillows on the floor beneath the girl.

She is ten centimetres dilated; the second phase has begun. It's hard to reach her now, she has retired into her own world but she pushes when Hilda asks her to. Another midwife appears. The girl hangs like a rag doll over the chair. Hilda is squatting on the floor ready to catch the child when it comes.

'Hold back! I can see the head now. Pant!'

The girl pants and squeezes the chair. Droplets form on her forehead and her bottom lip is bleeding where she has bitten it too hard.

'Would you like to see?' Hilda holds a mirror between the girl's legs so she can see the swirls of dark hair. The girl almost stops breathing, that's how unreal it all is. In a few minutes she will have a baby. Life will never be the same again. Hilda doesn't know anything about the girl's background, all she knows is what she can see here and now. And that is pure joy. The girl's face is lit up from within and for the first time in two weeks she smiles.

'What's that smell? It's not *me* is it?'

There is panic in her voice as she says it. Hilda can tell she is used to being in control but what's a little poo in the scheme of things? A good sign that the baby is on its way. Surely the woman should know that, she's a doctor, one of the famous ones too. Hilda has read about her in the paper, not just the local one, mind you.

'I've taken care of everything. Don't you worry.' Hilda sprays some air freshener to make the woman more at ease. She is concentrating very hard to push at the right time even though the epidural has made sure she feels nothing. After twenty hours she can't take any more. When the anaesthetist comes in the woman looks as though she could kiss her. The relief must have been even greater than the feeling of getting out of the wind on a freezing Malmö morning.

Her support person (her husband? He looks a bit younger) changes CDs to happy-sounding classical music with violins. Hilda recognises it as film music but she can't remember which film it is from. If she ever has a baby she hopes it will be easier than this. When the baby is posterior, with its back against the mother's, the pain is excruciating. On top of that, labour seems to go on forever. And now when it is finally happening the woman still can't push the baby out on her own.

The baby is too big. Hilda calls the doctor and after a quick explanation he tells the patient that they are going to have to cut.

'An episiotomy?' the woman says, dazed. 'I thought I was doing well.'

'You are but the baby has had enough now. It needs to come out.'

The woman nods, understanding. She is a doctor herself after all. But Hilda can see disappointment in the corners of her mouth. After all this time, all the pain, the pushing, the poos, she will still have to deliver with the help of a vacuum extractor.

The support person takes her hand and strokes it gently. There is so much loving in his voice as he leans over and half whispers, 'I'm so proud of you.' She kisses his hand and the sparkle in her eyes returns. It doesn't really matter, does it, how the baby is born? Hilda thinks. What matters is that it arrives safe and sound and she'll make sure of that.

The worry in the woman's black eyes speaks more clearly than her broken Swedish.

'I can not feel kicking. Why has my baby stopped kicking?'

Hilda takes her blood pressure and checks her pulse. Standard observations, standard results.

'I don't know. The baby is probably getting ready to come out. There isn't that much room to kick around any more.'

'But I already have three children. They all kick.'

Her husband stands by the window staring into the starlit sky murmuring something which sounds like prayer. The woman's eyes search Hilda's for an answer she cannot yet provide.

'Let me get a foetal monitor so we can make sure the baby's heartbeat is normal.'

Hilda fetches one from the store room and straps the pads onto the taut skin of the belly. The woman sinks back into her pillows and tries to relax. Instantly the crashing of waves on a deserted beach fills the room.

'There it is. Can you hear it? Sounds like a perfectly healthy little heart.'

'Thank God', the woman whispers.

The husband leaves the window and comes over to comfort his wife and thank Hilda. The ticking of the heart reverberates between the bare walls.

'Something isn't quite right, doctor. Take a look at this.' Hilda points to the screen where a little squiggly line shows the baby's heartbeat. 'It's becoming irregular.'

The doctor looks concerned. 'How long ago was she induced?'

'About an hour. The contractions are very strong now as you can see.'

The woman on the bed moans as her stomach ties itself into a knot. Her partner, a woman with short blonde hair and a wide mouth, wipes her brow with a cool damp cloth then hands her a cup of water before another contraction almost lifts her off the bed. She screams in agony.

'Is it meant to be this bad? Isn't there anything you can do?' She stares accusingly at Hilda and the doctor, almost as if she thinks it's their fault that she is in pain.

The foetal monitor starts beeping furiously. Something is seriously wrong and the woman's expression shifts from anger to fear.

'What's wrong? There's nothing wrong with my baby is there?' she almost cries it out.

The blonde woman tries to calm her down but there is nothing she can do. The decision has already been made. Within seconds the woman is being wheeled along the corridor towards emergency. They have to get the baby out otherwise it might not live.

Hilda swears silently inside as she sees them go. It happens far too often when they induce but they still do it in good faith. She hopes they get there on time. The last thing she sees is the blonde woman turning away from her lover and wiping her eyes as they get in the lift. She won't be able to be there for the birth after all.

Over the lake dawn colours the sky metallic blue. An old man walks his dog without a leash under the yellowing trees. Hilda runs a finger across her eyelids and stifles a yawn as she watches the day grow. Five women, five babies. It is time for her to go home and embrace the new crisp autumn day in her own bed. Without contractions, without monitors, without sudden vomiting. Without babies. The familiar lump of morning sadness treads on her bones.

As she looks up the last star blends with the milky sky.

Support

Heather Taylor Johnson

It wasn't out of rebellion that I snubbed straps and cups
and clasps and lace and it had nothing to do with women's rights:
I just never wore a bra.
It had something to do with whispers and flutters and freedom
and knowing that I was naked underneath,
feeling a weight that only I owned, that bounced
and made me proud,
loving the cold or a shot of tequila and feeling the shiver
end in my nipples, seeing its shape through my shirt,
catching contours through sunlit dresses,
see-through thin as cooing words in the wind.
Now I'm walking through racks of padded, underwire and sports,
sipping on a smoothie, filling my womb with berries and yogurt
and remembering the sunflower seeds in my purse
and I'm thinking My God! it's the size of an orange,
it's got tear ducts, a heartbeat, fingernails and toes!
What do I know except for this:
my breasts are heavy and hard with growth
and soon they'll squirt forth milk
and later like honey-coloured pure lily
they'll sweeten his tummy and tighten our grip
and what once was mine will now be ours
and this time I'll really understand what it means to be proud,
no shivers or alcohol involved.
I'll be a mother with breasts,
weighty with mornings, drooping with days, sagging with
    night-time feeds
and from this day forth, for the rest of my life,
I'll need a little support.

Indigofera

Stephanie Thomson

'What kind of legs do you want?' she asks me chirpily. I move to request clarification but I am too slow.

'There are just too many styles, leg-wise. The choices are infinite. What kind of legs were you thinking of?' The sales assistant inclines her head slightly. She is a willowy pale blonde in her mid-twenties with the kind of perfectly symmetrical, even features that could become anything under a make up artist's hand. She brings her face into the direct halogen aura of the crescent wall light under which we three are standing: she, my daughter and I. The mirrored wall on which the light is mounted reflects a complex dynamic collage of people and objects in which one element is the nether side of those same people and objects, as reflected in the opposite mirrored wall.

I connect with my daughter 'eyes-wise'. I'm baffled and I want it to show in my raised brows.

'Mum, she means do you want flares, bootlegs, straight legs, slim fit, or baggies . . . or what?'

'I *am* sorry. I've got it now. I'm just a tad out of touch with these things, Lauren. I grew up in the dark ages, remember?' My self-deprecation always wins Lauren's sympathy.

'Let's go with a straight leg for starters and see where that gets us. I think you might look great in straights.'

My aspiring fashion designer daughter is only twenty and a full head taller than me. Today she has the look of a zealot about her. Her green eyes are alight with passion. Her dark hair swept back into a neat ponytail, ready for business. She pats me on the arm reassuringly. She is responsible for my being here, in the chrome and Perspex vault that is the denim mega store Indigofera. On my forty-ninth birthday I am the uncertain victim of a Lauren makeover. I have not purchased a pair of denim jeans since I was in my twenties. I've promised to cooperate but already my sanity is under threat.

'Colour preference?' The salesgirl again.

'Oh . . . just denim will do. Denim jeans. Blue.'

'Yes Mum but they have special effects now: contrast, colour-washed, sparkle-effect, carbon, streaky . . . even pre-sunfaded and dirty denim,' Lauren enthuses.

'What? You are joking, aren't you . . . sun-faded? In my day denim was just basic blue!'

The salesgirl is clearly enlivened by Lauren's incantation of denim's latest hues.

'You know it's hard work harnessing the sun's awesome power. But for you and for the sake of denim, we did it. They cost a little more than untreated denims but they're worth it!'

'You mean you have to pay for denim that's already faded . . . or *dirty*?' I'm open-mouthed, looking from one earnest face to the other for a convincing reply.

'Yeah, Mum, dirty denim is the latest thing. It has real street appeal.'

'Lauren I am not paying good money for a garment that is already dirty! I can do my own fading and dirtying all by myself in the privacy of my own backyard if I want!'

'Mum . . . it's complicated now. Every style is part of a whole design story.'

'Mmmm,' I reply with an exaggerated sidelong frown. I don't want to disparage Lauren's chosen profession, but I do want to register a protest against such hype.

'It's the story of fit and comfort that interests me most. If I'm going to update my image I have to be as comfortable in my clothes as I am in my skin.'

''Scuse me for a sec.' The sales assistant turns and paces decisively along the wall. She swings open what reveals itself to be a mirrored door in the wall a metre or two along from where we are standing. She returns balancing a pair of jeans triple-folded across her crooked arm.

'Well, these'll work just bewdiful for you,' she smiles, handing me the jeans.

'Don't you mean beautifully?'

'Yes Ma'am. Bewdiful. These're tens. Try 'em for size. These denims have a bewdiful story to 'em.'

'To *them*,' I correct her, unable to help myself. 'Lauren?'

While Lauren takes up a sentinel post outside the fitting room I enter through the slap-shutting clatter of double swing doors with mirrored louvres.

'Was that sales assistant chewing gum?'

'No Mum ... I don't think so ... well, I didn't notice if she was.' I focus on finding my bearings in the smoky dimness of the fitting room. Lauren's voice sounds distant. *Lauren is right*, I muse while removing my stretch beige slacks. *It wasn't gum she was chewing. It was a piece of straw.*

I inhale as I pull on the jeans. Underneath the tobacco smoke, there is just a whiff of what I recognise, from a childhood spent at pony club, as saddle leather. I turn to look at myself in the mirror. The light is bad. But the fit is comfortable. Through the dim haze I'm puzzled by the fact that the mirror has thrown up illusory mountains behind me. They appear snow-capped. As I button the fly of my jeans the pale caress of a moon-washed Alpine midnight bathes me clean of city grime. I'm raw-scrubbed and restless, as if I've stepped from the heat of a tin-tub bath in the kitchen of some mountain ranch. I'm high on moonshine, swaying barefoot, trying to get my balance. It's Saturday night. I'm sixteen and I've just had my first taste of strong liquor. There is damp grass under my feet. And now the soft clink of a bridle ... the creak of saddle leather.

'Ma'am?'

I wheel around giddily. My sudden companions are a stately chestnut mare breathing steamily in the night air and an equally impressive dark male figure astride her. He removes his hat, a Stetson. He is lean hipped in comfortably loose denims. His stack-heeled cowboy boots are stirrup-worn on their sides and he wears a donkey brown suede jacket. Even under moonlight I discern that his face is tanned, his features chiseled. He's familiar but I can't place him.

'What brings you here Ma'am?'

'I've come ... I've come because this is where the flavour is ... but I'm not exactly sure where I am.'

'Marlboro Country. Come on up. I'll take us to a haystack that's still warmed through from this day's sunshine.' He removes his boot from the stirrup and I place my bare foot into the cold metal. He leans down, grabbing both my hands in his, helping me straighten.

'I'm a man who works with my hands,' he tells me when I am mounted behind him.

'I feel that,' I reply. As we descend into the valley I ask his name.

'Darrell. Darrell Winfield, Ma'am.'

'I'm Jean. My name is Jean.'

The honest smell of tobacco rises off the suede jacket he has laid out on that moonlit haystack for me. The trapped heat of the day cocoons us as we lie together.

'Try one.' He flips open a packet of Marlboro Reds that he has just taken from the back pocket of his jeans.

'It's the cigarette made for men that women like.' He cups his hand to give the struck match a chance against the night breeze. Heads together, he lights both of our cigarettes, flicking the spent matchstick away behind him in an impressively casual gesture.

'Why do you carry your smokes in your jeans pocket? Don't they get squashed while you're riding?' I ask him, lying back in the cradle of his suede arm, poking my finger through each of the magically backlit smoke rings in his expert trail.

'No Ma'am. Smokes 'n jeans belong together. They're made for each other ... like you 'n me. In Marlboro Country, where there's smokes ... there's denim.'

'Oh Darrell,' I giggle tipsily, snuggling in. 'Don't you mean ... where there's smoke there's fire?'

A sudden strong updraught of wind sends a shower of sparks flying out from behind our heads. We both leap to our feet. Without further warning the haystack explodes into a fireball singeing my eyelashes as I reel away from it, shielding my face with crossed arms. The doors of the fitting room swing open and I drop my arms to my sides, trying to regain my balance. Lauren enters.

'How are they, Mum?'

'Oh Lauren. They are really somethin'!'

'Some*thing*, Mum. You're talking weirdly. Do you need a coffee already?'

'Why? Are you suggesting I might needta sober up?'

'Huh? Mum . . . be serious. Let's have a look at the fit.' Before I can properly submit to Lauren's scrutiny the sales girl's head appears over the top of the louvered doors.

'Look, I am so, so sorry. I'm afraid you can't have those, they've been recalled to the factory. A faulty line. The factory forgot to sew the brand tags onto the pockets! We're not allowed to sell them unless the brand is clearly displayed. Only came in two colours though, so they'll be easy to round up from the shop floor. Yep, all those New Creek Blues and Madison River Browns have got to go back to Taiwan.'

'Shame,' I muse dreamily, 'they're special. And the fit is good too . . . like a well worn saddle . . .'

'Don't worry, Mum. I think they are a little too rustic for you anyway. The whole look is way too casual. I'd like to see you in something a little less . . . basic . . . less generic. And anyway, why stick to blue? Let's take a look at some designer jeans. Maybe something with stretch . . . more fitting round the hips.'

As I slip off the generic jeans to hand them over something falls out of the back pocket. I lean down to pick it up off the floor; a flip top pack of Marlboro Reds – squashed. I tuck it into my handbag like a guilty secret.

'Designer? Ohhh Daaarlings, why didn't you say so before?' The sales assistant croons as I hand the brand-less jeans to her over the doors. As she speaks I wonder how she can get away with this sudden parodic excess of schmooze. Back in my beige slacks Lauren and I follow her through a maze of displays. Lauren disappears behind a mirror-backed rack to investigate designerland for herself. Meanwhile the sales assistant pulls a pair of deep purple over-dyed denim jeans from the Perspex rack in front of us. They are decorated in a mass of whorls, curlicues, paisley leaves and hearts.

'They're Versace, of course. I adore the way the designer has used that whole sixties psychedelic visual vocabulary in this piece. Gianni was *really* onto something with these.'

'Don't you mean *on* something?' I quip.

'Mmhmm. They're a whole trip in themselves.'

I notice that the sales assistant is holding her breath. She opens her mouth minutely, enough to let out a muffled squeak.

'Here.' She passes me a neatly rolled joint. Her action seems to awaken a long dormant reflex in me. I take it without thought and draw back a good lungful before passing it back.

'You know these were designed in the nineties, right? But this psychedelic scrollwork is pure sixties! Each piece is individually hand embroidered. And look at these *darling* peace signs on the pockets, no two are exactly alike in proportion.' I look, marvelling at the gold hand-embroidered imperfection of the miniature peace symbols. 'The whole design is a precise copy of the doodles that some famous guitarist painted on his favourite guitar. Ummm . . . what was his name? Hendrix, I think.'

'Hendrix. Jimi Hendrix! Maaaan . . . I'm really flying the baby boomer flag now I suppose, but he was . . . wow . . . he was *God* when I was your age!' My exuberance alerts Lauren. She pokes her head first around the mirror wall and then her body follows. She is armed with a rainbow coloured arsenal of jeans on hangers. I meet my daughter's gaze excitedly, instantly fearing that I'm about to pay for this new breach of motherly decorum.

'*Muuum!*' Lauren admonishes me through her clenched teeth. 'What did you say '*man*' for? No one says that anymore. That kind of talk is not even from this *century*. You know that.' She frowns.

'Yes Lauren, I know. I just got a little carried away. This young lady just mentioned one of my heroes . . . Jimi Hendrix . . . and I . . .'

'Oh wow. Oh . . . *far out* . . . look at *those* . . . they are *divine*!' I'm quite used to not being allowed to finish my sentences. Lauren has just caught sight of the Versaces now draped seductively over the sales assistant's arm. 'Mum, you *have* to try these on. They are out-rageous.' She checks the brand.

'Versaces! They'll break the bank but it doesn't matter. They're *sooooo* sixties ... look!' She is holding out the bottom of one leg, the sales assistant beaming on. 'They're flares! You should relate to that, Mum.'

'Yeah man ... I can relate ...' I whisper vaguely. I am inaudible anyway, over the sound system. Hendrix. *Purple Haze ... all in my brain ... lately things just don't seem the same.*

We follow the sales assistant to a different fitting room on the opposite side of the store. I notice that all the shop fittings including display shelves, hanging racks and even the garment hangers are made of clear Perspex. This gives the impression that all the merchandise is suspended without corporeal assistance in the air; jeans floating in space. Or maybe this is just the effect of the dope? I can't tell. The sales assistant hands me the Versaces as we enter the vestibule of the fitting room enclosure.

'These Versaces will put you in touch with yourself. Reconnect with *you* ... go on.'

By the time I pull across the crimson crushed velvet curtain of the fitting room cubicle my head is spinning. Once inside I lick my fingers and extinguish in turn each of the three incense sticks that are clouding the air with patchouli-scented smoke.

''Scuse me while I kiss the sky,' I murmur, now trying to push my right foot into the trouser leg that my left leg is already occupying. I try to balance myself against the mirror walls of the cubicle but it's too late. I lean through the crimson curtain instead.

The hand that strokes my forehead when I come round is Lauren's.

'Mum, thank God you're OK. You took quite a fall.'

If the mountain ... falls to the sea ... let it be ... let it be. My right hand, which seems to have dissociated itself from my body, stretches up towards Lauren's face.

'Mum?'

If the sun ... refused to shine ... I don't mind ... I don't mind ...

'Mum! Snap out of it!' Lauren is clearly frightened.

''S OK. Chill, honey,' I reassure her, using her proffered hand to pull myself woozily to standing. It occurs to me vaguely that Lauren must have zipped me into the Versaces after I fell, for modesty's sake perhaps. The sight of her half-dressed stoned mother splayed on the fitting room floor must have shaken her.

'I love you.' I announce to the sales assistant who has appeared in the fitting room corridor. She tries to hold me at bay as I pull her face towards mine, kissing her on both cheeks.

'Stop that!' she chides me, pushing me gently away like a mother annoyed with an ingratiating, wayward child.

'Ohhhh. Don't be so aggressive sister. Peace ... give peace a chance ...'

'Yeah, well that's fine, whatever,' she sighs deeply, 'Peace and love don't sell any more. No. These days, peace and love don't sell jeans.'

Picking up my handbag from the fitting room I sway past an incredulous Lauren and the battle weary sales assistant. I am determined to declare my peace policies to a clutch of astonished Indigofera shoppers.

'Who cares about jeans ... you don't need them ... see ... you don't need them! Because ... because *all you need is looooove, da da da da da ...*' I'm singing now, loudly: over Jimi, over 'Purple Haze'. '*All you need is love, love. Love is all you need!*' I can't stop myself. I begin to unzip the Versaces. 'I don't need these ... these ... things ... designer peace-jeans ... diviner jean-pieces ... divine peace-jeaners ... jean-peacers! Oh Jimi-Jesus why did you leave us? Johnny-Beatle ... Paul and Ringo ... George, where art thou? Let me stop your guitar from weeping Georgie boy ... Hare guitare ... Hare Krishnaaaaa ... Krishna Krishnaaaaaa ... Hare Krishnaaaaa ... Hare Hareeeeee!'

I grab the Marlboro packet from inside my bag and begin throwing cigarettes to the shoppers like stem roses into a rock festival crowd.

'SEX!' The sales girl barks at me authoritatively, blocking my path through the racks. I stop dead in my tracks. 'It's *sex* that sells.'

Lauren meanwhile ushers me back into the fitting room, and helps me peel off the Versaces.

'These are definitely *not* you, Mum.'

'Sex sells jeans!' The salesgirl continues from outside the curtain, as if this is revelatory; a new dawning in her understanding. 'Sex and a certain association with danger . . . individuality . . . youthful rebellion.'

'Yeah,' Lauren is excited too. 'We've talked about this in design school. It's fascinating. We even made a visit to the Centre for Non-Verbal Studies to learn about clothing cues and fashion signifiers. So how do *you* feel about jeans and sex, Jean?' Lauren asks me, seriously, like some eager market researcher.

'*Jean*? Did you say your mother's name is Jean?' the sales assistant interjects.

I roll my eyes, fearing the obvious. The repetition of my own first name has brought me round entirely from the Versace trance. 'Jeans for Genes . . . jeans for Jean . . . Jean Genie . . . that is *so* cute! And such a cute name too: *Jean*. One syllable . . . a little bit feisty . . . a little bit sexy.'

'Mum was named after James Dean you know?' Lauren confides, keen to promote the discourse. Our sales assistant looks perplexed.

'Well I was supposed to be a boy, you see,' I step in, wanting to wrest back some control over my own story and my fashion destiny. 'My father was obsessed with James Dean. Went to the cinema to see *Rebel without a Cause* fifteen times in a row when it first came out in '55. My mother was pregnant with me in that year and they were convinced they were having a boy. So they'd decided on James as a first name and Dean as a second. When I came out a girl they got creative; took the "J" from James and dropped the "D" from Dean . . . so Jean I am!'

'These are for you, Jean. You *must* have them . . . they are significant.' The sales assistant grins, delighted with herself. 'I don't know why we didn't think of them before. Levi's 501s. Red tags: the jeans that James Dean made famous in *Rebel*!' She hands me a pair of crumpled worn-looking denims.

'These look so similar to the ones I tried on first,' I tell Lauren.

'Mum these are *not* the same at all. They're pre-faded for starters. And they're Levi's originals. See the red tag? They're authentic

Mum. Like you. And they shout rebellion, and sex. But quietly. They're retrosexual.'

'Retrosexual? Lauren you're making that up!'

'Muuuum. Denim was created before the female orgasm was even invented . . . even before the French started talking about the "little death!" – They're retrosexual . . . they're about sex like it used to be . . . in your day. Stop being so difficult.'

'Anyway, what's the big deal about the red tag? Should be white . . . with "I surrender" embroidered on it! It's just another gimmick isn't it, like the sun-fading?'

'*Messaging feature*, Mum. Designed to draw attention to your buttocks. Look up there!' Lauren points to the mirror-wall, where a giant projected digital image has appeared. I recognise it as the promotion poster for *Rebel Without a Cause*. It's the shot of Dean from behind: just his hips. He has his hands thrust into his jeans pockets. 'See? Dean presenting his hindquarters like a randy primate. He's taking it right up to all those businessman in a grey flannel suits . . . pure sexual display!'

'Hmmmm.' Lauren is circling me as I stand in the fitting room entrance for her perusal.

'You know Mum . . . no . . . I don't think so.'

'Whadda you mean *no*?'

'Maybe I was wrong. I think you might be a bit short in the leg to wear that looser, high-waisted style. The rise is too high on you. They make you look . . . dumpy . . . short.'

'How can you measure style in inches?' I ask, eyes narrowed, lifting my chin for defiant emphasis. 'I'm sick of you trying to tell me what to wear, restricting my choices. You don't understand me, Lauren. Nobody understands me.' Lauren gapes, incredulous.

'I'm sorry . . . I was only trying to give you advice Mum.' She is trying to control her bottom lip.

'If I were to take all your advice I'd be a no-person . . . a clone. I *am* short. I have *short* legs. Are short legs a big problem for you?' My pitch has risen to a yawl. 'I wanna live my life my own way . . . I just can't follow your tall skinny rules anymore Lauren. I wanna experience things . . . be myself at all costs, and if that means walking this world on short legs, then I'm damn well gonna do it!'

'Mum ... please ... calm down. It's OK. Short legs are OK with me ...' Lauren backs away, appalled, but I haven't finished.

'I wanna live my life as if I'll die today!'

The sales assistant, her timing immaculate, marches purposefully, smilingly into the fitting room entrance.

'I see where you're coming from Jean. The world needs extremes. Youthandasia jeans are a totally revolutionary limited edition premium lifestyle pop-fashion trendy icon brand targeted expressly for the Japanese market. Which addresses the shortness issue. Try them. But only if *you want to*.'

'*Euthanasia* jeans? Euthanasia? I wasn't serious ... I don't want to die *now* ... *today* ... Lauren, please?' I turn to my daughter, bleary from the first wellings of tears. She opens her arms to receive me.

'She's suggesting euthanasia,' I whimper. 'I'm not that old ... I'm not even sick ... it's only my legs, and they're not that short. They still work ... I don't want to ...' Lauren helps me back into the fitting room, snivelling and overwrought.

Once I am back in my familiar beige slacks I feel re-made, re-orientated. I am also ravenous and manage to convince Lauren to abort the makeover mission in favour of lunch at Cranks Salad Bowl, her favourite. She encourages me to order the spinach pie. 'Full of iron and Vitamin B, Mum. Useful in the prevention of early onset dementia.'

Over lunch I vow that next time someone asks me what kind of legs I want I'll ask for short, stretch beige. I'll tell them to hold the history. I'll pass on the drugs but ask for an option later on the sex. And when I try the stretch beiges on for size, before I ask how they look I'll demand the truth: the basic, clean, un-faded un-streaked non-contrasted un-embroidered truth.

'Do my legs look short in these? Because if they do ... I'll kill myself.'

Wardrobe Guises

Alice Sladdin

Royal wine cloaks with a long froth of ermine.
Fop's frock-coats.
Slutswear stretchy black micros.
Sarong sensuality.
Police-stern trousers.
A girlhood of faded sundresses.

Suburban Burlesque
True strippers laid bare

James Roberts

I was beetling along with Doug in his 1975 blue Volkswagen, trying to get to the Findon Hotel before 8.30. A weird mob occupied the backseat – Casanova, a Roman soldier, a baby and a chook. Doug kept his eye on the road and ignored them.

'I got into this business at Uni. My friends were working bars at night for eighty dollars. I thought two hundred dollars sounded a lot better so I started doing singing telegrams.'

We herbed into the car park beside a hot Commodore. Doug grabbed a mass of pink stuff from the seat and started stripping down to his jocks.

'I saw this as easy money, not performing as such, just put on a costume and be an idiot.'

He wiggled his way into the narrow tube of pink lycra that didn't quite cover the waves of curly hair on his manly chest. Somehow the thin shoulder straps looked insufficient. He adjusted the stiff net tutu on his sturdy hips.

'Be loud and own the situation. If you go in there thinking you look like a dickhead it doesn't work.'

Come to mention it, the goatee beard and black boots didn't really go with the pink tights, fairy wings and blue nylon wig.

We walked into the pub dining room. About thirty people looked up and laughed as Doug homed in on the victim, Rae. When he spoke his voice gained an octave and a sexual preference.

'*Have you ever had a singing telegram before? No-o-o-o-o? I can tell you don't want this one either.*'

Shrieks and laughter from the sympathetic friends.

He ushered her to a central chair.

'*I'm Sugarplum and I'm your birthday fairy come to wish you lots of birthday wishes.*' He swung his hips, an overgrown Shirley Temple.

'*Are you wishing real hard? You're probably wishing I'd piss off, right?*' There was a roar from the assembled guests. Rae turned red.

To the tune of *Beautiful Dreamer*, with suggestive asides to the audience, Sugarplum sang the telegram. Excerpts:

She's obviously a girl who gets around
That's why she knows every bus driver in town
But that's not the only time our gal's in disgrace
After one or two beers she's right off her face
But she loves a good joke we've been told it is true
Which is just as well Rae 'cuz this joke's on you

Hearty applause washed over Sugarplum and Rae before he led a stirring version of 'Happy Birthday'. Rae blushed for the last time as Sugarplum departed with a waggle of his bum that rivalled Marilyn Monroe's in *Some Like It Hot*.

Doug is a thirty-four-year-old contract teacher. He never knows from year to year if he's got a job or not, so he keeps doing 'grams on a part-time basis.

'It's also an outlet for performing. I s'pose I'm a bit of an exhibitionist.' Since Doug was again taking his clothes off in a public car park, I saw no reason to disagree with him. I wondered if he'd ever had any trouble.

'Only a couple of times. Once this big fat woman yelled, "We've paid for a stripper, we want a stripper!" She lunged out of her chair and tried to rip off my jewel-encrusted undies. I pushed her down and ran away, half-naked. Another time I was doing a chook in a backyard party for some biker types and about halfway through they started chanting, "Stuff the chook, stuff the chook." I got scared and ran off before I got stuffed.'

Tracey climbed out of her shiny Holden Astra. We were in the car park of a swank restaurant in an old bluestone mansion. She wore an elegant black dress, attractive make up and a nicely cut, soft hairstyle. In one hand she clutched a large CD player, in the other, a red and black suspender belt and stockings. Slipping off her shoes, she began wrestling the suspender belt into position under her dress.

'I'll change *anywhere*! It doesn't worry me no more!'

Inside, about twenty-five people at four tables turned as Tracey's powerful voice burst out, 'Hey, it's the birthday boy!' She swooped on young, blushing Darren and sat him in prime view wearing a dunce's cap.

'Hello everyone! I'm here to sing a telegram because it's Darren's twenty-fifth birthday!' she sang, encouraging shy Darren to much merriment from the crowd. A few stanzas:

You love fishing and never catch anything they say
But you're good with your hands and your tool they tell me . . .
Don't worry be happy . . .
When you drink too much you go very pale, my dear
And you tried to throw Jerry in a fountain but dropped her I hear . . .
Don't worry be happy . . .

Then she taught him to dance, demonstrating leg kicks, hip wiggles and pelvic thrusts. To the big-band sound of 'Big Spender', the duo strutted their stuff. Leering trombones announced the striptease.

Tracey started to bump and grind around Darren. Crossing her arms suggestively, she made short work of two hidden Velcro fasteners that ingeniously held her dress together. In one smooth movement she slipped it off.

Underneath, she wore black knickers and bra, suspender belt and stockings. She would have made a good model for Ruebens: bright eyes, lily white skin, and ample energy reserves on a rotund figure.

There were gasps around the room, nervous laughter and guffaws. Women snickered into their hands. Men chortled.

Off came the suspender, which she used playfully as an erotic fan belt around Darren's neck. I wondered how many people in the room could do what she was doing. If fat described her physical shape, it entirely missed her character: stout, bold, fearless.

Tracey, age twenty-three, weight 140 kilograms, has been doing Fat-a-Grams since she was seventeen. A professional seamstress by training, she works four nights a week.

'I wouldn't go out there every Saturday night just for the money. I get a real *buzz* out of it. The smiles I bring to people's faces far outweigh any leers or snide remarks.'

It was hard for her to grow up overweight, a condition caused by a hormonal imbalance, but she didn't let the taunts get her down.

'I think if you feel confident in yourself you can do anything. Some women judge me by my looks, thinking, "Oh God, I'd hate to be her." If they *only knew* what it was like to be me. I wouldn't change *for the world*, not at all!'

Most of the time Tracey gets a great response for her performance. But on a few occasions she has experienced the darker side of human nature.

'One time a slob in a pub tripped me up. I was lying on the floor while he was trying to rip my pants off. I just punched him in the face, kneed him and left. I remember feeling so annoyed that no one tried to help me.'

What riles her most is when people treat her with contempt. 'I did this 'gram at West Lakes, an eighteenth birthday at the parents' house. As I put my leg on the chair to take my stockings down, the kids pushed me backwards. I fell over and rolled down this slope towards the lake.'

'The parents couldn't believe it when I walked out. As I drove away the mother ran beside the car, trying to pull the aerial off. I stopped and said to her, "If you wanna touch it, go right ahead but you'll be on the *ground* in five seconds flat." I woulda *decked* her.'

Stout. Not fat, stout.

I raced out to Hope Valley to get there by 10.30. There were a lot of cars in the street and a blonde nurse in a white uniform standing outside the cream brick house.

Whether Kay Lee was waiting for me or looking around for grappling gear to climb the Himalayan driveway I couldn't be sure. She looked nervous clutching her little medical bag and adjusting her gold-rim glasses. 'I've only been doing this for two weeks,' she confessed.

We conquered the concrete slope and fronted the house. Through the vertical blinds we could see a sixtieth birthday party in full swing. That is, in full sit ... very well-behaved. Stan opened the door. Apart from his stunned expression he looked in pretty good shape. Kay Lee sat him down beside a table shouting with food. Cakes, sandwiches, dips, chips, savouries, a whole snapper; this wasn't a party, it was laying in for a siege.

'Hi, I'm from the *Artificial Insemination Association*. We've heard that Stan is turning sixty and this is his last chance to make a donation.' From the laughter around the room I recognised the sweet sound of anxiety mixed with relief. She drew a sizable plastic container from her bag.

'Stan, I'd like you to make a sample for us tonight ... if you could *just fill this little bottle* that would be wonderful.' The twenty guests sitting around the room roared their enjoyment. Unbuttoning his top shirt buttons to test his heart drew more laughter. Stan started to get into it, adding, 'Better check my blood pressure as well.'

'*And the rest!*' someone piped in, to raucous merriment.

'All your inoculations up to date?' she wondered as she pulled out a huge hypodermic syringe. It was tougher than I thought to qualify as a sperm donor.

After more medical testing, Kay Lee read the birthday telegram. The oohs and aahs from the group told the story well enough. In spite of being a Pom, falling asleep in front of the tele and making boring home movies, Stan was a good bloke. He tried to hand back the sample bottle.

'Oh, you can keep that for *later*,' Kay Lee said to hoots of laughter. They applauded as she left, the party coming alive.

'That was the *best* nurse I've done,' she said breathlessly. She looked slightly high, coming down off an adrenalin rush.

I found out the twenty-year-old agriculture student was doing 'grams because she loved the attention. When a Super Chook performed at her hen's night she was so thrilled she rang up the company the next day and secured a job doing casual work.

Her only regret is younger people asking her to strip. Older audiences are more sympathetic and an eighty-third birthday stood out as her favourite show so far. But every night's different.

'The next guy I'm doing has one leg,' she said as she got into her car.

From Hope Valley I raced across town to a disused shop on a Croydon main road. The ancient interior suggested a 1960s suburban butcher shop, a marked contrast to the sixteen young glammed-up Greek-Australian women lining the walls. There was more eye shadow in the room than oxygen.

In the centre sat the queen of the hen's party: solid, twenty-nine-year-old Marina. She was wrapped in a white sheet, made up with bright rouge cheeks, thick lipstick, outrageous eye make up and a feathered headband. She had the extreme look: as her friend Sally described it, 'Brides need to be overdone.'

They also needed male strippers.

In his tie and tails, Troy might have been suitor or servant. He wrapped his red silk scarf around Marina's neck, twisting it around in rhythm with the thumping music and pulling her closer. His pelvis had Elvis written all over it. To make sure his intentions were clear, he drew the scarf back and forth between his legs.

The tie came off, followed quickly by the jacket and shirt. Squeals intermingled with laughter, cheers and a dozen camera flashes. Underneath that modest exterior, Troy was built like a pocket Hulk. Lacking only the green skin, his sculptured body showed every muscle to its best advantage. For punishment, he took her hands and rubbed them all over his chiselled chest.

Still rocking that pelvis, he flipped off his shoes and dropped his daks to his ankles. More squeals. He swooned to the floor and demonstrated the lost process of impregnating lino. Hysterical laughter rocked the guests. Marina had to pull his pants and socks off so he could do an astonishing backwards somersault.

Freed of all clothing constraints except a discreet black G-string, he rubbed her hands over his tight, thrusting bum. The girls roared. He danced around the room, pelvis-rocking with everyone, including Marina's mother, who enjoyed it as much as her daughter's friends.

When the music stopped, they gave him a rousing round of

applause. Seeming almost shy now, in his evenly-tanned naked-ness, he read out the telegram. Excerpts:

Another sweet girl about to bite the dust
Today's the day to give in to your lust
So live it now, without any fears
'Cuz this is your last opportunity for the rest of your years.

Troy is twenty-four years old, works as a machine operator in a factory and does stripping telegrams part-time on the weekends. His impressive physique is the result of intensive body-building – up to an hour and a half every day.

'One reason I started stripping was because it cost me a lot of money for body-building. I wanted to get something back from it.'

The first few jobs required a couple of stiff drinks but after eight months he is comfortable with the job. Apart from the money, Troy enjoys hearing ego-boosting comments.

'I think it's important to look good,' he said, climbing into his car to head for the next job. Judging from the reaction of Marina's friends there was no doubt about that at all.

Doubling back across town to get to Newton by midnight I passed an ambulance racing the other way. Saturday night on the road was a dangerous time to drive but the show had to go on.

I sensed the dark house amid the jumble of factories. A heap of powerful V-8s jammed the drive and 'Foxy Lady' blared from the backyard.

Dave, one of four brothers at the buck's night, offered me a beer and a small pipe. I chose the libation. About a dozen bearded, tattooed guys sat around drinking from green cans. I noticed I was the only one without a checked shirt.

Tim, the twenty-five-year-old Buck, occupied a chair in the centre of the garage. He nervously stroked his goatee and pondered married life.

Tina arrived, accompanied by her boyfriend Tony. Standing aloof in a long black coat, high heels and stockings, she seemed over-dressed for the venue. That was soon to change.

Dave turned up the volume on the relentless blues number, 'Bad to the Bone'. Tina danced to Tim, backwards and forwards, turning to the circle but always bringing herself back to him. The men watched her steadily, intent. The word 'vulpine' came to mind.

She threw off the coat, then slowly took off her black bodice, dancing all the time. Next came her small skirt and shoes. Tim had to take off her stockings as she rocked to the rhythm.

'*Bad to the bone!*' wailed the singer.

'Bad to *my* bone!' joked Dave.

The quip cut the ice and some of the leers loosened into smiles. Tina flashed a grin. Probing for the best camera angle, the eldest brother crawled under Tim's chair and took some snaps looking up at her. Laughter drowned out the driving music.

Still dancing, she removed her garter belt. She had to nudge Tim twice to undo her bra strap – more laughter at his expense. Underneath all her clothes Tina was petite, evenly tanned and fit. In a final gesture she slipped off her G-string. Tony quickly threw her the coat. Under its cover she flashed the group and briefly kneeled over Tim. It was the last glimpse of a naked woman he would have . . . until tomorrow.

Afterwards, the only flashing twenty-six-year-old Tina did was with her smile. She enjoys her work, considering herself a dancer rather than a stripper.

'Most of my shows, I try to make them clean, respectable. I mean, a lot of strippers to me are disgusting. They're more interested in showing you everything they've had for breakfast, lunch and tea.'

She especially likes doing shows for older people.

'Afterwards, some of them get up and try it. They *really* spin me out!'

Her grandfather often comes with her to help with the navigating and crowd control. 'He's pretty embarrassing when he wants to be, especially when he has all the old ladies around him getting him drunk.'

Driving has been the big drawback for Tina's career – she has had three car accidents. Now she feels shaky on her legs and her knee threatens to go out. She works out in the gym three times a week but she can see the time when she will have to give it up.

'I tried modelling, but the agency went bankrupt on me. I want to get into fashion, my own boutique. I like clothes, especially Thailand clothes; they make a lady look like a lady.'

As Tina left one of Tim's best mates staggered up to me, loyal to the end. 'Will you put fifty dollars in his pyjamas so he can take the first bus out of town in the morning?'

I wandered outside through a cloud of pungent smoke. 'Purple Haze' swirled out of the speakers. It had been a long night of suburban burlesque.

Découpage

Glenda Inverarity

I wander into Rayleen's craft shop looking for something to help me bide my time in the evenings. Most of these shops only sell the raw products but she has many finished projects on display. I like the pink découpage photograph album with fairies. It speaks: challenging me to make one. I've always enjoyed decorating the front cover of my notebooks, so I think that découpage might be a good hobby.

I've never been terribly good at crafty things. My grandmother and aunt had been very crafty and made all sorts of things, from cane sewing baskets to lavender bags. My sister inherited that gene, but not me, too impatient. I start things but never finish; they look amateurish.

I am easily inspired. Last time I visited my sister, she showed me her latest quilt, the one that was featured in *Quilting Australia*. They paid her a fortune to publish the pattern. She'd never need to join a little craft group like this, she's too busy being president of the Victorian Quilting Association.

Rayleen is friendly and suggests that I join a class to learn properly. There is a vacancy in the Thursday morning group, at the tables in the back of the shop. I know this would be good for me. It will mean that I don't have to admit to anyone that I'm desperately lonely. All I have to do is pretend that I enjoy learning the fine art of découpage and I'll be part of a group.

I select a large placemat for my learning piece. The paper has nice Tuscan images that will suit my décor – an arched lion fountain, pedestals under pots with flowers and leafy vines – and sandstone background paint. I seal the paper on one side and wait for it to dry while I give the placemat its first coat of paint, before sealing the back of the paper.

They don't talk about their private lives. I'm glad because I don't want to talk about mine. I work out that most of them are from the other side of the railway line and older than me but I like their lack of polish. They try hard to shock the new kid in class with dirty jokes and funny stories. I'm not easily shocked and when I am I don't let it show.

Cutting out the lion fountain is easy but the flowerpots are tedious and I try to hold my tongue right as the sharp scalpel digs into my cutting mat. I feel all fingers and thumbs. I put the second coat of paint onto my placemat, brushing the opposite way to minimise the brush marks.

There's a good movie to go and see. They all love *Calendar Girls* and tell me I should see it. I don't like going to the movies, all those people talking, letting their newfangled mobile phones ring and rustling their sweet wrappers. I read the review so I know what it's about; I'll wait for it to come out on video and watch it at home. They say they want to make their own nude calendar, just for fun. I laugh but they don't.

The third coat of paint, brushed in the same direction as the first, takes time to dry, so I continue cutting the second flowerpot. It's tedious but I persevere. I buy a photo album with sticky pages to keep the pictures in, just as the other women do. I keep cutting.

One day there are some funny stories about condoms. One thin woman with fine grey hair tells how her husband left his French letters home when they went on their honeymoon, so they couldn't copulate. She describes one evening when he became particularly amorous and despite several cold showers, eventually had to satisfy himself, much to his embarrassment! She tells the story with such truthful graphic detail, we all laugh until tears stain our cheeks. I want to write her life history but she stops coming shortly after that.

My fourth coat of paint finally dries and I spend time arranging and rearranging the pictures on my placemat. It seems a bit bare so I have to go back to the cutting board for more leafy vines to decorate the top. I stand back to admire it and Rayleen makes some suggestions about what would make it look better. More pictures to cut.

Sport talk is boring. They love the gossip about how naughty Carey was to have that affair but he's a good footballer and that's what people should remember. His private life is his own and the media should leave him alone. Of course, Hookesey was an innocent victim in the fight that killed him. I don't open that can of worms. Yvette doesn't like football either. She gives them some anti-football ribbing and wishes there was less sport on television.

Glue, roller and Glad Wrap are added to my little box of découpage tools. I spend more time arranging and rearranging the pictures until I'm sure it looks artistic and clever. Rayleen helps again so it won't look like something from a grade three classroom. I start gluing the pictures on and make such a mess that it takes the rest of the lesson to wipe away the residue.

Julia brings a cake on her birthday, a big lemon cream cake with ingredients so evil that the cream is the healthiest part. Almost every week someone brings a recipe for us to copy and try but I'm not a very good cook. I tried Rayleen's savoury pinwheels once but they stuck to the tray. I have to serve them mashed and messy but they tasted terrific. Rayleen is an excellent cook and Yvette says she'll pose for the calendar when Rayleen writes a recipe book. Rayleen grins and says she's finally found inspiration!

I'm ready to seal my placemat now and I save money by using my painting brush. The first coat goes one way, the second the other way, the third back the other way. It starts to look nice and shiny. I tape the back ready for Rayleen to pour with resin. I find the tape doesn't stick very well but I think it will do the job.

John Howard is a liar and Mark Latham is the golden boy. They unanimously agree that he'll win the next election. This is a Labor heartland, so what else could I expect? John Howard's too chicken to call an early election, he needs time to find some dirt. Politics doesn't get as much talk time as sport.

The placemat looks wonderful, the resin is as hard and shiny as expensive ones I've seen in the shops. Unfortunately the resin drips under the tape and I have huge lumps of it on the back. It needs to be flat and smooth so I spend the lesson sandpapering the back. It's hard work.

They have some strong views about refugees who really should be able to speak our language and pass an English test before they come here. How do we know which ones are terrorists and which ones are genuine? The people smugglers should get jail for life but not at Australia's expense. That's not the way the tax dollars should be spent. The ones who come in boats are the ones that can't speak English, so the government should spend more money protecting the coast.

I buy a large piece of felt for the back of my placemat and I spend time cutting it to size and gluing it on. I only have to wait for the glue to dry and I'll have a finished piece of découpage. I was heavy-handed with the glue and some of the felt became hard instead of soft and smooth but it's not too bad. Maybe I could make placemats for everyone for Christmas.

Rayleen announces that she's selected the recipes for her book and her daughter will type them up but she still needs to find a good photographer. Helen says it's no use making a calendar because it's already been done and no longer a novelty. But nobody's done food in the raw. Old women displaying food in the raw in a recipe book, now that's a shocker! Their husbands are all dead but mine isn't and I say that I don't know what he'd think. They laugh and ask if I've learned anything from them yet.

Beetroot wedges and green rocket leaves on a bed of couscous in an earthy brown bowl are a good contrast for my lily-white wrinkled flesh. I hold the bowl between my legs while the photographer fiddles with the lighting and angles before the shoot begins. No, this year I think I'll give everyone a recipe book for Christmas!

Esteem

Alice Sladdin

There is a stranger in my bed.
He smiles and kisses
beyond our upright animosity;
we placate our bodies' whims.
We sleep together,
the dullard roars, the dark of a small town around us.
Under our blanket
we sigh
and push into each other's warm bodies.
The nights I please him,
he pleases me,
And we join at mouth and fissures.
Twitchy to indifference,
nauseous at the thought of a perfect shape
I falter.
He persists,
lost,
pays my dentist bills as bile burns tooth.

I bite
well
with these
and raise my hackles.
In the morning
he irons his own shirt,
is gone.
Me, at best,
dressing gown disadvantaged.
Or else fear has me
cowering under stale bedclothes
too conscious of my bladder
and white thighs
to emerge.

George

Rikki Wilde

He's on the doorstep. He is not as I imagined. Not as described. I had advertised in a queer-friendly newspaper's personals column for 'a mature, attractive male.' Admittedly I didn't spell out or stipulate what I meant by 'attractive'. I didn't want to put off potential suitors. I thought I should cast my net far and wide and do the sorting later.

The ad read:

Young, inexperienced camp guy, 18, seeks attractive, mature male. Reply Box 9989.

The guy who stood on my doorstep was not, in my humble, biased opinion, anything that could be described as attractive, even allowing for a certain amount of ubiquitous self-delusion. But you had to admit he had guts.

Later I found that he understood the psychology of my ad far better than I did, what it revealed about me: that I was naïve, easily influenced, easily dominated and probably easily discarded.

He was in his forties or possibly fifties. He looked pretty old to an eighteen-year-old. The fringe of grey hair around his large bald scalp probably made him look older than he was. He was short compared to me and weedy, if not skinny. He wore black-framed glasses and a heavy cable-knit cream turtleneck jumper.

I was expecting an Adonis. After reading his letter a hundred times, my fantasies were definitely out of control. He had described himself as attractive, mature, an English teacher at an exclusive Victorian boys school near Geelong. He had agreed to pick me up from the flat where I lived with my mother and sister at seven o'clock on Friday night. Then he was going to drive me the ninety-seven kilometres back to Geelong and had promised to return me to Melbourne later that evening, even though he would then need to drive back. He didn't seem to flinch at the idea of a three hundred kilometre round trip. He seemed to want me to visit him at home.

In hindsight, a more neutral locus for a first meeting would have been appropriate but I was desperate to get away from my suburban flat, even for a short time. I was astounded that someone would drive so far to spend an evening with me.

We drove to the unit in Geelong. It was a newly constructed homette that he had recently purchased – brown brick, very Seventies, very austere. Unfortunately it was located near the water treatment plant and sometimes an odour drifted across Verdun Street.

We both enjoyed talking about things we were reading. I had just finished *The Waves* by Virginia Woolf and I had found it mesmerisingly poetic. I had also recently read Quentin Bell's popular biography. We got talking about Joyce and he said *Ulysses* was completely incomprehensible. He had just attempted to read it in the new Penguin edition. He said I could have it as a gift; it bore his name. His name was George and he was originally from England.

He made a lovely salad that night with vegetable oil and vinegar and he spun some records that he had brought back from England on his hi-fi. There was Cat Stevens, Sly and the Family Stone, Little Feat's 'Dixie Chicken' and Steely Dan's 'Countdown to Ecstasy'. Some seriously funky stuff; I could tell he didn't like it much but he was trying to impress me. His DJ friend in England, who had given him the records, had to be a cool cat, judging by his musical tastes.

His bedroom was very spartan, austere and grey. No curtain covered the window that looked onto the blackened backyard.

He undressed quickly and methodically and lay naked on the bed like an already stiffening corpse. He was a skinny bloke, bald, with wiry grey chest hairs, knobby knees and a small flaccid penis. He wore a rueful smile. Under the harsh light of the naked light bulb he did not look inviting. But I was young and innocent and did not know what aroused me. I knew this guy before me did not.

I needed to learn what I found physically stimulating and I suppose you could say it was my ignorance that this guy was exploiting.

What annoys me now, what I did not know until a while into the relationship, was that George was an expert, a specialist, in helping ephebes like me find our true identity, what we really did want and what we didn't. And I discovered after a while that I didn't want him. He was totally selfish in his lovemaking – if unresponsiveness and coldness could be described thus.

It was very cold in the room. The unit was built on a concrete slab, which meant that it would be vermin free forever. He lay there passively, like a log. If his body had been erotically appealing perhaps this inertia would not have mattered to me. This guy would have needed loads of technique. He didn't appeal to me so what was I doing in bed with him?

Well, I liked him. He had driven me all the way to Geelong in the white Mazda. And, as I said, I craved any opportunity to escape my deadening, suburban existence. I admit it, I saw this guy as a meal ticket, a ticket to anywhere else. But I was not sophisticated enough, or I did not value myself enough to realise he was getting far more in return for his investment than I was.

I had been a very thin thirteen-year-old. I was not tall at that point, as my year eight class photo reveals – we were classified according to size, tallest at the back, medium in the middle and the short ones in front. When we had PE with Mr Wieniawski I was extremely self-conscious of my body, it seemed entirely without shape or curves, like a beanpole, as someone jokingly remarked.

I was ashamed to be so skinny. So when we went to the change room for PE period I hung back, disrobing very slowly, until most of my class mates had gone from the room. This strategy usually worked fine, except for the times when I was ticked-off by Mr Wieniawski for being late. But one day, no matter how slow I was, I noticed that Kevin and Billy, the class bad boy, handsome in that Troy Donahue kind of way, were hanging around even longer than me. Why wouldn't they go, so I could reveal my baggy stained underpants to nobody?

At first I thought they were hanging back to 'play' with each other but later I decided they wanted everyone to leave so they could go through the pockets of all the lifeless trousers to see if they could find any spare change. On further reflection, as no money was ever reported missing, maybe my initial impression was correct, or maybe no one left any spare change in their pockets.

They told me to get lost. What was I waiting for? Billy was naked except for his briefs. He shimmied up to me, dancing like a Turkish belly dancer, revealing his sculpted pecs and a protuberance in his white nylon briefs.

'Is this what you want? A suck on this? Go on, take it out of my undies and suck on it.'

I was shocked but turned on. I was sorely tempted to obey his command. But I thought it was probably a provocative joke at my expense and I hurriedly removed my pants to jibes of 'Droopy Drawers' when I revealed my yellowish undies. That was the whole thing about school. There was a lot of homoerotic stimulation but I was too frightened to be out – although later at school I was virtually out. (A branch of gay liberation from Melbourne University had infiltrated our school.)

But I digress. George would lie on the bed, a dead weight, and I would fool myself that I was enjoying the chore of trying to arouse him. Eventually he would make a feeble ejaculation. That first night, as George rolled over, I felt very frustrated and entirely sleepless. My thoughts were racing as George drew away and I pulled a thin blanket over myself.

Suddenly the whole bed shook. George's entire body, lying next to mine, had contorted in a massive wave from head to foot. I didn't know what to think but I was panicking: had he had coronary? In the darkness I was almost too afraid to speak but I managed to croak, 'Are you OK, George?'

He sleepily replied, 'Of course I'm OK. I was just drifting off to sleep when you spoke.'

'But your whole body just convulsed. I thought something bad was happening.'

'Don't be ridiculous,' he said. 'I always shudder like that before

I fall asleep. Most people do. It's something that humans have inherited from the apes.'

'What?' I said. I had never heard anything about this ancient mechanism before.

'Millions of years ago the primates would make one last tensing of the muscles to make sure they were safely located in the fork of the tree. After that, they would relax all the muscles and ligaments in their body and fall asleep.'

I closed my eyes and thought about how many hours there were until daylight.

Throb

James Roberts

Easter was looking resplendent in his best Sudanese Ambassador get-up, stolen from a costume shop. I hoped that my crumpled suit didn't show the stains from our night in prison. It always seems a poor introduction to a prospective business relationship to announce straight up that you have a criminal record.

Mr Rich Shoes came across the office wearing his shiny patent leather numbers, from the House of Ricardi if I wasn't mistaken.

'How do you do, gentlemen? Allow me to introduce myself– Marman Granthi.' He put out his beautifully manicured hand, complete with a big fat sapphire ring. His hair was jet-black and oiled and he smelled like an expensive car.

'Nguagua Rolpuita Marnuopi,' Easter said, shaking his hand. 'My friends call me Gua.' *Gua*. Where did he dig that up?

'William Teller,' I said. 'Bill, for short.'

'We don't get many visitors to our manufacturing facility,' Marman said. It made the factory sound like a NASA lab in a shining new tech park.

'I can understand that,' Easter said. 'It's not easy to find.'

'We go out of our way to be discreet.'

Discreet, eh? I wondered what the guy produced. Hookahs? Silk? Sandals? Guns? Maybe he made exploding hollow points for the AK-47s on the street. Maybe he made lava lamps filled with hash oil.

'How can I help you gentlemen?'

'We're buyers, Mr Granthi,' Easter said. 'We're on a fact-finding mission to Panga and we're strongly positioned to pre-order next year's forward supply.'

Marman tapped his fingers together. 'Tell me, what do you sell, mainly?'

Easter looked at me and I looked back at him in that way that tennis players do when they find they have somehow managed to bat the ball over the net: the ball's in your court, baby. The basic problem was ignorance – neither of us had a clue what the guy manufactured.

Easter coughed once. 'I sell . . . what sells.' He glanced around our cosy trio to see if this made any impact.

'Such as?'

'I am a buyer; I buy what sells,' he said. 'I don't buy if it don't sell. What I buy is selling. I sell buying.' Marman and I watched him as if hypnotised. It was like watching *Being There* on very heavy 'ludes. And it went on, as if Easter was himself on some kind of loop.

'There is no buyer without a seller, no seller without a buyer. If I buy, I sell. If I sell, I buy. Selling, buying, they are the one and the same to me.'

Marman nodded out of politeness, or perhaps it was putting him to sleep. I jumped in.

'He really is an abstract thinker, isn't he? It's a combination of the earthy feel for the product and tremendous theoretical reasoning, backed by a study of all the major philosophers. He can really move mountains, Mr Granthi,' I said. 'A tour of your operations would absolutely help him to identify the major sellers for our markets. And after that I promised to take him to the library for more Wittgenstein!'

We all laughed, even Easter. We'd just settled down when he said, 'Who's Wittgenstein?' That really cracked Marman up. He must've thought we made quite a team (little did he know). When he looked up, his face had relaxed and he was genuinely smiling.

'Gentlemen, I have to say I don't normally take visitors into the plant. But as you have come so far, it would be rude of me not to. You did say you were looking to pre-order?'

'If it sells, we are buyers,' Easter said.

'Well then, follow me,' Marman said. He turned and led us out of the office through a bland cream door into the factory.

The smell hit me straight away: the unwashed in large numbers. And the noise; a combined assault from drills, hydraulic presses and electric motors. The interior was dim and lit by too few fluoros and no daylight. It was difficult to see very far past the jumble of crates and boxes that rose up everywhere.

We followed him into the factory, weaving through the maze until we reached a more open packing area. He reached into a box and pulled out two pink plastic vibrators. I could fairly say it was the last thing I was expecting – guns or drugs would have been more likely. A lava lamp would have been more likely. But we made a fair show of examining them and Easter was the one who recovered quickest.

'Throb,' Easter said. 'Have they got *throb*?' I hoped this was a technical term he had picked up somewhere in his travels.

Marman paused. 'How do you mean?'

'My clients always ask me. You know, man, does it get your *juice* going?'

'Our products are very popular, sir. We have a high acceptance rate among our customers.'

Easter reached down to the nearest cardboard box and picked up a massive black dildo. He lifted it up and examined its shaft, running his hand over the surface.

'I've seen better in Mali,' he mumbled.

'I beg your pardon?' Marman said.

'This is one big mother but does it *throb*?'

Marman took it from him and placed it back in the box. 'That is a passive model, sir. We try to market something for every taste. Over here you will find our extensive range of powered products. Allow me.'

This was promising. I wondered when he was going to get to the good stuff. 'Do you have anything that *moans*?' I asked.

Marman paused in his tour. 'You must understand, Mr Teller, we have a very wide range of clients. We cater to many tastes.' He clicked his fingers and a factotum appeared from behind a stack of cartons and crates.

'Yes, Mr Granthi?'

'Mr Teller wonders if we have a model that moans?'

The man appeared to be a mass of shoulder gyrations welded to a hip replacement. His traditional cap was pulled low over his eyes and he bobbed and weaved like a cork on the ocean.

'We're working on it, sir. Working. Very hard. In development, it is, in R&D as we speak. Moaning.'

'I could move a *lot* of moaners,' I said. 'I've got a lot of requests from the Tri-State area. They've got chains and outlets there begging for something with a bit of real passion.'

Easter jumped in. 'As a matter of fact I also have many unfulfilled orders for *screamers*. What do you have in the screamer line?'

Marman appeared slightly uncomfortable. He adjusted his silk tie and swivelled his chin to ease the pinch of his collar. 'We've focused our business development on quieter models, Mr Marnuopi. All of our market surveys indicate a preference for less buzzing, you know. It's a distraction for some. A contemporary intrusion, unwanted.'

'Agreed one hundred percent,' I said. 'Who wants to get off to a *lawnmower*? But we're talking human sound, not machine sound. Big diff. We're talking *moaning* and *screaming*, not that sick *whimpering* the Japanese seem to go for. What is it with them, some kind of pain fetish or something? And *not*, I hesitate to say, not accompanied by the kind of roar that you might expect from, say, a double-overhead cam one-point-five litre Fiat with exceptional fuel economy.' I couldn't resist a glance at Easter. It was the rental car we'd just sold to escape a pair of dangerous barbers armed with razors.

'My friend is right,' Easter said. 'Who wants a supercharged turbo in the boudoir? The clicking of tappets and the thud of pushrods?' He was trying to be helpful but he was way out of his depth and it just confirmed why he could never work as a journalist.

'That was some time ago, *Gua*,' I said. 'That went out with the Village People.'

'As a matter of fact we do have some models with pushrods and others with a beaded cam-chain,' Marman said. You could have knocked me for six.

'Show please,' Easter said, going ahead with vigour and anticipation, looking back at me with a leer. 'I must see those at once.' He loved nothing better than proving me wrong.

Marman led us further into the factory. We came into a bay with perhaps twenty young boys sitting at low tables. Long black hoses hung down from the ceiling and supplied air pressure to drive the screwdrivers and riveters they worked with. Dozens of boxes of different sized screws, washers, bolts and nuts surrounded their workspace. The basic mechanism, a clockwork vibrator, was piled up in the hundreds around every table. The boys grabbed these units and screwed a power socket onto them, then covered the works with a plastic sheath and fixed it home.

'Good little workers, eh?' I said. Easter had stopped and was staring at them.

Marman picked up a model to show us. 'See the pushrods on this model? They provide periodic lateral expansion of the sheath.'

'You mean *throb*,' I said. 'Look at this, *Gua*. I believe this is what you were looking for.'

It took him a moment to turn around. 'Your workforce, Mr Granthi . . .'

Marman shook his head. 'I know. If they would bath more often it would please me. I'm sorry. And this is the beaded chain model.' He held up the works, showing a chain encircling a drive wheel at either end of the motor. 'The spherical beads transverse a vertical path along the length, over the top and down the other side. Our customers find it most pleasing.'

'They're very young,' Easter said.

'Ah, youth,' I said, 'It's wasted on the young.' Marman and I laughed. Easter turned to me with something burning in his eye.

'You're not that old yet, Gua, there's hope for you yet,' I said, slapping him on the back.

'Come on, chum, how many of these mothers do you think you can move?'

Easter dragged his gaze down to the vibrator in my hand. He took it and weighed it, turned it over. 'These mothers? How many can you supply?'

Marman rubbed his chin. 'With a significant forward order, I can gear up the production process to make whatever you need,' he said.

'Really?' Easter asked. 'How about ten thousand?'

Marman seemed eager. He nodded. 'We could accommodate that.'

'The workforce isn't too small?'

'We can always get more workers,' Marman said. 'That isn't a problem.'

'Excellent,' I said. 'I am beginning to see the potential we've got here, Mr Granthi. With your supply capabilities and our unmet demand, I think we can really *go* places.'

'There's more to see,' he said. 'The Phallus Centre is only one of our hubs.'

He took us down a narrow passageway through stacks of spare parts. Under a flickering light, a clutch of young girls worked at rows of wooden benches. Marman picked up a rubber mouth that one of them was working on.

'You see we have a range of models to accommodate all tastes. This oral unit comes in Anglo, Afro, Asian, and Arab. It has a vacuum valve to ensure optimum fit for each customer, regardless of size.'

Easter was looking at the girls. I nudged him with my elbow and said, 'But does it bite?'

Marman laughed. 'Not unless you want it to,' he said.

The girls kept working. None of them looked up or gave any sign that they were aware of our presence.

Easter picked up another mouth from the bench. 'What's this?'

'That is one of our newer models, you'll note the difference.'

Easter pulled back the lips. There was a full set of white teeth covered with wire braces. I whistled. 'That would sell like *hotcakes* on the convention circuit.'

'We get many of our sales at high school and college reunions. We hope for the same success in an older market with this one.' He picked up another mouth, reached inside and pulled out teeth.

'Dentures?' Easter asked.

Marman nodded. 'Fully customisable and serviceable with or without the teeth.'

'A fella could have a pretty good weekend in Dallas with this stuff,' I said.

'What's your unit cost?' Easter asked.

Marman smiled. 'Our costs are ours to know, of course. Standard commercial confidentialities apply. Our wholesale price on this is about twenty dollars.'

This time it was Easter who whistled. 'That must be a healthy margin. Your wage bill would be low with these kids.'

Marman shrugged as he led us away. 'It's true they don't earn much. But my costs are higher than you think. I have to look after all their living expenses. It's not equivalent to an American workforce.'

'They live here?' Easter asked.

'Yes, and I have to pay all their costs. I have to feed them, house them, clothe them and buy them medicine. It's a never-ending drain on my resources. The costs keep rising all the time. It can easily get out of control.'

'Costs,' I said, 'the enemy of profit. The splinter in the eye of every businessman. The bane of a market economy.'

Easter glared at me behind Marman's back. 'Are they orphans?' he asked.

Marman stepped over an oily puddle on the floor. 'Some of them are and I consider it a civic duty to take them in and give them an opportunity in life. I feel they are receiving a scholarship in life and I am their benefactor. There are different cases here – others are contributing to their family's income. They may be the only member of their family to have a job. Some are disabled or disfigured and this is the only work they can do. A few of them are working off debts from loans I made in good faith to their parents who defaulted.'

We came out through a crate canyon into another work bay, dingy and gloomy in the half-light and the smell of bodies and bodily fluids increased excrementally. I pulled out a handkerchief and put it to my nose. Easter gave me an unfathomable look, as if

I was a creature in a zoo from another planet, newly arrived and on display for the first time. I turned away. There were about half a dozen children scattered around the bay, hunched over their dirty work benches.

'You do employ cleaners, Mr Granthi?' I asked.

'Yes. I apologise for the odour here. These employees are on restrictions.' He picked up a plastic vagina. 'The pudenda units are a popular success in a number of our best markets.'

'How do you mean, restrictions?' Easter asked. 'I don't mean to pry, but we do have responsibilities to our suppliers . . .'

'They've broken the law, stolen from me. I'm trying to run a business and I can't do so if it is sabotaged from within.'

'Fair point,' I said. 'Employee theft is a *huge* problem for manufacturers right around the globe. What do they steal here?'

'Nuts, washers, screws, anything small enough to hide and sell.'

Easter picked up a tiny washer and held it in his big fingers. 'And how much would they get for this, would you say?'

Marman looked at Easter more critically. He put the vagina down on the bench and sighed. 'Mr Marnuopi, I realise it must seem harsh but it is the constant drain on our resources that undermines our profitability. A small theft committed over and over not only reduces the bottom line over time, it also erodes employee loyalty.'

He walked over to a dark bench and pointed to the girl behind it. 'For example, this thief was caught stealing a number of times. I gave her repeated chances to prove herself. She ran away, we brought her back, she ran away again, we brought her back and the next time she ran away she took these others with her.' He gestured to include the other children in the bay. 'Effectively, they are all criminals and by rights could be locked up in jail. As that would serve no one's interests, I have brought them back here to repay their debt.'

Easter was looking closely at the girl. Of all the children in the room she was the only one to lift up her head and look him in the eye. Her long black hair was matted into clumps of felt; it hung over her face in oily strands. It might have been the dim light but her skin appeared jaundiced and thin. There was no blood in her lips, they were as pale as the rest of her. Her cheeks were hollow and her neck was a narrow stick below her shrunken face. The lack of meat made her cheekbones stand out and her eyes protrude. Her experiences were etched in the poisonous expression with which she observed us. If she recognised Easter, she made no sign of it. Nor did she move her foot, which was shackled to her bench with an iron chain; the foot Easter had grabbed when she was dragged screaming past us in jail.

'Well, you certainly have them quiet and well disciplined,' I said. 'Better here than on the streets, eh? At least they're learning a trade. At least they're doing something useful for society.'

'Exactly how I think of it, Mr Teller,' Marman said. 'What kind of place is prison for a child?'

'No place,' Easter agreed. 'No place at all.'

Finding Ignacio

Henry Ashley-Brown

His flat, when I find it, is upstairs in a building made from unpainted Besser blocks. The ocean is not visible. The street is sketchily planted, narrow and grey, fenced with corrugated iron. I begin to wish that the sea would rise sufficiently to flood it with the life of water, perhaps up to his balcony so that he could moor a small rowing boat to the corroded zinced pipe that is the balcony rail, one day to sail away from this place, following the rhythms of tides and wind. If only I had known how idle wishes sometimes work perversely and diligently to come true.

He is quick to answer the door. I am hugged. His brown eyes are signalling that he is not only pleased to see me but that he is pleased with himself. He has been writing. He is lively.

'I'll close the window,' he says. 'Can you smell the fertiliser?'

The air does smell enriched.

'Blood and bone?' I enquire. 'I quite like the smell. I'm a gardener. I think of sheds. I like sheds.'

'You wouldn't if you lived here,' he tells me. The windows are dusty. There's a cement factory, he thinks. Over there, but he's not sure exactly. There are several amongst the many hot iron rooftops, flat and skillion, that could have evolved for the making of fertiliser and cement.

'I'm going to move,' he says from the end of the room where he has his desk, a computer and a printer under a streaky window. I am given the piece of paper that has emerged from the printer.

'Do you like the title?' It is 'Hupomnêmata'.

'What does it mean?'

He chuckles and does not answer.

It begins: *'The already said says something about me. About my absence. Of the full presence assigned to it. In this structure marked by self-presence there falls into the world my absence . . .'*

'Why?' I ask.

'My absence from class was noticed the other day,' he guffaws, 'so I became invisibly present!' For such a small person he has an out-of-proportion laugh. It is brief, like the bang of a champagne cork when the contents fizz impatiently into the world. He has written a lot more, each sentence slipping out of sense. I would not like to be his university supervisor. Ignacio seems to have specialised in a kind of slipperiness that connives with laughter.

The conversation somehow moves to Marcel Duchamp, Derrida, Barthes, the postmodern and deconstruction. He has taken over the interview. I am being quizzed. From time to time he seizes my paper and inserts a sentence. He becomes author.

'Help me with these,' he says suddenly, grabbing a cardboard box and standing on a chair. He removes a bare light bulb from its socket. I hand him the cardboard box. He has made a hole in the centre of the base. He attaches the box to the light fitting, replaces the light bulb and switches on the light. He smiles triumphantly. The box is now a lampshade. It has been deconstructed.

I follow him as he deconstructs the rest of his boxes in the same way. Square, some rectangular, a few with slits in the sides that project small crucifixes across the ceiling; he has replaced the former contents with light. Some of the boxes announce their weight. This pleases Ignacio. The contents, 'do I get it', are now lightweight. He promises not to tell anyone else. They can work it out.

I try to retrieve the interview. 'What's an early memory?'

A look of rage crosses his face. Is it because of the cliché?

'In the shopping centre, in Melbourne, not long after we arrived from Spain, three or four louts pushed us into a corner and told us we were dagoes and wogs and that we should go home. My mother was paralysed with fear. She was too small to do anything. They leaned into the pram and spat all over the baby's face. My mother shrivelled up after that, like a dead flower.'

I pick up the piece of paper he gave me before. He looks out of the window. There is a silence. I am shocked. I put my arm around him. My eyes fall to his writing. I read:

'Lost in the others fall-out. In the thought of others; in short pre-occupied with the flight of a self known to no other but myself. So intimate is the servitude this self keeps to hide it-self that as a consequence my looks belie my (r)age.'

Ignacio looks nowhere near forty and although he spends much time pulling the nails out of what appears to be solid in life, has a very strong set of rules about what is right and what is wrong. He intercepts my intention to sympathise. 'Beer?' he offers.

'I can do it,' I say, going to the fridge. There is nothing in the fridge except two small bottles of beer; they are not very cold. He must have bought them only a little before I arrived. There are no glasses. We drink from the bottles.

I have been seated near his deconstructed coffee table. He is watching me. There is no top on the table. I carefully put my bottle through the vacant space onto the floor without showing any surprise. Ignacio booms a large laugh from his small brown body. He is everything in appearance that a caricature of a Spaniard should be. He is short, black of hair, has a large nose and brown eyes. His skin is brown. I had never before met a person from Spain who actually looked like the Anglo-Saxon version of all Spaniards. Ignacio doesn't like his appearance. His siblings are tall and fair.

It is hot in the flat with the windows closed and no softening blinds or curtains. He goes into the kitchen and returns with some of his favourite books. One is about Marcel Duchamp. Is Ignacio about to assail me with jokes about books being 'food for thought'? I decide to enthuse about Marcel instead. But he has another book on Marcel, also in the kitchen, even better. My curiosity is aroused. I have to look. His books repose on a brightly coloured tablecloth he has found in an op-shop. The tablecloth covers the kitchen stove. The stove has been deconstructed. It is now a table.

'So how do you cook?' I ask.

'I don't.'

'Ah,' is all I manage.

'I eat everything raw.'

'Everything?'

'Yes.'

'Even meat?'

'I eat meat, but I prefer fish. I'm mostly vegetarian.'

Somewhat taken aback I recall that I ate raw fish in Japan. I also remember that my mother, anaemic as a child, was made to eat raw liver.

It is time to escape Ignacio's flat (for a while) and the smell of fertiliser, the gritty presence of cement dust and the heat. Drinking the warm beer has made me hungry and it is obvious Ignacio has no food. He has probably spent his money on the beer.

'Sarah's,' I say. 'Have you been to Sarah's in Port Adelaide, the vegetarian restaurant? Can I take you to lunch? I've been wondering if you could have a look at my Spanish homework?'

Ignacio likes the idea.

During lunch we discuss how we met. He's not quite sure.

'At Brook's,' I say, 'under the pin-ball machine.' It was my turn to surprise him. 'No,' I correct myself, 'it was at the Cargo Club. You were there as a performance artist and were making a salad. Brook was there too and he introduced us. It was later that I saw you again, under the pin-ball machine.'

He remembers. He had a bad back and Brook arranged for a mattress in the spare room but the pin-ball machine had been too heavy to move. Ignacio had to camp on the floor between the machine and the wall.

Brook is a garage sale addict, amongst other things, hence the pin-ball machine. 'The Pachinko', as I call it. I prefer the Japanese name, its onomatopoeia appeals. Brook also collects people. Ignacio has attended one of Brook's men's groups.

'Why?' I ask.

'I wasn't sure about my masculinity,' he answers. 'I had a tough time at school. Anyway, it was an opportunity to explore issues.'

'You were constructed by the school system and peer group pressure and wanted to reconstruct yourself?' He looks surprised. But I had not caught him out.

'Exactly,' he smiles. 'I decided to integrate my masculinity and my femininity and aim for androgyny.'

He is looking pleased with himself and also enjoying his 'Salad a la Sarah'. A plump olive is fixed to the end of his fork. Ignacio is having fun. Two young women enter the restaurant. The olive he is about to eat hovers in mid-air.

'Androgynous?'

'Mmm.'

'What does that mean sexually?'

There is a whoop of laughter that dislodges the olive. Eyes turn. He is infectious. People are smiling, even though they don't know what the mirth is about.

'It doesn't mean I'm gay, or bisexual. It means that I'm not caught in the 'either/or' of sexuality and sex-role stereotyping. Everyone's different, but not many allow themselves to enjoy their difference. They conform to an idea of how they should be and what they are permitted to do as male or female. They limit themselves. I have given myself the freedom to be me as long as I don't hurt others in the process.'

'So, as an artist you are also in the process of creating yourself?'

'Yes.'

'But surely,' I say teasingly, 'as Janet Wolff points out in *Aesthetics and the Sociology of Art*, even with the help of your favourite persons such as Marcel Duchamp, Derrida, Foucault, Barthes, you still end up becoming part of the history of art you are trying to avoid?'

'You've been peeking at my essay!' he accuses. 'Didn't you read the ending?'

'No,' I confess.

'You don't know my ending? I will give you a clue.' He scribbles in my notebook. 'It's by Barthes,' he adds. 'You can look later because when we go back to my place I want to show you my wardrobe. And you're invited to our end-of-semester presentation at the university. I'll send you an invitation.'

The two young women are interested in Ignacio. 'Do you have a partner or girlfriend?' is my next question.

'Now and then but most of them get a shock to find out that I'm forty and not the twenty-five I look. Anyway I seem to have been too busy.'

'Finding the self? Studying? Travelling? Working?'

'Yes.'

'Have you been to Spain?'

'Yes, it was wonderful. I felt at home straight away. I was accepted I was so happy. I found other people like me, who even *looked* like me, believe it or not!'

'But you came back.'

'Family. They're all here. I missed them.'

Stepping out of the seclusion of Sarah's and out of Ignacio's inner world, into the busy Friday afternoon world of shoppers and traffic makes me forget to look at what he has written in my notebook. I am looking at it now.

'Do you want to see my wardrobe?' He is laughing again.

Is another deconstruction awaiting, I wonder?

The wardrobe turns out to be just that – an ordinary wardrobe. It is full of costumes. They are extraordinary. I am completely distracted again, so it is not till lately that I find his note. Ironic, I think, but typical. Trust Ignacio to deconstruct my interview and turn me into audience.

'Made them myself.' A sewing machine reposes on the floor of the wardrobe. 'My alter-egos,' he announces, putting on and taking off, 'or sub-personas. There are many of me; more than Marcel Duchamp had. Want to come to the end-of-semester performance?' he repeats, 'I'll do you an invitation. I'll use my new paper. It's black. That's because I make it from old newspapers and the print colours it. But I have added more black, so I can use white ink. I'll send it closer to the date so you won't forget.'

The invitation does turn up, accompanied by a picture of his own face superimposed upon a Joshua Reynold's portrait known as the *Blue Boy*. I can almost hear Ignacio's chuckle.

It is to be the second-last time I see Ignacio. His new outfit makes him look slightly like an ancient Assyrian when he appears with his group. The spotlight picks him up in profile as he makes his entrance. He is moving but his body is perfectly still. He has done it again; still movement. I realise that he is on his beloved miniature silver scooter. The whole routine is accompanied by silent gesticulation, rather exaggerated, like a Marcel Marceau mime. It is otherworldly, ceremonial. The unfolding however, leaves it to the individuals in the audience to invent their own meanings.

'Going on holidays in a couple of weeks,' he announces when the show ends and I am making it known that I was really there.

He invites me to his raw food party and I go. It is at someone else's house. When I enter the kitchen I see at once that the stove has a tablecloth on it. He has apparently found a raw food group. Most of the guests look pale, unhealthy and unhappy. I am offered a plate of assorted sea things, strong smelling, impaled on toothpicks. I settle for the carrot and celery.

'Organic,' says the hostess.

Some people have grey skin, others bare feet and there is discussion about the use of juices to fight cancer. So many sick people are turning to the organic greengrocer for advice. Do I have a compost bin?

'Going already?'

'Ignacio, tell me, where are you going for your holiday?'

'It's a farm in northern New South Wales where you get food and accommodation in return for work. It's near a rainforest and a long way from cement dust and reconstructed residues from chicken farms and slaughterhouses.'

'Reconstructed?'

'Yes, into fertiliser. They're already deconstructed when they arrive!'

We say our goodbyes and I wait to hear from him. No one seems to know exactly where he is. It is Brook, the friend who had made the space for him behind the pin-ball machine in the spare room who rings with the news.

'I think I'd better come down to your place Brook. Is it alright if I come now?'

'He was found dead in bed. He'd been fasting and at first the doctors thought he had starved himself to death but an autopsy has shown that he died from a brain haemorrhage.'

Now, much later I return to his 'Hupomnêmata' and read:

'I will stand there, looking on at the audience directly and indirectly addressing them in a speech made up of the already said – a kind of self-portrait made to be seen and heard. My only confession is that I fear I will be compelled to avert my eyes. Listen to the fallen whisper, my absence as a place of presence that fills up the lack of me. Listen to the sound asleep emptying out of myself.'

'An autopsy!' I hear someone's muted exclamation, a snatch of guilty laughter after several drinks at a gathering of Ignacio's Adelaide friends. His body has been sent to Melbourne for cremation. We are aware of the full presence of his absence.

One of his friends has had a reverse mohawk to commemorate the occasion. He has shaved a strip of hair off his head, from front to back. It runs like a white line on a highway at night under headlights.

'An autopsy!' continues the voice. 'You mean he ended up being deconstructed? He would have liked that!' There is shock and reluctant strangled laughter seeping from the group. The sub-voce news escapes from hissing attempts at restraint. Soon everyone is laughing helplessly.

I am looking at what Ignacio wrote that day and come across something he pencilled in at Sarah's during our lunch. It is from Barthes: *'the birth of the reader must be at the cost of the death of the Author.'* The hand is firm and confident.

Somehow Ignacio has managed to have the last word.

Stanley Spencer's 'Resurrection'

Cath Kenneally

They're climbing out from under slabs
chubby and clothed
in florals and tweeds, cardies and singlets,
children hauling parents by the hand
back into the light of
the green English countryside
Mildreds and Georges
Stanleys and Glorias
Marjories and Freds and Sylvias
tubular limbs
tight-packed flesh
restored to cushioned springiness
wide faces blank
in unaccustomed sun
dazed, winded-looking

not euphoric
they crawl over the ground
like fat blind worms
reacquainting themselves
with touch and smell
oppressed again by gravity
all this upheaval caused
by unseen agents, lounging
somewhere on high
dangling their still-echoing trumps
everyone waiting for The Man
to say what comes next

Note: *The Resurrection* is in the Tate Modern Gallery, London

Nearly Blind

Patrick Allington

One day, in her fortieth year, the famous artist drove her jalopy to the end of a five-mile dirt track. When the vehicle's rusty radiator cracked in the heat she walked home, dragging behind her a bleached bull's skeleton that somehow held together like a museum display.

That night she threw most of the bones onto the pile behind the studio but she propped the skull on a table against a mud-brick wall. She set up a fresh canvas and began to paint, occupying herself with the cavernous holes where the beast's eyes had been. She added a wandering crack between the eyes, a fracture caused by the impact of a rifle butt or by the hard head of a rival bull. Through the night she fussed with a white blob of paint, trying to achieve a colour that was so brilliant it shone but that still revealed the slow torture that the wind and the rain had inflicted on the skull.

In the morning her face was cracked and peeling. When she blew her nose, dirt, sharp as crushed glass and moistened with blood, made a curious pattern on the tissue. Once the tissue dried she slipped it into her sketchbook to look at later. That day, and all that week, she painted with her swollen feet recuperating in buckets of antiseptic.

Her eyesight was perfect then. The sandpapered, cayenne curves of New Mexico were simple and raw and beautiful. But that was half a lifetime ago. Her world had slowly become murkier. As her eyes failed, she painted less. Her body felt bloated with inspiration that she could no longer release. She felt so heavy that she sometimes could not rouse herself from her favourite armchair but at the same time her friends became so alarmed by her weight loss that they tried to fatten her up with spare-ribs and Budweiser and chocolate mudcake.

She fought courageously but eventually submitted to her body's demand that she should no longer paint. She needed to free herself from the images that crowded into her mind. Rather than lose her gift slowly and painfully she resolved that she should finish her life's work with one act. She wanted to carry her imagination away in a golden garbage truck and dump it somewhere special. But she found such a termination impossible to execute at home. She needed a new place. She needed to make one last trip, somewhere far away. Somewhere different but the same.

'You're an icon,' Caroline announced at Sydney airport. 'An absolute bloody icon.' She dropped her cardboard sign (a crude drawing of a smiling daisy that said *Welcome to Australia!*) and grabbed the artist's fragile hand in both of hers. She shook so hard that the artist thought she might take off.

'That's how doctors talk: *you've got cancer ... terminal bloody cancer.*'

Artificial winds blew from aluminium grates embedded in the floor and the roof and walls of the terminal. They buffeted the artist from all sides, helpfully conspiring to keep her upright. 'So you're the hired help?' she yawned. 'Well, get me out of here. I'm exhausted.'

'Hired? You must be joking, I wouldn't dream of taking money. It's an honour to be working for you.'

'An absolute bloody honour?'

'Imagine: for a whole week I get to be your eyes.'

'Come on, girl, what are we waiting for? I'm dreaming of the hotel's hot spa.'

'No,' Caroline said firmly.

'No?'

'I cancelled that reservation. I'm not leaving you in some smelly hotel room, not even for one night.'

'It's the Hyatt.'

'I don't care. I've got the spare bedroom all ready. You're coming home with me and I'm cooking you dinner. I'll do a chickpea stew.'

'Wonderful.'

Caroline put her arm around the artist's waist and steered her toward the exit. They moved slowly, like lovers strolling beside a winding riverbank. The artist shuffled, her swollen, sweaty feet tight within dirty sneakers, her kneecaps creaking, her breathing laboured.

Caroline stopped suddenly and said, 'Can I ask you something?'

'What?'

'If you're blind . . .'

'*Nearly* blind.'

'But why did you come here?'

She smiled grimly. 'To look around.'

Study a photograph of the artist when she was a young woman, before she laid her head open on canvas upon canvas upon canvas. Find one that the photographer took, there are several in any decent history of American photography. Observe her neck as she looks away, her steely muscles pulling at unlikely angles underneath her taut skin. See a close-up of her bony shoulder, protruding like a camel's hump. Or focus on her back, the slight curvature of her spine and her dry-ice skin. Or her fingers, reaching like a fine vine across her chest. Raise your eyes to meet her steady gaze and acquaint yourself with the calm confidence of a master.

With each photograph a variation of the artist stained the paper. The photographer – her lover, her husband – had an engaged subject to work with and so it was when she painted. She visited the same place a thousand times, each time sketching the same squat hill, the same dry riverbed, the same mid-morning sun. But each picture was different, because she saw that the desert, far from being a discarded husk, was vibrant and alive. The photographer's genius was with frozen moments whereas her dusty landscapes flowed all the way to the sea.

Then her eyesight began to deteriorate. The hills stopped eroding and the rivers, for all she knew, were so full of water that they had burst their banks and washed all the beautiful bones away. She kept trying, but she could no longer tell if she transferred the image in her mind onto the canvas. She couldn't see if she was creating something radiant or something tame.

They flew into Alice Springs late in the afternoon. By dusk, the artist sat hunched in a deck chair, allaying the hard plastic with pillows and towels, while Caroline swam laps in the tiny hotel pool.

'For Chrissakes girl, how much longer are you going to be? I'm so bored.'

Truthfully, she felt quite relaxed. She gargled another mouthful of Wild Turkey and held the glass close to her nose to mask the putrid smell of chlorine. She swatted flies with her free arm. Caroline touched the wall and bobbed at the shallow end, looking up at her.

'Your face . . .'

'What about it?'

'It's beautiful in this light.'

'Hmff.'

'It's like a sketch on a piece of paper that's been screwed up and flattened.'

'God help us.'

'Are you sure you don't want to have a swim? It's lovely in.'

'Don't be ridiculous.'

Caroline swam another lap and then said, 'I was wondering . . .'

'What now?'

'What was he like?'

'Who?'

'You know who I mean . . . *him*.'

The artist sat back, opened her eyes wide and smiled. Caroline looked up at her, expecting a wise anecdote about the photographer, or a criticism, or even a risqué tale.

'What was he like when he was young?'

'My dear girl, I wasn't born when he was young.'

'Ooh,' Caroline giggled. 'What about when he was old, then.'

He had a black callus on his finger, she remembered, hard as granite it was. When he got too old to work he sat shaking in his favourite wicker chair by the bank of Lake Breckinridge, a rug over his knees. He couldn't even hold a camera but that finger still pressed an imaginary shutter. And every time it did his moustache would quiver. It was as if someone was tickling him but he couldn't laugh.

'Are you alright? Yoo hoo?'

'You can take me back to my room now.'

'But it's lovely outside.'

'I'm tired. And I've got nothing else to say.'

Budding artists, earnest enthusiasts like Caroline, were forever bothering her. Many of them made pilgrimages to New Mexico. They hoped that the distance they had travelled would overwhelm her. They dared to imagine that she would invite them in for dinner and perhaps offer them a bed for a night or two. All of them believed that they possessed unique insights into her mind. All of them knew her intimately.

One young artist, a tall lad with arrowhead sideburns, banged on her door one day, begging for advice, expecting to be told he was prodigiously talented. He held out his portfolio, all neat borders and plastic covers and shaded hexagons. She stood in the doorway and squinted at him. She was too busy for this and she disapproved of his grubby, ripped shirt. When he ran his fingers through his hair, which he did ten times a minute, he presented her with a full view of his underarm. She slammed the door in his face.

'But I'm thirsty,' he called out and then, in desperation, 'I think you're wonderful. You remind me of a nun.'

Despite her irritation she opened the door long enough to ask, 'Why a nun?'

The question startled the boy. It was something he'd overheard someone say at a gallery. He had no idea what it meant.

'I don't know,' he stammered. 'You're so ... beyond us all. Or maybe it's your sense of fashion.'

She snorted and slammed the door again.

He called out: 'Would another day be more convenient? I'd love a memento, perhaps a sketch. It wouldn't need to be any good, just something you're going to throw out.'

A couple of years later the young artist had a breakthrough exhibition in Chicago. He sent the artist an invitation to the opening. He scribbled: 'Thanks for everything! I'm playing with the big boys now' between the printed words and an image of a bewildered pig.

She rather liked the pig. It had wide, wet eyes. It seemed to have been crying but it looked too happily stupid to ever be heartbroken. She remembered the boy and thought that he had produced an excellent self-portrait. She stuck the pig to her fridge and gave its ears a tickle every morning.

She stood barefoot in the hot red sand and imagined that she was wading through a cool, pure river. The gentle current tickled the soft skin between her toes. She stood still and her feet sank slightly into the mud. A miniature crab nibbled her toenails. She squatted, leaned forward and the water was cool on her pasty lips. Caroline rolled down the window of the rental car and called out, 'For heaven's sake, close your mouth, you don't know what might crawl in. Wouldn't you be more comfortable in the car? I've got some lovely Bach playing. You could wind the window down and stick your head out, if you must.'

'Leave me alone.'

Suddenly, she knew that she was right to come all this way. She opened her mouth wide to taste the new desert. She guzzled more dirt than her lungs could hold. It hurt to swallow, but it was sweeter and thicker than molasses. She lay on her back, writhing and moaning with pleasure.

'Where are you when I need you?' she called out. 'Here's a photograph worth taking.'

Suddenly, the photographer was beside her. He stood, as always, self-consciously upright, expecting that strangers would equate his imposing height with his eminence. His soft eyelids began to blink as the dust swirled around him. He began fidgeting and flicking at himself with his hands to try and keep his suit and his impeccable white moustache clean. And then, almost immediately, he was gone.

'The desert is fit for snakes and other creatures that live in holes,' he complained as he faded. It was a parting shot but he smiled as he said it.

She lay on her stomach and hugged the ground. She kicked and swatted it and tried to bury her face in it.

'Oh God,' Caroline screamed, abandoning the Ford's air-conditioner and running to her side. 'Oh no, don't go, don't die, *not here.*'

'Calm down, girl. I'm exploring.'

But Caroline took hold of her back like she was a cat and lifted her out of the dust. She squealed, freed an arm and swung it as hard as she could. She barely connected but Caroline was so stunned she dropped her with a thud.

'I'm sorry, I'm so sorry. Are you alright? Where does it hurt? Can you feel your toes?'

The artist lay still. Caroline dropped beside her, drowning or baptising her with hot, flat Sprite. She shoved a finger down her throat to make her cough up the earth she had drunk. Over and over she said, 'Speak to me, speak to me.'

Eventually, she turned over, opened her eyes and pushed Caroline away. 'I'm alright,' she said. 'Just go away, will you, go for a jog, do some yoga, do something. I won't be long.'

She sat cross-legged on the ground. She stared straight ahead, her wide-open eyes staring through strands of sweaty hair, her lips joined, her arms loose by her sides. She sat there a very long time, fortified by the still heat. She knew that the sun was setting when the bright cloud ahead of her turned pale and when the air around her grew loud and heavy with millions of insects.

She stood up and began to paint the sunset. She didn't use brushes and canvas and oils, just the movement of her body and the cool breeze that sprang up around her. Caroline watched and fretted and thought that she was dancing wildly. But the artist could see the imprint of the movement of air she was leaving behind. The colours were bold and the strokes were graceful and precise.

She turned in wider and wider circles, her feet sliding across the ground, her hands reaching towards the fading light. She stopped eventually, not from exhaustion but simply because she had finished the painting. She stepped back and stared at her sunset critically. It was as big as the sky itself.

'It's your finest work,' she said to herself. 'You can't do better.'

28 *Point of View*

C h r i s t o p h e r   L a p p a s

It was 28's suggestion to begin this journal. 'Recording your thoughts may be therapeutic,' she said. 'Sometimes there are parts of ourselves that need to be gently teased out. We are protective, like an oyster shielding its precious pearl.'

But there are emotions inside my shell that I am uncertain about. I fear that if they escape, I will have no control over them. Just like the time I thought my son had lied to me. I blamed him for turning the power on to my work-shed. I started lecturing him, about safety and honesty. He hadn't actually done anything wrong; it was a misunderstanding, between him, his mother, and me. But I couldn't stop, not once I started. That shed was a dangerous place with all those power tools in it. Andre cried and the more he cried the angrier I became, and the angrier I became the more I yelled at him. I tortured his feelings and destroyed his innocence. At the same time I killed a part of myself. I killed that part of me that promised I would never do anything like that to my son.

Andre and I talked, after I calmed down. 'I'm sorry,' he said, as only a child can, a child willing to take the blame in order to keep the peace – and to protect love. It made me wonder how people can start out being so similar when it comes to emotions yet try so hard to become different. Trying so hard makes you forget and eventually you forget how to behave and how to forgive. If I could be like anyone in this world when it comes to forgiveness, I would want to be like my son.

Approaching her room from the corridor was like entering the scene of a murder. 28 was slumped backwards over the middle of the bed, her knees bent and hooked over the side, her sockless feet limp and motionless. Stepping cautiously around to her head, my eyes followed her arms to her hands and her delicately parted fingers dangling loosely. Her hair was spread like tentacles over the faintly patterned linoleum floor. Wearing tights and a loose shirt with long sleeves, she could have been a dancer in a dramatic pose. But was she dead? Her mouth seemed twisted, her face like an ogling grotesque mask. It took some time for me to realise that she was trying to smile. She must have sensed my concern and emitted an awkward, indecipherable squawk.

Keeping her head inverted while trying to speak forced the corpuscles of her face to swell. 'It's gravity,' she remarked. 'The weight of your flesh, especially your cheeks pulling down, distorts your face. Then the dizziness and the nausea nearly cause you to faint. But that goes if you concentrate, if you focus on just one object.'

I began to tilt sideways, first my head, then gradually my whole body, trying to relate, trying to assimilate.

'I'm just looking at the legs of the chair,' she informed me.

I tried to do the same.

'And at the skirting-board behind it.' She pointed. 'And at the dust on the floor, and a narrow strip of paper that seems to have found its way under there. I don't recall seeing it yesterday.

'As a little girl I used to bend over backwards from a standing posture, like a contortionist, and look at the world upside down while walking on my hands and feet. Then later on at school, in about year seven or eight, I became interested in gymnastics; I would have been content to spend the rest of my life hanging from bars, ropes, poles, swings, rings, trees, dining tables, doors, clotheslines, anything – you name it, I hung from it. Bat-girl! "She excels at gymnastics," the instructor said on my report card. "Pity she doesn't apply herself as enthusiastically to Maths and Science," wrote my house-master.

'It really is a different way of looking at the world, inverted like this. Not for everyone though, my younger sister would howl when she was hung upside down.'

I was beginning to lose my balance and was glad to have us both back to the upright position.

A soothing 'Mmmm' issued from 28 as she rose, scratching her head, 'It tingles, stimulates the scalp.'

She inquired about my son but I had little information to convey. Andre's condition is still the same, flat on his back, upstairs in the children's ward, tubes inserted in his nose and mouth, needles penetrating his veins. At every visit I smooth back his golden-brown hair and plead with his eyes for a sign. But there is no response, no sight of the striking blueness of his full-of-fascination eyes that once penetrated a world so fresh and alive for him. His eyes no longer scan intensely, no longer question, no longer weep. Andre, a twelve-year-old who only weeks ago had told me how grown up he had become – too old for Harry Potter books – now lay as if his life had ended, like a broken angel found fallen to earth. My hands, hard and rough, seem too large and too awkward to caress that angel, seem as if they would damage his tender skin and draw blood. If a stranger happened by, they would believe they were witnessing an intimate moment between two souls, one comforting the other in a compassionate exchange. But there is no communication between us, no awareness by my son of my presence, no matter how hard I try to believe there is.

This morning, two nurses arrived to wash Andre. I had spoken with them many times individually but now they arrived as a duo. I stood up politely. Little was said in reply to my greetings except, 'It's bath time.' My first reaction when they began to draw the curtain around the bed was to leave. The smaller, more frail nurse hesitated, fixed her uniform, checked the band that held back her dark hair and fiddled with the trolley of cloths, sponges, and a bowl of water; she was uncertain whether to begin while I was there. The taller one, much larger in all proportions, with a gentle, chubby face, knew the routine. She did most of the lifting and the huffing and puffing. Clearly an old hand at this, she grunted out monosyllabic commands and otherwise indicated directives by thrusting her dimpled chin about as if conducting an orchestra. I was in the way. And I felt uncomfortable. But I was glad I stayed. At the end I took a towel and helped dry my boy – his back, under his arms, around his neck. 'Have you washed behind your ears properly, Andre?' I dabbed his cheeks and eyelids as softly as I could. Each time I lifted the towel away I hoped that his eyes would open and he would smile.

These entries have been written in retrospect. 'Retrospect' is a word that 28 often uses. I like its power – it takes you somewhere quickly. 'History' is the opposite, both the word and its meaning are slow. So is 'yesterday'. Gradually I will catch up to the present. I have so much to write – about my son and about my strange encounters with 28, an intriguing woman. These pages are more a composition of her words and her ideas rather than my own and not always conveyed as eloquently and accurately as they deserve to be, but I will do my best to assemble at least some of her style and even a little of her eccentricity, perhaps something like this:

28

Different angles. Altered perspectives. A smorgasbord of languages and foreign styles. Making no sense, without words. Words forming on the page. Words twisting in the mouth. Unable to think any more without words. Words were designed for stick-on labels. Conveyor belts carry slabs of processed thoughts. But not from the soul. Soul thoughts. Soul-writing. At the end of the day, the language we employ, is of little consequence if meaning is not conveyed. The shade of a person's skin or the texture of their hair, the propensity of their nose or the configuration of their toes. Try looking at a human body, try looking at a tree, just try to look at any object, without forming words. Maybe, if we look at the world, and look at ourselves, without the usual words, then we will be able to construct soul-words.

Without warning – snap – like an acrobat or one of those beetles that click, her position changed, she was arching herself backwards on top of the bed with her navel pointing towards the ceiling.

'This is called kissing the sky with your belly.'

She held her position for three long breaths before gradually lowering herself down again to the mattress. Flat on her back, she brought her legs straight up – L-shaped – then continued until her toes came to rest on the pillow above her head.

'We must take a different approach, you and I, come at life from different angles. Be on the look-out for alternate signs.'

Her voice was muffled, her face buried beneath her thighs.

'You know, everybody is entitled to a different point of view. When I was climbing the stairs in that office building, before they brought me to this hospital, I was thinking about an obnoxious little dribbler back in the sandpit when I was just a babe, a tyrannical sand merchant who was chauffeured around in his high-tech, three-wheeled, carbon-graphite, space-shuttle. "This is my domain," he would shout from the sand – although perhaps not quite in those words. Then he would beat his chest and thump the ground, "Gruff!" Perhaps he was entitled to his views as much as I was to mine, even if I couldn't agree with his determined ways.

'I was taking the last few steps before drawing up to the second floor – or so the sign above the door informed me – when I stepped on something hard that scraped underfoot. It was a sharp piece of glass, part of a mirror, triangular in shape, smaller than the palm of my hand. I picked it up, able to see the reflection of only one of my eyes at a time as I tilted it from side to side. Turning the piece over, I read the remains of a few words scrawled in a cursive style on the back with some bits crossed out like the draft of a letter or a poem – ack, lac, refract – fragments like that. I think it was written to someone named Jack. I began to play with the idea that maybe my companion in the sandpit was called Jack. Maybe I was holding the shard of a poem written to him.'

She began gradually curling herself into a ball while holding an imaginary mirror to her face with one hand.

'I remember,' she continued, 'a day when he came to the sandpit with small paper flags – coloured blue, white, and red with vertical bars. He used them to crown the turrets of his castles. His mother was delighted when she returned that afternoon, declaring that her clever Jack had reconstructed the entire island of Mont-St-Michel, with its soaring abbey, fortified towers and even the humble St Aubert's chapel.

'The more I think about it now, the more I'm convinced that my dribbler was indeed called Jack. If I close my eyes I can see our parents and the caregivers introducing us and trying to teach us each other's names – and the names of all the objects in the universe. The problem was that the objects changed for me after that, they lost their identity. And Jack also became just a name and no longer my unique little dribbler. And then one day another Jack arrived in the sandpit, and later on in my other world away from the sandpit, an auntie gave birth to yet another Jack. Did this mean that all Jacks were the same, that my Jack was just a duplicate Jack?'

Rolling onto her side, propping her arm under her head, 28 now moved into a somewhat more comfortable position. Beginning by facing away from me, she methodically raised her leg in the air, up and down, like human scissors. Eventually she turned, repeating the exercise with her other leg.

28

Sometimes I assemble an idea that I think must be close to the truth, like the memory of Jack in the sandpit, then I wonder if I am just deceiving myself. So many stories and so many points of view. Which ones and who can you trust? It's like looking into two mirrors at once.

At some time, in the beginning, I believe I must have known what could only be described as an innocent truth, when I existed as a whole entity, before my personality began to split – multiplying until I was no longer certain who I was. As the years unfolded I moved further from that truth, each single part of myself opposing all the others, trying to manipulate, trying to win out.

I'm sure we are all fascinated with mirrors at some stage, crawling up to our own reflection, amazed by the ability of the other that we see before us – a miming toy, capable of imitating with precision our every movement. Yet some of us are disturbed by the presence of that other, mocking, competitive intruder.

I wonder what Jack was like. Perhaps, as a toddler moving into his second year, jetting about his parents' home in his little 'trotte-bébé', he was very happy. Happy bumping into walls, happy with his mother's soft but full breasts, happy with receiving all he demanded and happy in his infantile reality. Happy that is, until one day when he gazed into the long gilded mirror in his parents' bedroom. To anyone witnessing this event, it would seem that nothing unusual was taking place, just the normal outbursts of a child's laughter – the monkeying around, the fascination with arm and body movements and the many variations of distorted facial expressions. But perhaps Jack turned blue then white then red and began to shiver – a turning point that would change his life forever.

Gazing at himself, perhaps he realised that he was not the centre of the universe as he'd been led to believe, perhaps he saw something that resembled how others saw him. 'There are two of me,' he would declare, 'and I don't like that other one that I see, that blob that is at once inside me, yet outside me. It wants to replace me. That thing, as seen by others, could indeed be anything they fancy, anything they care to interpret me as. And how dare they! To think that who I am may be determined by them, and differently, depending on which one of them you listen to!'

He would be astonished by the idea, the unending possibilities and the uncountable perspectives overwhelming his infant mind. With his sense of self shattered, he would cringe at the notion that his appearance could and would be compared to others and by others and that he was who he was in terms of those others. 'I am not omnipotent,' he would shout, 'and this thing that I have become, this presence, or lack of it, is irrevocably common. What will become of my social standing, my position in life, my future? My God, I am one of them!'

I left her dangling backwards over the end rail of her bed, arms folded like the wings of a bat, her tone of voice deepening with the change of pressure from her new position. In a barely audible, low drone the words, 'Au revoir, Monsieur, take care of yourself,' faded behind me.

It is Sacrilegious to Desert the Body of a Book

Sabina Hopfer

The floor was moving under his feet, tricking his mind into a state of apprehension. He looked around, observing the merry crowd.

He remembered that this was not the first time he was defeated by a nausea that originated somewhere deep inside the earth, working itself to the surface and finally seizing his body. He believed he could hear a roaring noise underground, a forming of slow-moving forces – masses of land, or rocks, shifting somewhere deep below.

His body resisted at first, then withdrew from his skin, making itself smaller and smaller, disintegrating into a fragile, transparent substance the size of a tennis ball – waiting, vulnerable, as if inside a glass dome that could shatter at the slightest touch.

He thought about air; abstract, non-idealised and ungraspable. He liked its invisibility. So invisible would he be, so untouchable, yet flowing and never-ending light and every other creature dependent on him.

Suddenly a long, sharp fingernail relentlessly, shamelessly buried itself into his shrunken existence and forced his body back into solidness.

'Are you coming?' a cheerful voice invited him.

The nausea still lingering, he answered in slow motion: 'Where?'

'Anywhere. This country is large, somewhere where we'll have a good time.' Her look was intense, just like her fingernails. Her pastel complexion, untouched by the sun, betrayed her foreignness.

He didn't feel anything, only emptiness from lack of trust. She grabbed his hand, her nails digging into his palm.

'I'll show you a way out. I don't like crowds either.' She steered them through the smelly mass of human flesh.

He noticed her dress, a knee-length, jade-green kimono with red floral designs overlaid with golden beads. Like a mother she pulled him along. The walls squeezed in on him and the music, frenetic jazz, seemed to attack him from all sides. But there was the firm grip of her hand, which gave him unknown comfort.

'Do I know you?' he asked.

She laughed, not unpleasantly. 'No, we haven't met before, but that doesn't mean I don't understand you.' They had reached the door and stepped outside. 'I'm still learning, getting used to people here. I saw you standing in the corner, looking as if you needed some fresh air. So I came over to rescue you.' Her fingernails relaxed inside his palm and she looked at him as if waiting for him to take the lead.

'We are both foreigners, you and I,' she said eventually.

'I've lived here all my life.' He no longer possessed the curiosity needed to communicate successfully with other people.

'That's not what I meant. You can be more foreign in your own place than in a foreign country. Should we walk a bit?' She had a certain directness in being vague: vague about her motives and the role she wanted him to play.

'Okay,' he said, 'let's walk down to the river.'

'Yes, I'd like that.'

They walked without speaking, he with his hands in his pockets and she with a carefree, curious gait, looking at the buildings and the people they passed, her long red wavy hair bouncing freely. She had asked him to accompany her. He had never been anything else but an accompanier of people. Being dragged along was part of what he thought was the essence of life. *His* life anyway. The world held no temptations, no hopes and no desires for him. Books alone excited him. Books were his only passion.

'What's your name?' she asked.

'Paul.' They kept walking.

'Is that all?'

'Smith. Paul Smith.'

'Have you ever left this place, Smith?'

'I travel all the time, in my mind.'

A group of young people approached singing Irish songs, swinging beer bottles in their hands.

'And you?' he asked, while she turned to watch the group pass.

'They're having a lot of fun. I like that,' she said and linked her arm inside his.

He looked up at the town hall tower. The hands of the clock showed 11.30.

'You're not particularly interested in people, are you?' she said.

'What do you mean?'

'Those young people, isn't it a rare sight to see young people singing and being happy?'

'They're drunk, that's nothing unusual.'

She pricked up her ears. 'I think I can hear water. We must be close.'

'The river is usually quiet.' He tried to remember the last time he had walked and talked with a woman. His mother, last Christmas. He had walked her to church. She had asked him about his future, as if he was still a teenager with his whole life ahead of him. He was forty-two years old.

'And you?' he asked again.

'Me what?'

'What's *your* name?'

'28.'

'Beg your pardon?'

'My name is 28.'

'A number?'

'A number.'

'Very unusual.' He unhooked himself from her. 'And where do you come from?'

She cocked her head, threw her hair back, 'Do you really want to know?'

'Why not?'

'Is it that important to you?'

'You hinted earlier, saying you were a foreigner.'

'I suppose I did.' She shielded her eyes with her hands as if it was bright daylight. 'I'm sure I can see the river now.' She increased her speed and he fell behind. He was a steady, calm walker. People without destinations never hurry. She waited for him.

'You know,' she said, 'I always wonder what "having a home" means.' She paused. 'Do you sometimes feel like breaking away, leaving everything you know behind, to go somewhere you've never been before? Do you ever think of death?'

He looked down at his sandals. He had worn them for almost ten years. Her shoes looked new: red, lace-up ankle boots.

'Sometimes. Don't we all?' he replied.

'I'm from 28 Storeys. Eventually, I'll go back. Perhaps.'

'28 Storeys?'

'28 Storeys, my home.'

'Sounds more like a building to me.'

'Building is not bad, I guess. You *could* call a book a building.'

'A book?'

'A book.'

Was she insane? All he was certain about was that he was walking, late at night, with a stranger. He remembered he had done it once before, only then it had been a man who walked with him through half the city streets, talking about philosophy and how to change the world. The man had just been released from prison after a ten-year sentence for murder. His first walk back in freedom. In the end they shook hands, wished each other good luck. He never saw the man again.

'Let's sit down somewhere, shall we?' she said, leading him by the hand across fresh grass. They had arrived at the river. They were alone.

'A book,' he said, sitting down next to her. 'You said, a book.' He looked at the darkness of the water, how the gentle ripples caught the light of the moon. The moon was full tonight.

'I jumped out of a book. I'd had enough of my job, needed to leave for a while.' She took off her shoes and stretched herself out on the grass.

'Your home, or a book? I'm confused now.'

'Both.'

He didn't say anything.

'You should come and visit one day,' she continued. '28 chapters of my life: up 28 storeys. I jumped out of the book yesterday, the day it was launched.'

He thought for a minute. 'Yesterday was the twenty-eighth.'

'My birthday. I thought it'd be a good opportunity to start travelling on my birthday.'

Something started to shift inside him. For the first time in years he felt comfortable inside his body.

'Who's the author then?' he asked.

'It's quite amazing, Smith, to be here, talking to you.'

'Tell me, who's the author?'

'My creator, you mean?'

'Whatever. Author, creator . . .'

'My creator is CL.'

'What does that stand for?'

'CL, that's it.'

'Female or male?'

'I've never thought about that, that's an interesting question.' She fell silent.

He was intrigued. He wanted to know more. Maybe he had finally found someone who was passionate about books – completely insane perhaps but passionate.

'How come you ended up at the pub?' He hadn't asked so many questions in years.

She sighed. 'Oh, I just walked by. I heard people cheering, so I went inside to see what was going on. And then I saw you.' She suddenly stood up. 'You know what? Moonlight is good for your body, the best cleanser, better than washing yourself with soap. Have you ever tried?'

'Tried what?'

She started unwrapping her kimono. Usually indifferent to what was happening around him, he now became agitated. 'People may walk past, they could see. I wouldn't advise you to do that here.'

'Fear and inhibition, Smith, create enemies.' She pulled down her knickers. 'If we are not afraid of foreigners, foreigners won't be afraid of us.' She stood naked now in front of him. He watched the

125

moonlight play with her nakedness, the shadows enhancing the few cavities on her immaculate porcelain skin.

'Come on, Smith, it's good for you.'

'I'd prefer it if you called me Paul, it's less formal.'

She lay down on the grass, rolled from one side to the other, then stretched out her arms, slid her legs apart and closed her eyes. 'Paul, I'd like you to try. It revives you in a way nothing else can.'

He looked around. He couldn't believe that he was considering it. He slipped out of his sandals and took off his shirt. When he was down to his underpants he pressed his back against the grass, holding his breath.

'Your underwear, too,' she said without looking at him.

'I'm quite fine, thank you.'

Any minute, he was certain, an old acquaintance would jump out from behind a bush, laughing at him hysterically. A dirty, embarrassing joke, like they used to play on him back in his uni days. But nothing of that kind happened. So he pulled off his underpants.

'Mother,' he would say next time his mother asked him about his future, 'I'm going to take a moon bath, with lots of moon bubbles. Wanna come?'

'Feeling anything?'

'A little.'

'It takes a while, especially with beginners. You need to relax first. Focus on the spot between your eyebrows. And then feel your body sink further and further into the ground. If any thoughts cross your mind, let them drift past like clouds.'

They lay motionless, two naked figures stretched out on the grass by the river, caressed by the light of the full moon. Stars sparkled in a clear night sky. A shooting star crossed.

'Have you ever thought about freedom, Paul?' She didn't open her eyes, didn't move. 'What it means to be free?'

He cleared his throat. 'I don't know. Books give me a sense of freedom, the freedom to think. I suppose I'm glad to live in a country where I can buy any book I like and not be imprisoned for reading.'

'As long as you have the money.'

'There are libraries.'

'Freedom is more essential for me,' she continued. 'For me, it carries a notion of responsibility. Sometimes I think the more money we acquire, the less free we are. Money for some reason makes humans either lazy or greedy. And greed creates enemies, enemies create fear and fear creates more enemies. Ultimately, terror is the result. So, can we ever really be free? Free in life, I mean, not in death?' Here she turned her head to look at him.

'Well, in that case,' he said, 'are we free now, lying here naked?'

'Not if fear holds you in its embrace.' She rested her hands on her stomach. 'The important thing is to understand that we can never be absolutely free. Not within the boundaries of our bodies and the body of the society we live in. The need for travel, I think, is our need to jump into what we think is absolute freedom.'

'What if a child appeared and saw us naked?' he asked, ignoring her last comment. 'Isn't it irresponsible of us to lie naked in public, aware that a child might see us?'

'Why?' She rolled over on her stomach. 'A child is innocent, a child doesn't know fear or inhibition, not until you teach it. A child copies. It would most likely take its clothes off and lie next to us. That's where the problems start. Children don't only copy the good but the bad just as much. Ideally, children would make the best ambassadors and politicians.'

He couldn't deny that he enjoyed talking to this uninhibited, insane woman. Even though he would have preferred discussing issues of freedom with her, dressed, over a cup of tea or coffee perhaps. He wondered how much longer they needed to bask in the moon.

'Let's breathe together,' she said calmly, rolling on her back again. 'Breathe in . . . breathe out . . . breathe in . . . breathe out . . . breathe normally now . . . imagine your heart filling with the light of the moon . . . imagine swallowing the moon . . . its fullness . . . its calm cool light spreading through your whole body . . .'

They were breathing together, in synchronisation, quietly. They lay peacefully next to each other, comforted by each other's closeness, content with the soft ground underneath them, content within themselves.

'I like you, 28,' he whispered and squeezed her hand. A streak of sunlight tickled his eyelids and the croaking sound of a crow penetrated his ears. He opened his eyes, blinking, irritated. Aware all of a sudden of his nakedness, he jolted up as if stung by a bee, his left hand clutching a tuft of grass.

There were no people to be seen in the vicinity, even though the sun had already risen quite high. He dressed hastily, almost jumping into his pants, afraid that someone might see him. He ran his hands through his hair and looked at the flattened ground, the imprint where she had lain.

He saw something shimmer in the grass. He bent down. It was a golden bead from her dress, the shape of a grain of rice but bigger. He picked it up and looked at it. It was warm. While holding it in his hand, he could feel her spirit, hear her laughter and see her face. A bead that contained her essence. He smiled and put it in his pocket.

He went down to the river and washed his face. Refreshed, he headed back towards the city. At the first café he came across, he ordered a strong black coffee and watched the gradually increasing crowd of people file past. He finished his coffee and headed for the mall, to the largest bookshop in town. He went straight up to the counter and asked for a new release with the title *28 Storeys*.

The sales woman raised her eyebrows. 'You won't get that book in a hurry, Sir!'

'What do you mean?'

'Haven't you read the papers today?' She pointed to the newspaper stand by the door. 'Have a look!'

Confused, he hurried over to the door and with a swift movement picked up the daily paper. The front-page headline screamed at him: *Newly released novel withdrawn from shelves after main character goes missing. Angry author claims that his character is in breach of contract. 'It's sacrilegious, she just took off without my permission!' he said yesterday. Gabrielle Gordon reports.*

He swallowed hard. Without reading the rest of the article, he stumbled out of the shop, down the street, twisting the golden bead feverishly in his pocket.

Lovers

Petra Fromm

I drove along the highway, enjoying the feeling of being in complete control. In control of the car and for perhaps the first time, in control of my life. I could begin again. Already, I loved the new house. It had that lived-in feeling that houses have when they've been, well, lived in. Its rambling rooms and mellow dignity suited me perfectly. Never in my life had I had so much space, ideal for entertaining. And once settled I would take a lover. My thoughts tracked in two directions, simultaneously contemplating the possibility of a new man, whilst becoming aware of the surrounding landscape. In my peripheral vision faded vegetation masqueraded as trees, while a faceless man whispered in my ear, 'Let's go somewhere.'

A lover had said that to me once, running the tips of his fingers along the base of my spine. 'Let's find somewhere private,' was what he'd meant. Strange how each affair begins so bright with desire. I tried to remember his face but it eluded me, only the huskiness in his voice remained. Had there been so many lovers that I could no longer tell them apart? I probed deeper into memory, searching for a clue. The voice was so familiar . . . was it Bryan? No, it couldn't be. His face at least I would remember.

Again, the landscape caught my attention. Stunted trees desperate for water took on the same significance as my worn out affairs. They too had grown from seeds bursting with energy. The inability to put a name to the voice was really beginning to irritate me. The face flickered in my mind's eye, obscured, transitory, like the trees barely glimpsed. *Damn*, who the hell was he? How is it possible to become aroused by the memory of a faceless, nameless man? For the first time in over a month, I wondered what happened to Bryan.

Bryan and I met in my second year at university. He had almost finished medical school. Over the next few months we lived out of overnight bags and it seemed inevitable that we'd move in together. We found a tiny flat within easy walking distance of campus and hospital and settled down to play house. I loved the warm feeling of coming home after lectures, of dividing my time between studying literature and romantic dinners for two. The glow lasted for another year.

Bryan began to talk about what he'd do after his internship, making plans to go back to his home town and take up practice. It was characteristic, the casual assumption that I would go with him. He spoke of marriage and babies. To begin with I was flattered; my mother's daughter thrilled at the thought of being this man's wife. I tried the shape of it on my tongue: 'Doctor and Mrs Morecroft.' But contemplating my own plans, a degree with honours, I realised that I'd be tied to the university for several years at least. Only then would I be able to think about establishing a career and I wanted to write. When I reminded Bryan of this, he assured me that I wouldn't need to finish my degree. Once in practice, he'd be making enough money for both of us, or perhaps he'd specialise. Gynaecology or paediatrics would be more lucrative than general practice. We began to quarrel when I pointed out that it was important to me to finish what I'd started, talked about my goals. 'No problem,' he said. I could always write from home if that was what I really wanted. The next day he came home with a dress. Simple, elegant, black: the kind of dress a doctor's wife would wear to dinner parties. The label told me all of this and more.

From that point on we began to fight in earnest. I was angry with him and that made me feel irrational, vulnerable, out of control. We made each other miserable until eventually I told myself that separation was best for both of us. He disagreed but by then we disagreed about everything. The truth was that I didn't feel capable of continuing the relationship, refusing to make a commitment that demanded giving up my own identity. I would not give up control of my life, did not want to become absorbed into his to the exclusion of my own. Until the day he left we continued to make love and each time was more fulfilling than the last. In the end our lovemaking took on a poignancy and desperation that left me ravaged.

He made no attempt to see me or call, so I assumed he got over our separation. I waited for the passage of time to take away my own sense of loss, without any noticeable effect. Sometimes I wouldn't think of him for a day or two. When I did think of him I'd become angry again, although now the focus of that anger was directed more towards myself. Naturally, this was worse when I was alone. I considered dating again but knew somehow that this would only make the vacuum I was living in harder to bear, a new lover would only suffer by comparison. I had trouble sleeping. Sometimes I could swear that I felt the touch of his hand on my skin. My first love, his caress had left an indelible imprint. Occasionally, it would seem that he was lying beside me and the thought would comfort me until I fell asleep. But more often the image of him would arouse me and I'd be unable to sleep at all. Recollections of his mouth on my lips, my breast, demanding surrender. That surrender was the sweetest thing of all, for then we were truly one being. His breath in my mouth at the moment of our passion's release, held balanced in a place where time did not exist, the intensity almost unbearable. Bittersweet.

It was twelve months before I let my guard down enough to allow another man into my life, or my bed. I lived alone and poured everything into my writing. Surprisingly, my novel was published during my Honours year. Pain is such a marketable commodity. I gave up university to write in earnest and for the next four years became so absorbed that there was no time to regret the change of plans. A country cottage and an increasingly reclusive lifestyle seemed appropriate. My second book wasn't a huge success although my editor was reassuring. We both got excited about my next project. On the surface life was good. But while my friends settled for marriage and children, I'd been unable to stay in a relationship for more than a couple of months. Sometimes it took that long before the man I was with began to make plans for my life as well as his own, began to show a hint of possessiveness. Sometimes it took only a week, however the moment seemed inevitable and with practice it got easier to say goodbye. I find it strange how one relationship can set an immutable pattern.

On my twenty-sixth birthday, almost paralysed by solitude, I decided to go back to university. I returned to the city and was lucky to find a great lease-property immediately. A new house to mark the beginning of a new life.

Settling back into study was remarkably easy, although naturally there were differences. The cute boy in the library had acquired a permanent frown and receding hairline and I could afford both coffee and cigarettes. The coffee shop hadn't changed much and my morning routine began there. I sat outside, at a large round table under a striped umbrella, trying to roll a cigarette and read at the same time. A stranger asked if he could sit down. I nodded assent without taking much notice. His bag landed with a thud on the other side of the table, then he dragged a chair next to mine. I glanced up, wondering why he'd moved so close, wishing that he hadn't. As soon as I looked up, he began to talk.

'Do you work here then?'

Lighting the cigarette, I kept my response flat, indifferent.

'No, study'. My head went back into the book.

'It's cheaper rolling your own is it?'

'Mmm.' I glanced back up, noticing the empty tables around us. I could only assume he'd sat there specifically to talk to me. I hoped that he wasn't trying to pick me up, I just wasn't feeling very pick-up-able. I looked at him a bit harder, coming to the conclusion that I didn't fancy him at all.

'I'm studying music,' he volunteered. 'Classical guitar.'

'Really? We don't see the music lot much, they don't hang around with us. We hear them, but we don't see them.' I wondered if he'd take the hint but was disappointed.

'What are you studying then?'

Ignoring him was an option but there was no real reason to be rude.

'Arts. Literature actually.' I feigned concentration on my book but could feel his eyes on me and glanced up in time to catch him staring at my breasts. He looked away then, in a casual, unhurried manner that made me instantly want to slap the complacency from his face. Anger clawed its way from the pit of my stomach into my chest and I panicked. Shaking, I swept my things off the table into my bag. The book went in crooked, bending the cover. Small white filter-tips scattered onto the cobbles. But all I wanted was to get away before fury dissolved in tears, irrational, out of control. I ran, eyes blinded by salt and water, not looking where I was going. I didn't feel the side of the van when it hit me, only the pain exploding in my head as I hit the road.

'It's alright nurse, I'll take it from here.'

The smell of disinfectant suggested that I was in a hospital. I tried to sit up but my head felt like a construction site. A jack-hammer was busy chipping bits off the inside of my skull. I settled for opening my eyes, slowly, one at a time. I felt . . . disoriented . . . confused by a surplus of stainless steel and that voice.

'Well hello, fancy meeting you here. Can you see me?'

Yes, I could. But what I saw didn't reassure me that I was conscious. This had to be delirium or fantasy, the crisp white coat, the stethoscope. It was all there.

'Where am I?' How disappointingly predictable. I felt as though transported to the set of a soap opera. Must follow the script.

'You were hit by a van. Nothing too serious, just a few bumps. You were lucky. I want to examine you now so I'm going to help you sit up.'

How strange, I have two bodies. One recoils in pain as his fingers push my hair to the side. The other body also hurts when he touches me but it's a different kind of pain, not located in my head at all. For the second time that day my eyes swim with tears.

'Sorry, did that hurt? You're going to have a whopping bruise I'm afraid but there's no sign of concussion.' His hands and voice are incredibly gentle.

What a wonderful bedside manner you have Doctor Morecroft.

'I thought you were in Rosemont.' The only coherent thing I can think of to say.

'What, doctoring the local kids? I was for a while but well, long story. For another time, when you're feeling better.'

That remarkable smile. Boyish, lopsided, it pulls me towards his mouth as he speaks.

'I think you'll be fine to go home by this evening. Is there someone we can call?

I shrug.

'No, not really, I just moved back here. But I can get a taxi, I feel much better already.'

'Don't be silly', the smile broadens, 'I knock off at six, I'll take you home myself.'

Part of me just wanted to stay next to you and drive. Something about being there, a feeling of belonging, in that place, with you. Able to see everything from inside the car without touching any part of me. People, places, time – all meaningless. Insignificant in their being separate from the moment. A different world. I feel safe here, cocooned. You're making it happen, you're real. The only real thing. Your smile, your words, your touch. Just you. We're wrapped in a bubble. Seductive. Addictive. The car stops.

'Would you like to come in?' I try to keep anticipation from my voice.

'I can't, I'm on call later. You know how it is. But have dinner with me tomorrow night . . . please? Our special place, about 7.30. Shall I pick you up?'

His fingers brush my cheek. I can't imagine saying no.

'7.30's fine but I'll meet you there.'

Once again the touch of his fingertips, then his lips graze my own as he murmurs, 'God, I've missed you.'

I float through the front door, ignoring the unpacked cartons still littering the floor. An hour later and I'm soaking in a hot bath with a glass of red wine. The first sip but already I'm intoxicated. The pain in my head has completely disappeared. So time had not healed, nor would it. I know that now. No one had ever touched me like him. I realised then why my anger was so over-powering, illogical. With him I had never been in control, it was always an illusion. Had I not sent him away I would have become the slave not only of his desire but my own. When we made love I knew this. Eventually I would do whatever he asked. And still my body argues his cause. It whispers to me. *Anything for his touch.* My body's a traitor but what can I do? After all, I have to live in it.

The following evening I take the never-worn black dress from my wardrobe. It slides over my body like new skin. Peering into the mirror I wonder what he will see? My dark web of hair hides the bruise. Green eyes gaze incandescently at me from the glass as I check my make up. Minimalist chic. I am ready.

7.40. He's sitting at the bar, an open bottle of red wine and two glasses at his hand. I pause in the doorway, willing him to look up and he does. It still works, the silent communication, that strange connection we always had. His smile reaches across the busy restaurant, wrapping me in its familiar, sensual comfort. We kiss. Old friends greeting one another, polite, on the cheek. Bryan's gaze traces the contours of the dress and his smile intensifies. He signals the waiter, who shows us to a table and pours the wine. I don't need to look at the label, or the menu. Bryan orders for both of us.

'Will there be anything else Doctor Morecroft?' The waiter's professional courtesy irritates me. I want him to go away.

'Thank you George, no. This will be fine.'

We sip the wine, the sudden gulf of silence almost tangible. Then we both speak at once.

'So, how've you been? No, you first.' I giggle, feeling girlish, light-hearted.

'I read your book.' His expression grew solemn. 'Phillip was me, wasn't he? It made me cry.'

A flood of talk then, I couldn't seem to stop and nor could he. We talked through the best scaloppini I'd had in years. Bryan had tried settling down in the Rosemont practice but realised that he needed the challenge of a busy hospital. So he came back six months ago, to the place where we began. At Bryan's request the waiter brought us coffee and cognac. We lingered, sipping slowly, reluctant to dissolve the moment. The other patrons had left. The staff had cleared the tables and dimmed the lights but still we lingered.

'I think it's time that I took you home.' The resonance of Bryan's voice was both soothing and incredibly erotic. 'Perhaps I should give you a quick check-up, just to make sure there are no complications from yesterday.'

I remember this game. 'Oh, I can think of at least one complication. I have a pain. Would you like me to show you?' I allowed everything I was feeling to show on my face and he was immediately out of his seat, helping me out of mine. As I stood, I felt the tips of his fingers at the base of my spine. Shifting his weight closer he whispered, 'Let's go somewhere.'

My legs were jelly as we said goodnight and made our way to the door. Bryan held it open for me but before I could step through, the waiter interrupted.

'Excuse me Doctor Morecroft, you have a telephone call.'

Annoyance flickered across Bryan's face.

'Thank you George. Is it the hospital?'

'No, Doctor. It's Mrs Morecroft.'

'Just tell her that I've already left will you?'

Once again his hand in the small of my back, steering me out of the door towards his car. No, Doctor. It's Mrs Morecroft. I thought of all the lovers whose faces I'd painted over with his. I thought about the men I'd punished because he let me walk out of his life. I thought about his wife, who could have been me, ringing restaurants and being told that he'd just left. I thought about the years I'd wasted wanting him. I didn't move. The car door was open now. Bryan just held it there, watching me.

'Darling, I can explain. I was going to tell you. Just get in the car, I'll fix everything, I promise.'

And just like that I knew and so I told him.

'Doctor Morecroft, I think you already have fixed everything. I feel better than I've felt in years. Completely healed.' I kissed him on the cheek, turned and walked away. In the taxi I gave the driver my address and leaned back into the seat. Tension curled down my spine and then, like smoke, simply drifted away from my body. I felt wonderfully free.

The Window Winder

S t e f a n   L a s z c z u k

About ten years ago I used to do some labouring work for a friend of mine. Not real work. Just a couple of days of cash-in-hand odd jobs. I didn't really have much clue as a labourer so he mainly had me running errands. It wasn't a particularly memorable period of employment for me but there is one job that I will never be able to forget. It was the last job I ever did for him. And then I quit, because after that job life was never quite the same.

The last thing I had to do one particularly sticky Friday afternoon was to return a ladder he had borrowed from this bloke who owned a recording studio. Truth be known, I don't know why he borrowed that ladder in the first place. It was a piece of shit. Like the music this bloke listened to, it was heavy and metal and old. The steps were actually jagged, sharp even. You couldn't even stand on it unless you were wearing a decent pair of boots. It would literally cut into your feet. It was a virtually useless ladder. But if my mate hadn't bothered to borrow it ten years ago then I never would have seen what I saw that day. And I wouldn't understand beauty and tragedy and the way that sometimes they are the very same thing.

My street directory is from 1985. This bloke's recording studio was on a street that didn't exist in 1985. I had to guess where it was from studying the blank spaces on the outskirts of my directory. My mate had described the building for me.

'Big and wooden,' he said. 'Number 35, Lovers Lane.' And he'd given a cheeky wink.

I'd driven all around where I thought Lovers Lane could be and I was about to give up when I came across a post without a street sign on top. I remember hearing once that Lovers Lane was apparently the most stolen street sign in the English speaking world. I don't know how they worked it out, or if there is a list of the most popular stolen street signs somewhere as a matter of public record. All I know is that I remembered this inane fact as soon as I saw that signless post and so on a hunch I turned left down that nameless street and scanned around me.

If it was Lovers Lane, I thought to myself, it was a damn insult to the name. There were no parked cars with necking teenagers anywhere. It was all dirty industrial graffitied buildings and poorly designed car parking spaces with overgrown weeds pushing up through gaps in the badly laid concrete slabs. There were bars over the factory windows and a slight bitter smell that leaked in through the open gap of my own, slightly open window.

And then I noticed a large wooden warehouse-looking building at the far end of the street. Thinking that it must be what I was looking for and thinking at the same time, as I pressed my foot to the floor, that the bitter smell was starting to become *un*-slight, I reached down to wind my window up. I drive an old panel van – it's old enough to be my street directory's father and the driver's side window winder has always been a bit dicky at the best of times. I should have known the day would come when it would fall off.

I suppose I should have slowed down before looking for it somewhere under my legs on the floor. I suppose I might have taken my foot off the accelerator, perhaps even applied the brake, perhaps even, pulled over to the side of the road. But for some reason I didn't. I don't know why. Perhaps I thought I would be done in a second. Perhaps it was because no one was around, the street was deserted. Perhaps I just couldn't be bothered.

I remember the girl's face the most because she had just turned to look in my direction. She had a wonderful smile. The sort of smile someone smiles when they know truly in their heart that someone else loves them. I remember thinking she looked as if she'd just finished kissing the man in her passenger seat. She was truly the definition of starry-eyed. But her starry eyes immediately clouded over with fear as they met my own panicked ones and her recently kissed mouth broke open wide into a silent gasp, over which the screeching of my tyres was effectively 'dubbed', making it look like some sort of dodgy B-grade movie scream. She had her left hand on the wheel and her right arm hanging out the window. I saw the knuckles on her left hand turn white and I winced as I watched my car ram into her right arm, flattening and crunching it into her side door.

I remember the immediate thought that stormed into my head faster than one of those Japanese bullet trains: *what were they doing kissing like that just before pulling out into a public road, for fuck's sake?* But the sight of the ladder flying off my roofrack and towards the young girl's side window was like the end of the line for that particular train of thought. Put simply, I was immediately rendered unable to think. Only able to watch. Watch as the ladder crashed through the side window. Watch the knuckles on the young woman's left hand turn even whiter as the ridiculously sharp, jagged ladder steps sliced through the skin, muscle and bone of her slender neck and then straight on through the skin, muscle and bone of the slightly thicker neck of the stunned young man sitting next to her. Watch their two heads, whose combined age was less than my own, fling into the back seat of the car. Watch the remaining bodies slump forward towards the dashboard and cascade blood against the front window which, perhaps surprisingly, was still intact, like some inside-out macabre car wash.

I don't remember getting out of my car. One minute I was sitting there and the next I was standing at the other vehicle's rear window, witnessing possibly the greatest tragedy I would ever see in my life. I was stunned. There was nothing I could do but stand there with the window winder in my hand. I stared down at it and then back at the two heads lying at opposite ends of the back seat and in a sudden fit of frustration and anger I suddenly threw the window winder at their car.

'Stupid bloody thing!' I yelled. 'You stupid bloody thing!' At the time it was necessary to blame the deaths of two young people on a window winder. As time has passed I have learnt to accept my own responsibility. But it hasn't been easy, not by a long stretch. In fact I doubt whether I could have come to terms with it at all had I not seen what I saw next. Had I not seen what I saw next, I think I would have maybe just gotten back into my car and driven off a cliff.

I must have thrown the window winder both particularly hard and freakishly accurately. It went in through the driver's side window and bounced off the column shift gear stick just behind the steering wheel causing the young couple's car to shift gears and roll ever so slightly back from the twist of bumpers and crash metal. It must have rolled about three feet. I didn't try to stop it. There was no point doing anything and I was still too shocked to think clearly. I stood and watched their car roll slowly into the slight dip between the road and the carpark. I happened to be looking right in the back window and I gasped as I suddenly realised I was staring at the young lady's head on the back seat. I gasped again as I realised that she was actually staring right back at me. I couldn't take my eyes off hers and I swear she was looking at me as if to say: 'What were you doing reaching for a dropped window winder while you sped down a public road for fuck's sake?' I also swear that what happened next is true.

There hasn't been an overwhelming amount of research done on how long a human can retain consciousness after decapitation. There aren't a lot of research volunteers, as you can imagine. I remember reading once that a guillotined head managed to wink nearly thirty seconds after it landed on a linoleum execution floor, as an agreed sign to a curious doctor that the decapitated mind was still active. I don't know exactly how long it was between the time the ladder went through the window and the time I was standing watching as the car rolled backwards into the dip. It could have been ten seconds or it could have been ten minutes. I haven't a clue. I was in shock. All I know is this – as the car slipped into the dip with not enough momentum to get back out the other side, it rocked back gently and settled. This gentle yet sudden rock seemed to be all the impetus the young lady needed. I could see the strained look on her face and the desperation in her eyes as she willed her head to roll along the back seat, closer to her lover's.

And then somehow, ever-so-slowly and awkwardly, it did. I had that sinking feeling you get when you play pool and you've ever so gently nudged the eight-ball over to the pocket and it's slowing down as it approaches the lip and you're hoping it's going to keep moving for that last millimetre and drop, but in your heart you know it won't. In my heart I knew her head wouldn't roll all the way across the seat. But fortunately, hearts can be wrong. Not only did the young girl's head reach her lover's but they managed to end up with their noses pressed against each other's cheeks. I couldn't see the look on the man's face but seeing the look in that girl's eyes was as close as I reckon you can get to actually seeing love. I stood back, eager not to intrude on their final moment together, but I was unable to look away completely. It was too fascinating. The two heads were were pouring tears out as fast as their necks were dripping blood. I think I saw the girl mouth the words 'I love you' but I couldn't be sure because my own eyes were welling up and it could have just been her last gasps of breath. One thing I can be sure of is that what happened next was a conscious decision between the two heads. I've never been surer of anything else in my life.

Gently, yet firmly, they manoeuvred their lips. It was as if they simultaneously decided to leave life together, with a last kiss. But it wasn't just a pressing of lips between two severed heads. It was a kiss that could have been the model for all kisses. A greater kiss than any screen kiss, than any first kiss, than any kiss of any two people in history. Not only their eyes were locked. Every muscle on their draining faces seemed to have the final mission of making the kiss work. And work it did. For a good few seconds those two kids would have out-kissed any couple in any car in any Lovers Lane in the whole world. And then the last blood drained from their necks and the kiss stopped.

I reached for my mobile phone. Obviously I would only bother calling the police. When I'd hung up and wiped my eyes I decided to take one last look at the couple's car. I peered in through the front window at the bodies of the young couple but I could only hold my gaze for a few seconds before I had to turn away again.

It was too much. I headed back to survey the damage of my own vehicle. But I stopped, stopped dead in fact. Because I had to go back and see something. See if my eyes had deceived me. I went back to find that they hadn't. There in the front seat, the bodies of the two young people were slumped, still bleeding, only less furiously, against the front windscreen. The thing that freaked me out though, the thing I can never forget to this very day, the thing that keeps me awake all night sometimes, is that the two of them were holding hands.

'Come on', I hear you say. 'That's not so strange. Their muscles probably just seized up at the point of death and locked together.' But here's the thing. I distinctly remember, as I think I told you before, that I smashed the girl's right hand into the side of her car with my own and that at the time of the crash, in fact right up until the time of her decapitation, she had been gripping the steering wheel with her white-knuckled left hand. There is no other way to explain the fact that those bodies were holding hands other than to say that these were two rare people whose love for each other was so strong during life that they were able to physically reach out for each other, even after their heads had been separated from their bodies.

And so whenever I think about life and death and beauty and tragedy, I know now that they are all forever entwined. Sometimes you just have to take what life gives you and try to remember that it is possible to find beauty in the worst tragedy. And I remind myself of three important things:

the human mind is capable of really amazing things
there is love after death
electric windows are a good idea.

Your Hands, Madam

John De Laine

use them
to wash hair from
the shore
of your brow.
use them in collaboration,
to show Vivaldi
still matters.
remove the long white gloves
and use them,
to say no to one more
wine.

Cupboard Love

Stephanie Thomson

Standing at the kitchen sink in her white towelling dressing gown, Stella prepares. Her cheeks, pale from unquiet sleep, begin to take on pinkness despite the clinical fluorescence of the kitchen light. She turns each of the taps to a precisely titrated point so that the sink fills with water just as hot as her hands can stand. 'Asbestos hands,' Steve always calls her.

'Stell can take it hotter than anyone I know,' she'd heard him tell his boss Ray. Even at twenty-eight Steve is dumbly innocent of innuendo. For Steve things are only ever what they seem.

Alert for any surprise hinge-creaks she inches open the door of the cupboard under the sink and feels for the plastic squeeze bottle of detergent. She doesn't need to look down at what her hands are doing. Years of placing that bottle back in the cupboard just so – just there, where she wants it, have turned this ritual into pure instinct. She looks fixedly ahead through the rising steam and the now condensated kitchen window, out into the starless night.

Stella walks across the red and white tiled floor of her kitchen in measured footfalls. With a balletic sweep of her arms she swings apart the double doors of the china cupboard, forgetting to listen for creaks this time. From the cupboard she removes a stack of pristine white dinner plates. *Ten.* She counts them in a whispered incantation, running her index finger down their cold rims; marking their existence.

Returning to the sink she plunges the plates into the sudsy water. Letting the hot tap run slowly into the other free sink she rinses each plate, checks for soap streaks, and then stands each one upright in the wooden draining rack. She glances at the wall clock which hangs above the humming refrigerator. 12.00. Midnight's potential shortens her breaths. This is no rehearsal. It's the real thing. She feels bionic. The so familiar choreography of these pleasures is danced to excess in midnight's stillness.

Careful ... careful. One of the plates clacks against the chrome spout on its way from wash to rinse. *Don't want to wake up Steve.* The problem is always the same. How to keep silent and still acquiesce to need? When she has polished each plate to a cold gleam she picks up the stack from the draining board and retraces the precise trajectory of her steps back to the china cupboard. *Five*, ending with the right foot forward.

Replacing the plates in the cupboard Stella carefully transfers the ten matching white bowls into the waiting crook of her elbow. When these too have been numbered, washed, drained and polished she starts on the side plates, then the saucers and cups, then the serving dishes, salad bowls, tureens and casseroles until every piece of china has been returned to its place in the cupboard. When she pulls the plug to drain the sink she covers her ears and averts her eyes. The sucking wheeze of that water draining away sounds like a universe of spent pleasure whorling down into some foul vortex. With closed eyes she turns on the cold tap to wash away the remaining froth.

Stella looks up again at the kitchen clock. 2.00. The stupor of completion settles on her: something between satisfaction and sedation. Flicking off the light switch she feels her way along the hall in darkness, her hands making the slightest frictional hiss on the walls. She steps neatly out of her slippers at the bedside and slides into bed beside her husband. His mouth is open. He turns towards the wall with a sigh and the flicker of a smile, subliminally registering his wife's presence. Turning back to face her in the milky pre-dawn, ropy tendrils of Stella's long dark hair have strayed onto Steve's pillow. Their scent feeds his dreams. It's more than enough.

Some men could turn dangerous. She'd met the first one when she was eleven. How proudly her parents had announced to their old neighbours that they were trading up to a sparkling triple-fronted bungalow in a new housing estate on the outer fringes of the comfortingly shabby suburb she had come to know as home. She'd been riding her bike that day – freewheeling down the dusty road that separated this new, barely known world from the scrubby wasteland on the vast Adelaide plains that threatened its ragged borders. Aged eucalypts and sighing peppercorn trees stared down stray cacti, thorn bushes and the odd clay-clodded paddock of cabbages or potatoes. Only Italian market gardeners with tin sheds for houses and sacks for internal doors lived out there.

Paddocks of yellow sour-sobs and a brisk spring breeze had felt to Stella like a call to adventure on the day she encountered the man in the red Holden. She had put on the rose-sprigged cotton dress that her mother had said was 'Only For Best.' Although Stella was only eleven, the firm curves of her body, her strong limbs and long dark hair suggested a robust thirteen.

The man in the red Holden must have seen Stella from way off. Riding towards him, absorbed in her vigorous pedalling, she saw him only when the cloud of dust that was his aftermath died back to nothing around the suddenly stationary car. He'd pulled over onto the wrong side of the road. Her side. As she'd approached the chrome grin of the car's front grille he'd called her to a stop. She'd noticed first that the car boot was open. She recalls staring impolitely at the strangeness of his glossy black curls, olive-tanned skin, and darkly stubbled chin.

'Can ya help me get it on properly, sweetheart?'

It was childish obedience that induced her to squat unnaturally beside the driver's side tyre and push ridiculously on the hubcap.

She can still remember the outrageous contrast of his olive hand with its fuzzed shadings of dark hair on her winter-pale thigh. The rucked up folds of her best rose-patterned dress. The surprising stubbiness of his fingers. A thick gold ring.

Stella has retained only fragments of whatever happened next; a potent little cache of freeze frames. The cold vinyl of a back seat. Her bicycle being lifted into the boot of his car.

'Anyone ever tell you you're bewdiful? What's your name, gorgeous?'

'Stella.'

'Christ. That's my Nonna's name. You know what it means?'

'Uhuh. Star.'

'How old didya say you were, sweetie? Jesus!' A fifty cent piece. Her bicycle being lifted out again. Nothing after that. Nothing of the bike ride home.

What had she done to awaken this strangeness in a stranger? What was it in her that had obeyed the menace of it?

The red and white tiles on the kitchen floor, the white curtains at the windows, the white faux wrought iron front fence have been the markers of Stella's terrain since her marriage.

'Home-making is in your blood, Stella.' Everyone says so, even her mother whose standards are impossible. When she was a young girl, even younger than eleven, she had pored over *Better Home Making* by Beryl Conway Cross. This volume had been given to her mother as a wedding gift in 1955, to help prepare her for life as a young bride. In the introduction Stella read, 'All lives are pleasanter if surrounded by beauty, whether of flowers, colours or of form and face ... so this book deals with each kind of beauty, as well as the more practical chores, such as laundry.'

Home is Stella's religion. She knows it's unfashionable choosing a path so fiercely askew from that of more modern, career driven women. At home she can believe in her own dedicated selflessness. There are needs to attend to. But there have been no children yet. She sometimes wonders if God has denied her babies because she'd never cope with their mess.

At home Stella can arrange things. One income doesn't allow for extravagance but she has a knack for making things seem more precious than they are. How would the silver-plated candle stick look if repositioned on corner of the piano with those wooden framed photos placed diagonally opposite, as though in conversation? No. Too contrived. Let the candle stand alone, in the centre. The photographs can go elsewhere. And on the wooden dining table ... a bowl of lemons? Or grapes and green apples? Flowers? Yes. Yellow flowers.

Lately Ray has been making a habit of coming round after work without his wife.

'Ray's just like a father to me Stell,' Steve professed this morning after telling her that Ray would be 'Over again tonight with a few beers.'

'Jesus, look at this place! Like coming into a bloody art gallery ... and always spotless, like a hospital. Stell's certainly got a feel for it, you lucky bastard. Mandy's got no flair in the home department.'

'Yeah mate. I knew I'd landed a prize when Stell took me on. She's way too good for me!'

'Ya c'n say that a-bloody-gain mate.' Ray is usually more careful with his language around women, especially women like Stella.

'Is he treating you right sweetheart?' Ray asks when Stella reappears in the lounge room with a couple more beers. 'Cos if you're having any trouble with 'im, you let me know pronto.'

Stella parts her lips, about to assure Ray that Steve is indeed treating her right.

'Eh ... eh love? Ha ha ha! Eh Steve ... whad'ya reckon you lend me your missus for a while? Eh?' Steve drains his beer, smilingly dumbly at Ray.

'I know how to treat a woman right see ... bring out her talents.' Ray, winking beerily at Stella, rises from his seat. 'Got a few messes of me own need cleaning up too! Ha ha ha!'

Ray has positioned himself next to Stella, sliding one burly arm around her waist. She looks down at the arm, noticing dark hairs drag against the white rough-woven linen of her blouse. Ray's meaty hand presses her hip bone painfully into his sweaty bulk, geeing her up in rhythm with his laughter. She pulls her head away from Ray's leering grin while registering the warmth of Ray's torso and thigh against her own. Placing a hand on his chest she holds Ray gently at bay before twisting elegantly out of his grip. In the kitchen she washes her hands. At the sink she studies her own reflection in the window. Smiling, tilting back her head, she undoes the top button of her blouse. Seconds later she refastens it. She sets about wiping up the rings of beer from the polished laminate of her kitchen bench top.

Steve and Stella. Even at the time, she knew that she'd been responding to something about the sibilance of their twinned names when she'd said yes to him. They'd both been nineteen. Steve was gentle, steady and believed that a man should provide for his family or he wasn't a man at all.

'I know one thing, he adores you and he'll certainly never do you any harm,' her mother had said. Even so, Stella knew her mother had misgivings about the differences in their intellect. No, more than that, in their 'capacities', a word she was fond of using. And true to her mother's prediction, in their twenty years together Steve had never pushed Stella into anything.

Except maybe last Christmas. Ray had given Steve a larger than usual Holiday Bonus as a 'reward for loyalty'. Steve had gone ahead without asking her and booked a five-day holiday in Surfer's Paradise. Stella and Steve had never been on a real holiday and he'd meant it as a surprise but Stella had found the airline tickets on the top shelf of the wardrobe while refolding his jumpers. She'd always imagined, if they ever had the money, that they would go to Sydney.

Ray's furniture factory turns out reproduction Shaker, Victorian or Federation desks, chairs, tables and beds out of cheap pine. It continues to puzzle Stella that even after eleven years as a carpenter Steve often suffers cuts, blisters or drill burns on his hands. When he arrives home every evening he is raining sawdust. Stella is at the front door. First she brushes him down. Then Steve peels off first his checked flannel shirt if it is winter, then his t-shirt and jeans. She is there to take his things and muss his brown curls to dislodge the wood shavings which fall in soft beige splinters and finely serrated ringlets onto the polished red surface of the porch. This in itself is surely an act of love; she'd got that right, hadn't she?

'You sure you're not making yourself a slave to the housework Stell?' Steve asks her on occasions, always after his evening shower. Then, sometimes, he is allowed to touch her, run his hand down the length of her hair, or stroke the inside of her pale thighs with the backs of his newly scrubbed fingers.

Kelpie Cringe

Alice Sladdin

Master calls enticingly
Here girl, here, to me
He has a new young bitch, just free of puppy fat.
Heel.
Sit. Still.
Stay.
Drop.
Be quiet, he advises, not Speak Up.
Roll over.
Fetch.
Get back! he barks.
Play ball.
Lie down.
Come behind.
He wants her to play dead.
She is irritating him like a cringing kelpie.
He may want to play, to command,
but she cowers,
tail down and does not jump for joy.
Perhaps he wants to murmur 'Good Girl',
to encourage her to rise.
But she is cringing.
Maybe he'd like to placate her fears,
see her bound, extended.

But her anxiety cripples her.
He might like to see her lope with confidence.
Instead she skulks indoors
and 'round the confines of his yard.
He cautions her, sabre rattling,
and wants enjoinment, not enjoyment.
She can only hear menace in his calling.
So although he was going to master this new little dog
    gently gently,
with a pearl choker and other tit-bits,
she flattens herself, cringing from his touch.
His calls turn harsh.
His stroke turns to spank;
he gives her a whipping.
He delivers the final kick in the guts;
propels her from his hearth.

Good Girl

Amy T Matthews

'My cock's fifteen inches long,' Harry told us earnestly as he leaned over the counter. I concentrated on tying my apron strings and didn't look up. Harry was small and greasy. He had a slippery grin and you could smell him when he entered a room.

'That's not what I heard.' Tori strode to the kitchen, brandishing a fat black texta. Harry snorted.

'Like you'd know.'

'Know what?' The Chef emerged from the office.

'Apparently Harry's got a fifteen inch cock.'

'Harry doesn't have a cock.' Chef took the texta off Tori and began writing on the whiteboard. We scrabbled for our pens.

'Right, Ladies. Today we have a Pumpkin and Coconut Milk Broth with Fresh Thyme.'

'Can we have a taste?' Mark asked coyly.

'Only if you blow me. Then we have Roast Hahndorf Venison on a bed of Celeriac Mash with Caramelised Shallots.' Chef had a thick Manchester accent and it took a minute to understand what he was saying.

'You can taste that if you blow *me*,' Harry said, leaning further over the counter.

'Fuck off.'

'For dessert we have Steamed Lime and Ginger Puddings or Date and Kahlua Tarts with Coffee Anglaise.'

'You wrote Trat again,' I handed him the duster. He had a problem with the word tart. It never came out quite right.

'First table's in at twelve fifteen,' Tori announced, clapping her hands like a school teacher. 'Marky Mark, you've got the Dempseys. You might want to start chilling a pinot for them. Angel, come here.'

Angela, I said silently, *my name is Angela.*

'You've got the VIPs today.' She jabbed an acrylic nail at the floorplan. 'Mr Hardcastle and company. He's the Chief Executive of The Montgomery Hotel. Very, very important. Be nice.'

'Angel's always nice. Aren't you Angel?' Chef tossed me the texta. 'If you could arrive at work on time you'd be the perfect employee.'

'Sorry.'

'Trouble getting Lily in childcare again?'

'Yeah.'

'Must be rough on a two-year-old.'

'Yeah.'

'You've got Hardcastle, huh?' The Chef ambled back to the oven and took out a tray of bread rolls. He was a huge man. Six foot four and as wide as a rugby player. Compared with him everything in the kitchen looked like a child's playset. 'I used to work for him in Mexico. Total wanker.' He put the tray on the counter and handed me a tea towel. 'Careful, it's hot.'

'Who is he?'

'Used to be a bigshot in the Montgomery chain. Chief Executive in Tokyo, Paris, you know, all the important places. Then he fucked up. Don't know what he did but it must have been bad. He got sent here. No offence but Adelaide's like the arsehole of the world. Who'd want to run a hotel here? Who even *comes* here?'

'You did.'

'Not by choice. What comes with the venison?'

'Celeriac mash and caramelised shallots,' I replied without looking at my pad.

'Good girl.'

Mr Hardcastle was late. I folded napkins and stared out at the courtyard. It was a damp and mulchy September day. The white cedar was blossoming. When the wind blew the honey-scented petals rained down.

'Don't you look blue,' Mark cried, slapping me on the bum as he walked past with the bottle of chilled pinot. I tried to smile.

'Still worried about Lily, pet?' Tori asked, checking her makeup in the bar mirror. She bared her teeth to check for traces of lipstick.

'A bit.'

'Don't be. Kids are tough.' She sighed at her reflection. 'I'm looking old. Do you think I need Botox?' She pulled at the skin around her eyes.

'Listen to her!' Mark squealed as he glided back to the bar. 'Men pop their buttons over you, Tor. You've got the perfect body. Doesn't she, Angel?' *Angela.*

'Yeah.' I didn't think she had the perfect body at all. She was so thin she had to buy her jeans from the children's department. She had no bum to speak of. Her only feminine attributes were her enormous round tits. They stood straight up. Like doorknobs. There was some debate over whether they were real or not. Chef said yes. I said no. Harry said 'Who cares?' She was just a stick with breasts. I knew for a fact that she was so underweight she hadn't had a period for more than four years.

'I'd fuck you, Tori,' Harry said as he came into the bar for a drink.

'Fuck off, Harry.'

Mr Hardcastle arrived an hour late. He was dour and unsmiling, completely oblivious to my chirpy hello. I swallowed and struggled to keep my expression bright.

'Just this way, Mr Hardcastle. Right by the window here.' I kept grinning as I watched him lead his eleven guests to the table. He was a square man with a face so tanned it looked like my wallet.

'Can I get anyone a drink?' I sang happily as I unfurled the napkins over their laps. Part of me cringes every time I do that. Some people jump, uncomfortable with having your hand near their genitals. Others, men, give you a smile to say ... what? *While you're down there ...* Hardcastle waved a hand at his guests. I got half a dozen requests for mineral water.

'Absolutely,' I cooed as I handed Hardcastle the wine list.

'I'll have Lowenbräu,' Hardcastle snapped as he took it.

'Me too,' the man next to him said hastily.

'Absolutely, I'll be right back.'

'Bring the menus. We're hungry.' *Absolutely. I'll carry them in my* other *two hands while I get your drinks.*

'Tori?' I called as I punched the order into the computer screen. 'Can you menu them? They're restless.'

'Sure but I'm not specialling them.'

'Angela?' Chef called from the kitchen. I swore as I pressed the wrong button for the third time. *Goddamn touch-screens.*

'What?'

'I've got some Duck Rillette for Hardcastle's table. With compliments.'

'I've just got to get their drinks.'

'*Now*, Angela.'

'Alright!' I stalked towards the kitchen and reached for the platter.

'Don't you want to know what it is?'

'Duck Rillette with Toasted Sourdough and Cornichons?'

'What's Rillette?' He slapped his tongs against his leg.

'Coarsely shredded duck bound with duck fat. A kind of rustic pâté.'

'Good girl.'

I smiled widely as I placed the platter on the table. 'Compliments from the Chef.'

'Where's my Lowenbräu?'

'Coming!' I trilled. Smiling, smiling, smiling. They didn't have menus. *Why didn't they have menus?* I looked around for Tori but she was at another table. I snatched the tray of drinks from the bar and trotted back to Hardcastle.

'Where are our menus?' he demanded as he watched me distribute the mineral water.

'Coming!' I poured the Lowenbräu into a frosty schooner and set it before him.

'NO!' he roared, leaping to his feet. The tray trembled in my hand and my smile contorted into a grimace. The table was silent and watchful. The man next to Hardcastle stood, picked up the beer and put it back on my tray.

'Mr Hardcastle pours his own beer,' he said softly, with a nervous glance down the table. 'Just bring him a Lowenbräu and a glass.'

'Not that glass,' Hardcastle snapped.

'A wine glass,' the man told me.

'OK.'

'And menus!' Hardcastle sat back down with a *thwump*.

I took a shaky breath and went back to the bar. The nervous man followed me and caught my elbow.

'Just one menu. Mr Hardcastle usually orders for everyone.'

'All twelve of you?'

'Yes.'

'I can do that.' I scurried back to the bar, collecting a solitary menu on the way. I heard an echoing 'NOOOOOOO!' and looked up. Tori stood frozen, caught in the act of distributing menus to the table. I sighed and ran back down there with the beer.

'Just Mr Hardcastle,' I hissed. She lifted her nose and subjected the table to a withering glare. She shoved the menus at me.

'Menu your own table in future.' She pranced off, enormous breasts bouncing. I turned back to the table with a plastic smile and presented Hardcastle with his Lowenbräu and wine glass. As he poured it I placed a menu to his left.

'I'll just let you know the specials.'

'No!' He waved a curt hand. 'Don't confuse us with specials!'

'Sorry, sir.'

'We want wine,' he snapped as I began to walk away.

'Yes, sir? What can I get for you?'

'I haven't tried this Marlborough sauvignon blanc. How is it?'

'Fabulous, sir. The Marlborough region produces some of the best sauvignon blancs.'

He rumbled deep in his throat and flicked a flat black stare up at my face. 'I probably won't like it. Bring a Nepenthe as well. Just in case. And I want ice.'

'Yes, sir.'

I presented him with both sauv blancs and placed a glass of ice before him. He sputtered as he stared at it. The nervous man jumped up again and grabbed the glass of ice.

'No, he meant an ice bucket.'

'Oh. Of course. I have one right here,' I gestured towards it. Hardcastle glanced at it and sputtered more violently.

'What is it with you people?' he bellowed. I gaped. He snatched up the ice bucket and rattled it. 'I want it *full* of ice and water.'

'Yes, sir. I'll do it as soon as I've poured the wine.' *You twat!* I thought, *don't you know that wine is supposed to be chilled, not frozen?* I smiled and uncorked the bottles. I poured him a taste of the Marlborough. He sniffed it and glared, then tasted it and slammed the glass back on the table.

'Don't serve that!'

'No?'

'It's not fit to be drunk.' He glowered at me. *I didn't make the wine, you old fart. I didn't even put together the wine list.*

'I'll take it away, sir.'

'No. Leave it on the table. I'll have to pay for it anyway. Serve the Nepenthe.'

'Yes, sir.' I fixed my smile and began pouring the wine.

'I'd like the other one,' a woman said.

'Pardon?'

'The other one. I prefer New Zealand whites.' She raised a plucked eyebrow. I sighed and reached for the other bottle.

'No!' Hardcastle boomed. 'You can't serve it.'

'I prefer it,' the woman returned, locking gazes with him. He turned a seething glare on me.

'I forbid you to serve it!'

I chewed on my lower lip, unsure what to do. The woman solved my problem by reaching for the bottle and pouring herself a glass. *Thank you, God.*

Four other people asked for the New Zealand wine. The woman passed the bottle down to them. Hardcastle glowered.

'I want to order.'

'Yes, sir. What can I get for you?'

'We'll have three fishcakes, four prawn and chicken salads, two beef carpaccio, three pig's cheek ravioli, two chicken livers and two rabbit and speck tarts.'

'That's sixteen entrees sir?'

'Yes. Put them in the middle. Then bring two of every main course. In the middle.'

'OK. I'll just go get you some bread.'

'Bring butter. No olive oil.'

'Yes, sir.'

The Chef slapped his hand on the counter as the printer spat orders.

'Angela!'

'Yes?'

'What the fuck is this?'

'What's what?'

'Sixteen entrees and eighteen mains for twelve people? I tell you people every fucking day *check your orders before you send them through.*'

'I did. That's what he ordered. He wants them all to share.'

'Share?' His eyes narrowed as he watched me pile bread rolls onto a lacquered tray. 'That many plates won't fit on the table.' He hurled his tongs across the kitchen and I jumped.

'Can't you put more than one thing on a plate?'

'It will look like shit. I don't work my guts out to put out *shit.* Do I?'

'No, Chef. But that's what he wants.'

'Angela?' Tori called. 'The childcare centre is on the phone.'

'Can I call them back?'

'We'll have to send out half at a time,' Chef snapped as I left, weighted down with bread.

They had finished both whites. Hardcastle ordered another Nepenthe.

'Not that other one!'

'No, sir,' I chirped. The nervous man followed me back to the bar again.

'Look,' he said, rubbing his bald patch uncomfortably, 'I'm paying for lunch today. Could you bring another bottle of the New Zealand wine? Most of the people would rather drink that.' I could feel my stomach twist.

'Of course, sir. Whatever you want.' I watched him walk away and had to resist an urge to hurl the empty bottles at his back.

'Angela? The childcare centre is on hold. They say it's urgent,'

Tori waved the phone at me. I pressed the line and reached for the touch-screen as I spoke.

'Angela speaking.'

'Ange? It's Mary. I really hate to do this but you're going to have to come and pick Lily up.'

'Why?' I cleared the screen and pressed again. Every time I pressed the screen the wrong item lit up. *Fat fingers*.

'She's got the 'flu, Angela. She has a really bad temperature. You know we can't take them when they're sick.'

'She was fine this morning,' I lied. I had dosed her up on baby aspirin before we left home. To get the temperature down enough so that she wouldn't look sick. It must have worn off.

'You have to come and get her.'

'I can't. I'm working.'

'I mean it, Ange. If you don't come I'll call her father to get her instead.'

'No!' My heart leapt. 'I'll be there as soon as I can.' I hit done on the screen and rubbed my temples fitfully. I just wanted to sink to the ground.

They ate their entrees slowly. They ate their mains even more slowly. I kept an impatient eye on the clock. Childcare called three times. The first time I didn't take it. The second time I had Tori tell them I wouldn't be long. The third time I had to call my mother.

'Please, Mum. This is an emergency.'

'I'm on the golf course.'

'Mum, *please*.'

'Honestly, Angela, you're a mother now. You have responsibilities.'

'I know. Like paying my rent.'

'Well,' she huffed, sighing gustily down the phone. I could hear the *thwack* of a golf ball in the background.

'She's sick, Mum. She's your granddaughter.'

'It looks like rain anyway,' she conceded. 'But you have to pick her up by five. I'm meeting Max for drinks.'

'Are you working or not?' Chef hollered from the kitchen.

'Yes!' I ran to get the food as he pounded the bell for the fourth time.

By the time Mr Hardcastle and company finished their nineteen desserts they were well and truly drunk. They moved on to ports and then ordered beers, as a cleanser. I remembered the wine glass and didn't pour Hardcastle's Lowenbräu. He rewarded me by not glowering. The restaurant emptied until only my table was left. The daylight faded and my chest tightened. Four o'clock. Four fifteen. Four thirty.

'I have to go,' I told Tori urgently.

'Not likely. I'm not looking after that mob.'

'That's the spirit, Tori,' Chef sneered from the kitchen.

'You go out and do it, then.'

'I'm too pretty to be a waiter,' Chef retorted. Harry laughed like a hyena, jaws snapping. Tori threw her pen at him.

'It's your job,' she reminded me as she disappeared into the office.

At five fifteen my mother called. I hung up on her. I closed the bar on the table at five thirty and delivered three rounds of drinks. My shoulders throbbed and my feet ached. At six the nervous man came up to pay the bill. It came to nearly two thousand dollars. He handed me a gold credit card.

'Thanks for today. It was great.'

'Was it a special occasion?' I noticed his name was Bryan Brown. Like the actor.

'Mr Hardcastle is leaving us.'

'Oh? Where's he going?'

'To manage The Montgomery in Hobart.'

'Oh. Such a pity we won't see him here again.'

'Yes. Thanks again.' He handed the slip back to me. He'd left an eighty dollar tip. I smiled.

'It was a pleasure.'

I ran to open the front door for them. 'Thank you. Have a nice evening. Thank you.' I paused as Mr Hardcastle lurched towards me. His dark face was flushed a dull brick red. I could smell the beer on his breath. He put a meaty hand on my shoulder. His nails were neatly clipped and buffed.

'Did he tip you?'

'Yes, sir.'

'I'm sure it wasn't enough.' He sagged a little on the end of the pristinely manicured hand.

'It was very generous, thank you sir.'

'You did a good job today.' He fumbled a little and slipped something into my hand. 'Thank you.' He disappeared outside into the gathering gloom. I looked down at the crumpled bills in my hand. All fifties. I wandered back into the restaurant.

'Tori. They've gone. I'm leaving now.'

'Is the table cleared and set?'

'No but the evening shift starts in fifteen minutes.'

'I want the table cleared and set.'

'OK.' I hummed a little as I drifted back to the table.

By the time I finished polishing the last rack of glasses Megan had arrived. She straightened her tie in the bar mirror and bared her teeth to check for lipstick.

'How was today?'

'Fine.' I fondled the slippery bills in the pocket of my apron.

'Hey Megan!' Harry yelled from the bar as I was leaving.

'What?'

'Did you know I've got a fifteen inch cock?'

'Fuck off, Harry.'

Chinese Boxes

Vanna Morosini

The woman kneads pasta dough, soft and yellow, sensuous like living skin. Kneading and rolling, she stretches it into a thin sheet, springy, with small stretch marks and bubbles. I can still see the clean white linen tea towels, the white flour, her strong, muscular hands and fingers pushing and stretching, rolling the pasta sheet vigorously on the long rolling pin. Then the memory stops like a broken piece of film. I don't know what happened before or after. But even though it is small, this memory is suffused with light.

The woman making pasta was my grandmother.

All I have now of her are fragments – recollections, both mine and other people's – anecdotes, objects that were once hers. A lot has gone. Her presence has been erased from the house where she spent the last forty years of her life. Most of her garden has died, my grandfather reluctant to waste water on ornamental plants. The pot plants she lovingly tended, their luxurious growth barely contained by the confines of their pots, have disappeared. Even her kitchen, the centre of her world, barely contains traces of her. My memories of her are like pieces of a puzzle that I try to fit together. I shuffle and reshuffle but each time the story comes out differently.

The epicentre of her world was her kitchen. It was always spotless; the floor shone, the sinks glowed silver and the bench tops were always immaculate and free of clutter. There were never any dishes left lying around. Everything was immediately cleaned, dried and put away. The cupboards were full of neatly arranged tins, boxes and bags of food – rice, pasta, spices, coffee beans, some dried herbs, all ready for whatever dish she had it in mind to prepare. Her saucepans and other cooking utensils were stacked in neat rows, everything ready to hand. I still stack pots the way she did, putting the smaller ones into the larger ones in decreasing sizes, like a series of Chinese boxes.

The smells of rosemary, olive oil, garlic and white wine always remind me of her. Her dishes were legendary among her family and friends. Only the best quality food was allowed into her kitchen and she would travel for miles on her bicycle or on the bus to purchase just the right kind of coffee, the best cuts of meat, the freshest cheese or bread. As a small child I often accompanied her on these expeditions. Sometimes her sister came too and they would sit on the bus gossiping loudly in Italian. Embarrassed, I would sit behind them, staring out of the window, mortified at their exuberant laughter, their wild gestures and sudden loud exclamations. I was acutely aware of the silence of the other passengers, their grey heads turned resolutely away, bodies rigid in their seats and stiff with the waves of disapproval I imagined flowing in our direction.

The shops we visited on these trips were a cornucopia of delights. They were often filled with the rich aroma of freshly ground coffee and colourful displays of yellow and white cheeses, pink ham, pancetta and plump sausages. White tubes of salami hung in rows, and silver pots, pans and coffee makers dangled from the ceiling. Home made biscuits, fresh eggs and round, flat loaves of bread along with jars of multicoloured pickled vegetables and black olives covered the counters. Tins and packets of produce lined the shelves in the corridors and along the walls and if we stood too close to the counter our toes would knock against the oblong metal bricks of bulk olive oil stacked beside one another along the floor. The shopkeeper had to peer out from behind all the produce piled on his counter to serve his customers.

Food was taken very seriously. The shop would be full of women buying and sampling, discussing the best produce in serious tones with the shopkeeper. Items were discussed, analysed, sampled and assessed until finally a judgement was made about their purchase. The shopkeeper would make suggestions, sliding from meat counter to cheese slicer, offering samples and nodding sagely until his customer had decided what she wanted.

I would lean against the glass counter, while we waited to be served; watching the shopkeeper through the glass, his white apron, stretched so tightly over his bulbous stomach that I could see the faint depression of his belly button outlined under the snow-white fabric. The shop would be a cacophony of sound, with loud chatter and bursts of laughter from the women surrounding me, many of whom knew my grandmother and each other. Occasionally a hand would descend to ruffle my hair or pinch my cheek, which stung for moments afterwards from the strength of the broad, calloused fingers. If I was lucky I would be allowed to explore the shop, shyly at first, conscious of the flitting glances of many pairs of ever-watchful eyes. My favourite place was the corner where large plastic drums full of dried beans were kept. There were many different varieties: small brown lentils, round chickpeas, mottled borlottis, large, flat broad beans. With a swift look around to check nobody was watching I would plunge my hands deep into the bins. I could never resist the smooth, almost liquid feeling of loose beans running through my fingers.

When it was time to leave, the shopkeeper would always have something for me, a golden cube of cheese or a sliver of salami curled into a cigar, held out delicately with the tips of his pink sausage fingers. On tiptoes I would reach up for my prize, the glowing shiny moon of the shopkeeper's face suddenly visible as he leaned forward, his features creased in a wide smile. Despite my sudden shyness, my lips couldn't help but smile back. As we left the shop, my grandmother's string bag bulging with odd shaped parcels, the shopkeeper would always sing out *Arrividerla Signora*.

It was like leaving someone's home. There was nothing impersonal about it. Now, as an adult, I can't help looking over at shopkeepers when I leave their premises. They rarely look up or acknowledge me in any way. Despite this, I can't help feeling impolite when I walk out without saying anything.

My grandmother's day began early. One morning before daybreak I remember waking up hearing voices in her kitchen. The bedroom door was ajar and a streak of yellow light from the hallway fell into the still dark bedroom. Curious, I got up and wandered towards the voices. I climbed the steps into the living room slowly, still blurred with sleep and walked, blinking fiercely, into the sudden brightness of the kitchen. My grandparents stood huddled over the kitchen bench, arguing in tight whispers. The kitchen smelled strongly of fresh coffee. When they saw me they fell silent. My grandmother turned sharply towards the stove and over her shoulder told me firmly to go back to bed. But I wanted to stay up. I was tired but also intrigued by this strange, early morning world. Outside it was still dark but the birds had already begun to twitter in the trees outside the kitchen window. My grandfather reached for me and slid me onto his lap. My grandmother said nothing more.

Later, we went outside to farewell my grandfather as he left for work. The morning was crisp and clear. A soft breeze gently rustled the foliage around us. At that time, just before dawn, the world seemed to be unfurling itself. The stars were still bright in the sky, which was only just beginning to lighten from a deep navy blue. The air smelled fresh. My grandmother and I stood at the top of the driveway and I waved as the headlights of my grandfather's car disappeared around the corner.

The rest of the day was spent in the house or garden, cleaning, washing and cooking. My grandmother poured her energy into creating a clean and comfortable home. Her activities occurred around me and formed the backdrop of my day. The warm smell of freshly washed laundry, having to tiptoe across a damp, newly mopped floor to reach the back door, lifting my legs up from the carpet as she whizzed the vacuum cleaner around me while I sat immobilised by morning television. Her work seemed endless.

We often fed the chickens together, pouring their wheat into a long feeding trough my grandfather had made. Sometimes they were allowed out of their run to fossick and pick over the remains of last season's vegetable garden. I always looked for my chicken, Henny Penny, the largest one of all. My parents had bought her for me one Friday night at the Central Market. I had seen her in a glass case in a pet shop window, bundled under a heat lamp with all the other cheeping little balls of fluff. She went to live with my grandmother's chickens and grew to be enormous, strutting around her domain and aggressively ruling her roost. If I tried to pat her she stood her ground and gazed at me with her unfriendly, beady eye. I knew if I persisted she would peck me. Henny Penny was friends with no one.

After lunch all chores stopped while my grandmother watched her 'story', as she called her favourite daytime soap opera. It was a ritual religiously observed, even when my grandfather retired a few years later. She sat leaning towards the television, anxious not to miss a word. Strangely, given her tenuous grasp of English, she managed to understand the convoluted plot lines very well. In the ad breaks she hurriedly explained the characters and their latest dramas to me with disapproving shakes of her head and shocked whispers as though it was all happening to real people.

I have a photograph of us, probably taken when I was about four. She is clasping my hand, smiling at the camera, her other hand on her hip. Her dress has a bold pattern, black with comet streaks of white, her slender waist encircled by a narrow belt. The dress is sleeveless and v-necked and her arms and legs are slim and muscular. She looks young and fit, her brown curly hair blown by an invisible breeze as she smiles into the lens. I am standing awk-wardly, my leg raised as though I'm about to run off, face screwed up against the bright sun shining in my eyes. In the background I can see the climbing fig she planted just beginning its journey up the wire mesh supports near the back door. Later, it grew like a jungle vine, so thickly covered in leaves that objects could be lost in it forever. Now it's gone, replaced by green polycarbonate sheeting. My grandfather tore the creeper down after her death because the debris left by the living plant irritated him.

I have one other piece of the puzzle from around this time. We were in the garden and she was weeding, or picking vegetables, or watering – probably doing all three. I was with her and the sun was shining. She was teaching me a song and we sang it as she worked. I remember my hands were caked in red soil, beating a rhythm as I slapped my palms against the dirt. My fingernails were tipped with black crescents, packed with earth. When we finished she tilted her head back and laughed and I clapped, her audience of one.

She used to tell me stories of her life, about her childhood, her family, the people she had known. That was when the meaning of her words was clear and transparent to me. There was no pause, no need for translation.

As I got older I stopped listening. I slowly stopped being able to understand her stories, my language skills vanishing as I moved into adolescence. She became more and more insistent, trying to get me alone to listen to her reminiscences or hear her complaints, most of which I had heard before and now could only vaguely understand. Angrily, she would lift her sleeves and point to faint purplish bruises on her wrists and arms.

'This one was because of you . . . and this one,' she said as she jabbed her finger at another bruise, 'was because you didn't call . . .' She went on, pointing to other marks on her flesh, her stigmata. I glanced into the living room at my grandfather placidly watching television and imagined their bitter fights. In the same insistent whisper I would plead that she go away for a while, perhaps to stay with her sister but always she shook her head, irritated, silencing me with a dismissive wave of her hand.

I began to switch off to her endless rambling. I had left her world and had gone somewhere she couldn't or didn't want to follow. I tried to talk to her of my friends, or school or my hopes for the future. She listened disinterestedly, struggling to understand my English. Finally we had almost nothing in common, not even a language.

When I moved away to study in another city I very rarely saw her. She started to send me letters regularly. They arrived through the post, landing on the hallway floor with a thump. The envelopes were fat and covered in her scrawled writing, my address often misspelt. Just by looking at them I knew they were from her.

In my room, I opened the first few she sent me. Inside I found pages and pages of dense script, written on almost transparent airmail paper, all in Italian. I couldn't understand any of it. She knew I couldn't but she wrote anyway. So I just stacked her letters in a drawer, unopened. It was painful for me to open this drawer, soon overflowing with fat envelopes. I wondered what it was she was trying so desperately to say that she kept writing into a void, to a person whom she knew couldn't understand her.

When I did finally learn to speak and read Italian fluently, years later, I re-read her letters. What I found in them shocked me. Most of them were bitter diatribes against the people in her life, both past and present, including myself. They were litanies of blame. Towards the end, they became almost incoherent, with unfinished sentences and constant repetitions, the words running off the page.

When I think of her now, this is the piece of the puzzle that throws everything out of focus. Before I read her letters I simply dismissed memories that didn't fit easily into the picture of the kind and generous grandmother I knew. The glimpses of another side of her troubled me, so I left them out.

But later I wanted to find the real woman hidden in the shadows. Those discarded shards of memory that had never fitted came to seem important. I began to dredge them up; the way her manner could change in an instant from sweetness to vitriol if she didn't get what she wanted, my surprise and alarm at her rare bursts of vindictiveness, which disappeared as swiftly as they had appeared and left me feeling confused and disorientated. I thought of examples of her careful manipulation, her use of guilt and small deceptions, her self-interest, her fear and desperate compliance with my grandfather's often unreasonable demands. Her anger at me when I refused to pacify him as she did. But after all my sifting and sorting, shuffling and re-shuffling, weighing up her love against her bitterness, her nurturing against her manipulation, her fear against her anger, I still couldn't make all the pieces fit together.

The last time I saw her was at the viewing of her body at the funeral home. No one cried except my grandfather, who blubbered like a baby, tears squeezing out from his closed eyelids. My father, brother and myself looked on silently, dry-eyed, at her lifeless, wax like figure stretched out in the open casket before us.

She lay with her white hands folded on her chest, fingers entwined. She looked small and fragile. The dead flesh had retreated from the bones of her face, giving it a sharpness that it had never had in life.

I remember that the funeral service a few days later was elegant and tasteful, my father's eulogy beautifully written. As her coffin was lowered into the open grave, her sister stood beside me and whispered, 'Next it will be me.'

I never did cry for her. Instead, I grieved for her with a frenzy of cooking. I found myself drawn to continental delicatessens. I sampled, assessed and weighed up my purchases after long discussions with shopkeepers just as meticulously as she had done. At home I started to make more and more complicated dishes and to master techniques I never had time for before. I hunted for the long, thin wooden rolling pin I needed to make hand-made pasta. I painstakingly taught myself from a book propped open against the fruit bowl, rolling the dough furiously to get it to the right shape before it dried. I carefully pressed and moulded the plump little pillows of stuffed ravioli. I separated them with my little pasta wheel and dropped them into the bubbling pot of salted water already waiting on the stove. My speciality became ravioli stuffed with ricotta, nutmeg and sweet potato. It was a dish my grandmother never made: *Ravioli del Nuovo Mondo.*

Hungry

Chelsea Avard

hungry women
frighten.
Enormous mouths and breasts
threaten to consume
smother and swallow
in one gulp
mean mouthfuls
scissor and slice
promise to bite
tiny incisors and hipbones
hungry women
frightened

The Core

Emmett Stinson

Withered, brown, and sailing past the rubbish bin rim –
The core's subtle hymn to the arm still flailing
Through its arc, trailing. The extension of the limb
Ties the failure back to him – the cause, the failing.

Psychiatric History

Dena Thorne-Pezet

Like all remembered summers, revisited and reworked so many times they are almost learned by heart, that one seemed endless. The finding of John McDonald's near-naked body, tied and bound with twine and wire and sealed in the big old water vat near the greenhouse, seemed to bring it all to a sudden and unexpected end. My sister and I recall that we were not overly concerned when we first heard that he had gone missing. He was not a friend of ours. He had once peed himself at the park and mutely kept his pants on all day, despite our taunts, till the damp soiling had dried and disappeared. Even during the holidays he wore regulation school Plimsolls on his small feet and his hair always needed cutting. Once, I laughed out loud when he sobbed openly after I'd told him he smelled of digestive biscuits and hen feed. I was a young, callous boy and youth has its own reasons, carries its own pitiless conceits.

I remember that time seemed to expand, the days growing bigger, hotter and longer, the school holidays seeming to extend way beyond our brightest hopes. We spent most of our days messing around the farm with no escapade or mission beyond us. We liked nothing better than to spy on old Starkey, creep around the outside of his greenhouse and watch his comings and goings. We knew that Dad never liked Starkey, whom he'd inherited as an allotment tenant when he'd bought the farm and the outlying vegetable gardens. He said he couldn't get rid of him, the dirty bastard. He told us to steer well clear; told us that we had to be careful. Occasionally though, there were other kids at the greenhouse with Starkey: his niece, his neighbour's boy, or sometimes someone unnamed and unexplained.

Generally though, people said Starkey was more to be pitied. Grimy, withered, he seemed to neither have nor care for anything, apart from his Geraniums; ugly fecund plants with heavy, foul-smelling blossoms like small fists and thick, ropey stems. He said he sold them for a fortune at the markets. He grew the plants from shoots nursed in small murky jam jars which he kept in straight lines on the old dresser in the greenhouse. Jars that were alive with sticky roots that necrotised in the water like dark, dead nature.

These days however, I am mostly alone during the holidays. My work keeps me very busy. I have no children, my father is dead and my sister lives abroad with her family. I get ready for them well in advance, like most of the lonely, the lost or misplaced; those who may have quietly gone astray. I make sure I'm preoccupied and busy. Not with the buying of gifts, the drawing up of guest lists, the juggling of persuasive invitations but with the filling in of those long, vast hours when even the most steadfast might be seduced by the hard sell of the season. Rostering myself onto as many shifts as possible, I pick up cover for those with ties, obligations and family, places to go, better things to do. I make myself popular with the ward clerks, making their jobs easier, filling in the gaps at the clinic, dealing with the spill out of the institutions over the peak periods.

Even years on, we both still remember Starkey clearly. He had improbably long fingers like string beans, scoured, lumpy, dirty with soil, bragging that with them he could unpeel a woman like a piece of fruit. Old Starkey: permanent stubble rusting his face, orange twine around the waist of his overcoat even in summer. We thought we could both still picture him. Old? He must've been no more than forty-five at the time, not much older than my sister and I are now. Some truths just seem to bend, to accommodate time and perspective.

I remember that we never went in that greenhouse with him but were often in there after he'd gone home. I can still feel that place now, dry, airless, overwhelming. The whole of it full of the bitter tang of those fusty plants, more dead than alive. My sister and I thought we knew the ins and outs of that greenhouse. What he kept there and what he did. Every night he left the key under a pot outside the door and we'd use it to let ourselves in on those long, light, northern summer evenings. We never found anything special when we rummaged through his things. All we ever turfed up were old newspaper cuttings, bits of the orange twine he had around his coat, lengths of old wire he'd bent out of shape and those dirty books my sister was scared of. Mostly nothing happened and we'd end up catapulting one or two panes of glass just to bait him. But sometimes we'd catch him looking at his dirty books and touching himself, his penis, tuberous and menacing, poking out of his pants. My sister would run off and usually drag me along with her. But now and again I'd stay and watch as he grunted away, his hand busy, the pressure in my groin only an afterthought.

My strongest memory of the early weeks of that summer is of the hefty grey rat one of the dogs caught and half-killed. It lay in the yard, split in the middle, its entrails pooling out pink and meaty in the afternoon sun. I'd finished it off, flattening its busted but twitching body with a shovel and then scraped it up, knowing it would be useful for something. Together my sister and I wrapped the rat in an old sack, buried it behind the hay shed and minded it until it was soft and maggoting, digging it up every day to check on its progress. We reasoned that once it was ripe enough we'd take the key from under the pot, sneak it into Starkey's greenhouse and leave it in the drawer of the old dresser, in with his dirty books, the guts of it smeared across the pages. One evening, the air noisy and fat with flies, my sister's skin rose-budding with bites, we catapulted the greenhouse trying to flush Starkey out so we could plant the rat. We weren't sure he was there, it being so still, so quiet. But eventually he came running out with his trousers open, his penis sticking out of the dark slit in the front of his pants pointing alternately from left to right as he moved. Terrified, confused yet delighted, my sister had shrieked at me 'Run Dan, run!' and she'd leapt over the wall and run back up the path to our field. As I started to run I turned and saw something shadowing in the greenhouse, through the glass and the geraniums. I knew it couldn't be Starkey as he was still near the greenhouse door fumbling with his trousers. I was sure I saw the small outline of another person but Starkey's face was a map of anger. I was afraid, so I just turned my back and ran after my sister. In the flurry I dropped the rat. She tried to make me go back for it, our prize, but I told her I wouldn't.

Fact often gets lost with the imagined or barely comprehended and time plays tricks on the best of us. What knowledge we had of that particular period was gleaned only from the snatched bits of whispered information shared between my parents and later the hard talk of the school yard. We do know, though, that the police came for Dad one wet Thursday afternoon as the Laburnum trees rolled out their deep yellow carpet towards the beginning of autumn. It seems that he was probably one of the last people to see John alive. Agreeing with the police that he wanted to cooperate, Dad told them that, yes, he had seen John in our top field early in the afternoon of the day they believed he'd disappeared. John was throwing stones at the horses, Dad said. In his own uncomplicated vernacular he told the police that he'd caught John roughly by the shoulder, shaken him and ordered him off his land. Dad agreed with the police that, yes, he was very angry with the boy; this was not the first time he'd caught him bothering the horses. But he maintained he did not go after John and never saw him again after that. Dad did admit, though, at the end of further questioning and probing by the police, that he thought he'd made a mistake. He suddenly remembered that he had seen John, just once, later that day, alone near the greenhouse.

The police felt they had enough evidence to detain Dad further and seek corroboration of that last sighting. This took time. I remember they held him overnight, somewhere in the city, while other possible witnesses were sought out. The next day they came to the house in the early evening, just before teatime. Two of them, a man and a woman. My sister and I were questioned, even my mother, who quietly worried the twisting dishcloth in her busy, pale hands the whole time. Unfortunately no one else had seen John near the greenhouse that day. There was no one who could confirm his movements or the events of that early evening. That last sighting of John was never corroborated, although Dad maintained it all the way through. When hard-pressed by the police towards the end of his second day of questioning he had to admit that, yes, he had seen and spoken with the boy that day. He'd had some physical contact with John, he supposed. And yes, he had assaulted him shortly before his disappearance, if that's what they insisted on calling it. Of course, Dad said, he recognised that orange twine they had in the small polythene bags. It was hay-banding and was all over his farm. He used it for all sorts of things. The wire? Well, that was available anywhere.

To a child even disjointed events can appear sequential and have their own specific chronology and prescribed way. What happened over that early autumn may have unfolded smoothly and spread squarely across days, weeks or even months but it seemed uneven and incoherent to me. I took no time and at the same time, took forever. It could not have been long before the police understood that Starkey occupied the greenhouse and it must have been hours, rather than days, before they arrived to pull it apart, limb from limb, and to take Starkey away for questioning.

Tonight is Christmas Eve. Exhausted, having just finished a heavy clinical session, I am looking at my life under the harsh glare of the psych ward lights; a series of am's and pm's on a timetable pinned to the wall in a ward corridor. I run my fingers across the sum of it. Neatly blocked-in boxes, huge tracts of time filled by nothing more than blue marker pen, emergency contact numbers and medication schedules. I have time before I'm next on so I make for the car park at the side of the hospital near ER. It's still quiet there; the carnage, the compliments of the season probably won't roll in until the bars begin to empty, until the Christmas spirit hits the roads. I head downstairs through the guts of the building to the lower ground floor, past surgical supplies, the incinerator, the morgue and out into the empty car park and the night. I struggle to light a cigarette. The wind coming off the dark lake, fed by a tributary from the sea, is heavy and thick, weighed down with the sour trace of salt. It blows into my eyes and my hair, across Christmas Eve and into Christmas Day. I look at my watch as the twenty-fourth ticks over to the twenty-fifth; 11.59 pm to 12 am, 12 am to 12.01 am. The tick, tick, tick of isolated instants, the past and the future almost grafted together, with only a short-lived fissure in between for the present to glimmer momentarily.

My sister and I thought about John a lot all through the following months. She told me that she was there when the police peeled back the lid of that water vat and fished out his thin, damaged remains. When they began draining the putrid water she said they covered their mouths with handkerchiefs as they pulled John's body to the surface. I knew this wasn't true but I liked to listen to her just the same. She said that grown men had cried at the mess of his almost unrecognisable face and the purplish green tendrils, which sat behind the wire pulled tight around his quiet neck. He'd been in there for a while she reckoned, when they found him, but she said they couldn't be sure. She said that she'd heard Mum say that they could tell straight away that John had been interfered with, the bruising at his thighs and his lack of clothing were all pointers to it. Eventually though, with Starkey gone, us back at school and the days growing shorter and darker, we seemed to forget about the greenhouse, Starkey and even John.

A siren wails clearly in the distance and having drained my cigarette, I throw the butt into the huge industrial waste bin near one of the hospital fire exits. Before I go back I look over the lake, the inky bank of trees blocking out the sight but not the sound of the wintry sea beyond. The last full moon of the year hangs closely, precariously on the skyline, a vast eye in the sky watching, inspecting, knowing some truth it can never blurt out. I have to look away like a child caught lying; turn and walk slowly back to the hospital entrance. The siren gets closer and closer and sucks up the quiet of the night, becoming bigger and louder with my every step. When I open the fire doors the wind gusts out at me as though fleeing from a vacuum. It screams up and down the lift shafts and the stairwell in that familiar but ungodly way, like some summons from the dead, pounding me as I try to push through it. I put my hands to my ears, my mind full of wailing sirens, and try to keep out the noise and preserve what space there is left inside my head.

On reflection I can see that after so long, I am not as clear as I'd like to be about that time. What is clear to me is that when Starkey was released after his initial questioning he hung himself efficiently in the greenhouse. He put a bag over his own head, emptied his pockets, having taken off his shoes beforehand and placed them neatly together by the door. We never heard how long he'd been hanging there, dangling lifeless and cold in the dark, his bent head pressed close against the flat brick of the wall. It was Dad who found him that Christmas Eve; cut him down and wordlessly laid his rigid corpse on the floor amongst the dried up, frozen leftovers of those geraniums. He didn't remove the hood. He said he'd known at once who it was so there was no need. When the police arrived all Dad could say was that he knew he should've razed that greenhouse to the ground the day he first set eyes on it.

Looking back I can see that for a while I got confused about the last time my sister and I had been spying on Starkey; the day we'd had the rat and he'd come out and shouted at us. Sometimes it's still difficult for me to jostle things absolutely straight in my head. I know that Starkey did come out and he did shout at us. My sister did run away and try to make me go back for the rat but the bare, simple truth is that I lied as a boy and I continue to lie as a man. I did go back for that rat. The place was completely silent and I imagined that Starkey had gone or would be locking up so I thought I'd steal a look through the dirty edge of a broken windowpane and moved in closer. Through those stinking plants I saw that Starkey was still there and I could see what he had been so busy with. His trousers still open, Starkey had his hands firmly on the head of a small thin boy who was kneeling whimpering at his feet, like a bitch waiting to whelp. I could tell from the hair and the Plimsolls who it was and I watched quietly, hardly breathing, listening to Starkey's grunting until it stopped and the boy's whimpering began again. With a shame that can still make me gasp for air I felt myself grow hard and for the first time make my own pants wet. Then, leaving the rat and the greenhouse, I walked home in silence turning it all over in my head, knowing I would say nothing, knowing that I never could.

The Teeth of the Ghost

Dominique Wilson

Sadiki heard her baby scream. She smiled. They had started to cut him. She held her breath. Another scream, then another. Three in all, one for each of the diagonal slashes on his left cheek that will eventually scar and mark him as a member of the tribe. She pictured her husband and sister holding the babe, laughing with the barber as he performed the ceremony. She too had held babies and laughed in celebration but it was forbidden for the mother to attend her child's 'outdooring', so she stood at the entrance of her hut, watching the sun scorch the savannah, and listened to the drums and the screams of her son. Soon they would come and fetch her. She had stayed inside with the child for seven days after giving birth, as the laws of the Ghana people required, in case his soul decided to return to the spirit world. She had fed and cleansed him but had not cuddled him or talked to him, for he was not of this world yet. But this morning, even before dawn, she had heard him sucking on his fist and she knew that he would stay.

The rhythm of the drums quickened, and an elation of voices echoed through the valley, undulating through the village and across the river to disturb a lone secretary bird. Sadiki entered the hut and wrapped a bright blue and orange bandanna around her head, then stood still and listened. The drums slowed, the chanting stopped. She held her breath for an infinity. Silence. Then once more her baby's scream, indicating that the twelve cuts, the rays of the African sun, were being etched on his belly. The drums and songs rang out in primal acclamation. His little body was being bathed now in the large calabash filled with an infusion of warm water and medicinal herbs. At last she could rejoin the tribe. Together with her husband they would present her son, Makalani, to the community. Makalani, the name given to him on this day, the day his soul was reborn.

Fannah skipped along the trail leading out of her village. Her name meant 'happy', and everything about her justified such a name. Behind her, her mother and aunt walked, whispering to each other. Fannah liked this time of day when the rocks were still in shadow and the ground had yet to bake under the sun of Yemen. To her right the land sloped down into the sandy, barren wasteland that was the Rub al Khali desert, where a girl such as she could die in a day and even the thornbush refused to grow.

When they had set out this morning, her mother had said 'Where we are going you will be given nice things to eat,' and Fannah had wanted to know more. Her father had told her to be quiet and children did not argue with their fathers. A young goatherd came towards them, driving his flock before him. The women and the girl moved off the path to let him pass and the women lowered their gaze but Fannah stared at a little kid bleating pathetically, until her mother jabbed her in the back. When the goatherd had passed, the women each took Fannah by the hand and quickened their step. Fannah smiled at them but the women did not respond. The mood had suddenly become sombre.

They hurried on in silence until Fannah saw, a short distance away, a tent where a group of women sat. All, Fannah realised, came from her own village. As one, the women began to trill. The women rose, clapping and dancing, coming to meet them and Fannah felt her mother and aunt's grasp tighten. She became afraid and looked to her mother for reassurance. Her mother looked towards the swaying women and trilled in response. Like crows swooping on a morsel the women enveloped Fannah and she cried out to her mother but her wails were silenced by her shame as her clothes were ripped from her body. She was passed from one woman to the next, then stretched out onto the carpet within the tent. She struggled until she realised that two of the women holding her down were her mother and aunt. A veil of disbelief shrouded her. She closed her eyes in shame and sobbed as her legs were pulled apart. She screamed when she felt the knife rip at her clitoris, then tear into more flesh as thick hot liquid ran down the cheeks of her buttocks. As she fell into darkness, Fannah's mind echoed with the squawking of crows and the bleating of goats.

She woke to excruciating pain. She tried to move but her body ached and her legs were tied tightly together. She could smell herbs, damp earth and blood. Around her the women smiled and patted her cheek and told her of the secrets of her sex and how to please men and give them male children, as they ate fresh dates and sweetmeats and sipped tall glasses of mint tea.

Tokabanalai sat under the breadfruit tree. He didn't notice the dense undergrowth of the jungle around him, where amongst the dappled light delicate water vapour coiled upwards between the trees and exotic birds flitted through the ancient canopy. He had been born on this island of Tanga, married and had children here and now he was to become a member of the Sokapana, that secret society of men who had travelled to the Underworld and then been reborn. Tokabanalai prayed he would have the courage to meet with the Ghosts, not weaken and cry out, for this would anger them and he would pay for his cowardice with his life. Ngaffkin had cried out and his widow was mocked by the village for having had such a husband. From the taraiu, that sacred camp where only men can go, Tokabanalai heard the bellow of bullroarers and pipes that announced the arrival of the Ghosts. He rose and walked towards them.

Grotesque fishlike warriors, their bodies red and yellow, with false beards clenched between their teeth, thrust him into a frenzied battle where spears tore at his flesh and bullhorns burst his eardrums as rivulets of hot blood mingled with the sweat excreted from his skin until he fell, shuddering, his body emptied of his soul. The Chief whipped him pitilessly on the back and legs, then rubbed soot into the weals. His soul attempted to re-enter his body but the Teeth of the Ghost hooked little pieces of flesh from his back, which his uncle then cut off with the knife he had sharpened that morning and he knew that to cry out would be to anger the Ghosts, so he willed his soul to return to the Underworld.

He opened his eyes to this world, surrounded by the dancing, stamping feet of the Elders. Sat up, ignored by all. He knew this was because he was not yet reborn. He grabbed a handful of soot and rubbed it into his bleeding body, ignoring the wounds that oozed in disapproval. Daily for the next thirty days he would cover himself with more soot so that those in his village could not see him, or speak to him, for he had been swallowed by the Ghosts. Then on the thirtieth day the Ghosts would vomit him up and he would have the scars made by their teeth on his back to prove that he had been to the Underworld and been reborn. The village would rejoice and he would be feared and respected by all.

Padmini stood under the shower, letting the water wash the dust that was Bombay from her aching body. Tomorrow, she would be going home. Back to Melbourne. To a place where bodies were whole and babies were fat and happy and mosquitoes were harmless. Where the air smelled fresh and winters came every year and missing fingers were rare.

It was the missing fingers that she had noticed first, that day so long ago when, fresh out of her year's internship, she had followed her mother's advice and volunteered to work here. In this city choking on life and exhaust fumes and death and colour. Doctor Padmini Mukkadam. She thought she could save the world, back then. 'Go and see where you come from', her mother had said. 'Work in India for a while. *Then* you will be a real doctor.' She had been offended by her mother's words, felt all her years of study, of sleepless nights and frenzied shifts had been trivialised but her mother had just repeated 'Go to India,' and so she had come. And the first patient she had seen was a man with half his fingers missing who wanted a certificate saying he no longer had leprosy, so he could work. Leprosy. Just a word, in that safe cocoon she called home. But here ... here she saw the missing fingers, missing noses, missing toes until these mutilated bodies blended and unified and infested her nightmares and her thoughts and her soul. Mutilated bodies. Children burnt from unattended cooking fires, rickety toddlers with swollen bellies and fontanelles that never closed, women with perforated wombs and mutilated genitals, dried up faces that looked like disinterred mummies yet still breathed and suffered and could smile at her still. Smiles. Gifts from those who had nothing to give yet gave freely, asking nothing in return. Mutilated bodies feeding lice and fleas and rats and eventually cockroaches, shyly invading her heart, the seconds of her days, the eternity of her dreams.

Padmini stood under the shower, letting the water wash away her tiredness. Tiredness from working long hours, from fighting local authorities and arguing with religious leaders who nodded and always said yes but forgot all she said because she was a woman and therefore not important.

Jasmine linked arms with her friends, blatantly ignoring the stare of the drunk unfolding himself from the doorway. They danced down Swanston Street, three synthetically sexual butterflies in oversized wedge-sandals and too-short minis, young breasts absconding too-tight tops, long hair coloured and crimped and straightened and tied. Whispers, giggles and daring. Today was Jasmine's day. The day she confirmed her individuality and defied the wisdom of those who would fetter her to their suppressive realities. In her backpack the symbols of private school autocracy, in her wallet an ID card that ridiculed adult sobriety. She turned into an alleyway and climbed the metal stairs, her handmaidens close behind.

The sterility of the room silenced the girls. A bored, pasty wannabe asked for ID, then ignored it. 'Sit over there,' she told Jasmine, pointing to a bed in the middle of the room. Jasmine's handmaidens surrounded her in awe. Held her hand, grimaced and giggled. The wannabe grabbed Jasmine's tongue with cold metal forceps and Jasmine gagged. She felt the tip of the felt pen mark her tongue and the astringent liquid run down her throat. The handmaidens winced and looked away. Jasmine looked out the window at the Air India plane flying in a holding pattern above Tullamarine airport. The piercing canula punctured the underside of her tongue and she tried to stand as her salivary glands spurted in protest but the wannabe pushed her back down and one of her handmaidens whimpered. As the canula gored its way through the muscle Jasmine embraced the fogginess enveloping her mind.

'You look so cool! Yeah . . . so cool! Your dad's going to kill you!'

Jasmine smiled gingerly and shrugged.

'Thoo late now,' she said as she wiped a dribble of spit from her chin.

Fashion Chest

Emmett Stinson

Opens her chest only to find a cavity,
A vectorless tornado of moths
Devouring cutlets of clothes,
Mere vests where vestments had been.
So now the Thinker's thinking, the Moved Mover moving:
Are these phony fabrics my heart, moth-eaten by desire?
Without rhyme or raiment, the swarming cloth-eaters
Mimic a moving scarf around her neck,
Noose-like, now shimmy torpidly torso-ward
Into a slithering silk chemise. Under where
They warm the genitals, they balloon
Into bell-bottoms – now a southerly sashay into
Socks, shoes.
Their wings are pulsating tiny
Ventricles, beating on torso and neck. This second
Circulatory system vomits blood
Outside the body in a slow
Trickle of red paint falling off
White roses.

The rustle of their wings
Sounds like
'Eat me, eat me' and the Thinker
Sees a body that was hers, coated in
Soggy, crimson moths, and revolted by her own
Compulsion begins to eat her own skin,
Finding layer
After layer of blood and moths,
Moths and moths all the way down:
Where's the heart now?

Accommodation Wanted

Henry Ashley-Brown

He was dancing. He was singing. The windows were open, the music loud and the translucent white curtains drifting, trailing languidly in the warm evening breeze. *'Boom boom, boom boom, gonna get along without you now. Boom boom, boom boom, gonna get along without you now ...'* He twisted to the rhythm, surfed the beat, his black Cubano body at one with the music.

Mrs Theodosiopoulos lived in the apartment opposite, across the yawning void, above the straining top of a tree that came from the gloom of a courtyard far below. She had made herself monitor of unwanted noise and took it upon herself to shout it down. *'Boom boom, boom boom ...'* she heard and launched herself rotundly towards the window energised by righteousness, tensing her abdomen, ready to direct a chest full of volume.

Then she stopped. Briefly she saw him, as the curtains exhaled, dancing naked, his muscled torso glistening with sweat. The curtains sighed and fell back across his window. She decided to wait just a little longer. *'Boom boom, boom boom,'* rattled through the air. She regarded herself in the mirror, felt nervous with sudden excitement at the thought of losing a little weight by joining the dance class at the Snaz Latino where he taught. She smiled. *'Boom boom,'* she whispered and began to dance.

On the other side of the courtyard he was also smiling as he danced about in his new apartment, happy in his new accommodation, enjoying the re-created early twenty-first century décor. The day before he hadn't been quite so happy. Thinking about what a disaster his life could have become made him flinch, so he shook the feelings off in the dance.

As he moved about he looked at the strange old-fashioned

furniture, the homely utensils, the wind-up clock, the books he had not read because they had never been his. This style, 'New Cuba', was nearly as old-fashioned as the newly liberated Cuba. He felt at home. He must look at the photographs too. He couldn't believe his luck. What's more, he and James had become friends. They had a lot in common.

James also felt that the previous day had happened long ago. It was only yesterday that he had put his arm around his wife Eva in the gardens near the central fountain that gushed its four streams, Eden-like, to the north, south, east and west. He had waited weeks to get entry tickets. It was where their wedding photographs had been taken. It was supposed to be a surprise but instead of being pleased she had turned on him, shouting 'I don't love you, I don't love you, I don't love you.' He was stunned.

A child had wailed. People nearby turned, staring. She was still holding the real apple he had given her. It looked bizarre, the clutched green apple, partly eaten, gesticulating in front of her red dress. Follow the bouncing ball. It danced angrily to the hysterical storm in her voice as she went on and on.

He found himself looking at her as if he had never known her. He wondered if what was happening was real, as a policeman and a policewoman quietly but firmly eased them out of the gardens and shut the gate. They stood there preventing return. Then he noticed the Japanese tourists watching, capturing images. Did they think they were watching buskers? So together they had gone their solitary way.

Waking up in the spare room the next morning, James had groaned. Eva's heels were clicking across the floor of the family room. He caught a glimpse of her in jeans that didn't reach her hips and a tight blouse that didn't reach her waist. The blouse was Fuschia, or was it Thai Ruby? The high heels were Split Pomegranate.

His insides lurched hot with yesterday's shock and shame. Via the shower, hoping she might have left by the time he emerged, he got himself to the stainless steel European Cubano style kitchen with the granite-topped bench. Eva was there, so he read the previous day's paper instead of attempting to share breakfast.

He was supposed to be placatory, cajoling, affectionate. Eva was waiting. Looking up, he saw only that one of the goldfish was dead. It was floating bloated upside down in the water. The 'Accommodation Wanted' column was sparse. Perhaps in today's paper there would be something.

As he read, Eva's voice was in the background, scraping backwards and forwards as she walked, like shingle under the chop of water on a pebbled beach. When they had first met he had found her voice attractive and soothing. Often when they had talked their voices would blend comfortably in conversation. At night they had murmured in each other's arms. Now her voice was harsh with the hiss and collision of stones and he didn't answer. Their relationship had ended. His knowing had arrived without thought.

Eva had stopped talking. She was looking at him. She had been trying to prod something out of him, some response. James had become aware of the strange immediacy of each moment. She shrugged, put water in the percolator. She put the percolator on the stove; she lit the gas under the percolator in the stainless steel European Cubano style kitchen.

She took a saucer from the shelf. The cup clattered sharply on the saucer. He heard a teaspoon rattle on the saucer. She opened the refrigerator, took out the milk and put some in the cup. She put the milk back into the refrigerator. She put bread into the toaster and got out the Vita-Lite margarine with Omega 3 for health. She went back to the refrigerator, put back the Vita-Lite and took out the fig jam. The jar clacked on the hard granite bench.

She scraped the margarine onto the toast that was on the plate with the delicate flowers around its edges. Then she put the jam on and cut the gritty toast in half. The knife snapped sharply onto the plate as it bit through the crust. Between each movement and sound there was emptiness. He did not look at her. She did not look at him. She poured her coffee and stirred her coffee and drank it.

'I'm having an affair with someone who's a man,' she said and left.

Her perfume was still in the air. Her golden northern Italian hair had shone briefly in the light entering the door. Eva was more beautiful now than when they had married five years ago. James heard her staccato footsteps clatter across the foyer to the lift. There was the faint ding of the lift bell, then silence. He was pale but he smiled. *'Boom boom,'* he sang to himself, *'Boom boom, gonna get along without you now. Gotta along without you before I met you, gonna get along without you now. Gonna find somebody twice as cute, cos you didn't love me anyhow ...'* He began to dance, throwing off his shirt, kicking off his shoes, hauling off his jeans, his socks, his Calvin Klein briefs.

Ambrose the dog barked, leaped about excitedly. The noise drifted across the dark well of the deep down courtyard he had never visited. A warm breeze played with the white translucent curtains that overlooked brick wall and the desperate top of a tree seeking light.

Melissa Mladenovich, who had been on night duty at the city hospital where she was ward sister, levered herself out of bed swearing and moved to a shouting position at her vibrating window, which was shut when she slept because it opened onto the fire escape. She feared intruders. She hurled it open and identified the source. About to shout, she stopped. She liked what she saw.

James's perfect white body was an antidote for her despair about the carcasses she was trying to hold together in the geriatric ward until new accommodation could be found for them. A hirsute letter 'Y' ran enticingly in a dark line from his nipples to his navel and onwards. She wanted to run her finger along it and say 'Yes!' So *nice* to see a *young* person, she decided.

The music swept into her room.

'Boom boom,' she sang softly. His curtains ran out of breeze and blocked her view. *'Boom boom,'* she continued to sing, looking at a picture of her husband, who indulged in large doses of carbohydrate. *'Boom boom.'* Melissa Mladenovitch tapped her foot, took a few rhythmical steps, smiled. But across the way, the music suddenly stopped.

James had been prodded by Ambrose's cold, wet nose. The dog

lowered its head and ran to the door. Its ears were down, it licked its lips and whined. He needed to be taken out urgently. James dressed quickly, put on Ambose's leash and headed for the allocated dog zone, which is where he met Adan.

Adan, in another apartment, in another part of the city, had groaned when he felt the skin above his location implant begin to tingle and grow warm. It was compulsory viewing time. He had to watch the usual picture of scars made during unofficial attempts to remove implants. Then came the affirmations and success stories of the elderly who had moved to new accommodation.

Finally the camera visited the Ruddock Centre. Distressed illegals who had refused to co-operate by volunteering their accommodation were being repatriated, weeping and struggling, to countries who were signatories to the Treaty of Returns. Dogs were treated better, Adan decided. If only he were a dog. He would run until he couldn't think about it. He decided that a jog would be the next best thing, dressed quickly and left.

James sat in Permission Park near Ambrose's favourite group of self-flushing plastic trees and checked the paper for Accommodation. Ambrose had already made friends with someone who was trying to jog through the zone. James was used to people who talked to Ambrose and completely ignored him, so he did not at first look up when he heard the greeting. The man was black. His sweat shirt had a neat line of damp down the centre.

'Is this your dog?' he was saying. 'It was following me. I'm Adan.' Ambrose was enjoying the man's attention. 'He's beautiful. If only people could swap accommodation with dogs.' Ambrose wagged his tail with delight and slobbered on Adan's knees.

'Are you on a "Swap or Leave" visa?' James looked interested, had spoken impulsively.

'Yes, I don't know what to do.'

'But you know what you don't want to do!'

'Yes, I was hoping to swap with someone my age, not with an old official or someone sick, or . . .'

'Exactly! Do you have any problems with health or crime? Do you have dependants?'

'No, only problems with my girlfriend. Too possessive. Nothing else. You can check. Are you saying you're interested in swapping with a Cubano who comes under the Treaty of Returns: the Swap or Leave treaty?'

'Yes.'

'*You* must have *big* problems!' Adan was interested.

'My wife and I have just separated.'

'So you want to swap accommodation, full swap, everything?'

'Yes, I don't want to be married any more. A swap ensures divorce and I'm a citizen, so there won't be any problems for you. On the contrary, you'll gain instant citizenship. I assume you're healthy otherwise you would have been sent back under the terms of the Treaty of Returns.' The two smiled. Adan nodded his agreement.

'Do you dance or sing?' Adan asked, laughing. Both felt uneasy, surprised but relieved that so much had been decided so quickly.

'When it's something special, like today.'

'I teach dance. If you like I'll help out if you want the job.'

'It's okay, I have a job. They'll have to get used to my new image though!'

Adan liked his new accommodation, liked dancing in his new white body. '*Boom boom, boom boom.*' He had reached the framed photos at the end of the room. Astounded, he stopped. There smiling back at him was a picture of his difficult girl-friend Eva.

On the other side of town James was enjoying his new accommodation in Adan's fit lithe black Cubano body.

'*Boom boom,*' he sang. Ambrose leapt and barked, '*boom boom, gonna get along without her now.*'

Maybe a new girlfriend too he wondered. The doorbell rang. He danced to the door and opened it.

It was a woman, very attractive with two large suitcases. Her jeans didn't quite reach her hips. Her blouse was a Fuschia colour, or was it Thai Ruby? And the high heels, Split Pomegranate. Her hair in the light of the foyer glowed gold. A deliciously fresh fragrance drifted in the air.

'I've left him!' she said. 'I told James I'm having an affair with someone who's a man.'

The Last Men

Emmett Stinson

'One could well say of the event horizon what the poet Dante said of the entrance to Hell: "All hope abandon, ye who enter here."'
– Stephen Hawking, *A Brief History of Time*

9

They had left the land where it was hard to live, for they needed warmth. Rex Erection made a quick phone call, gave the good word and with a wave of the hand, prestidigitated a weekend getaway to Florida in a typical gesture of opulent charity. And he that hath not charity . . . so Rex delivered the three pale New Englanders from the bondage of northern ice and snow, having done everything but bear them himself on his very own back. But the flight on his father's jet had seemed miraculous enough to justify Rex's initiation into the canon of holiday saints, if not his anointment as the get-away-from-it-all saviour.

'Perhaps he could be the saint of inebriation or of suntans,' Peter had remarked.

Matter favoured these suggestions because although Rex did have a hippie beard, the only other similarity between him and the Son of Man that Matter noted lay in his proclivity for prostitutes. Betrayal rears the only head it has: the ugly one. Not that he wasn't grateful, mind you.

You can keep your judgments to yourself.

8

Matter's lips meet the cheek of the lion's bust. He expects its marble to be cooler than the ambient air but a dull warmth reveals it as some sort of plasticated, plastery, papier-mâché-cum-ceramiclacquery-faux-finish-übersubstance. Nothing as it seems. Matter alights on a folding chair to reach the cheek while Virginia Dentata kisses its obverse, two and one half inches away.

– FLASH –

Blind and unbalanced, Matter feels his world slip briefly into uncertainty.

'Those kisses weren't synchronised!' bellows Peter Diameter, savouring the Kodak moment. Wry lips curl catlike. Polaroid spits forth issue. Matter, catching the fountain's lip short of the stream of lion-slobber, locates his centre of gravity right before he's hurled headlong to bottomless perdition. Virginia descends and jogs to the table even as Matter follows her behind. *Behind's her best angle*, Matter thinks.

But the font of all this discord is Asshole, being as you know the drinking game where the seemingly simple object is to run out of cards first and the order in which you disappear from the game determines your rank in the next hand, such that the winners of the previous hand gain not only your best cards but also total domination over your body and soul which manifests mostly in the form of forcing you to drink more alcohol and kiss ass but as you continue to lose and be the asshole this situation grows more grave because you are unable to run out of cards and stay in the game the longest exposing you to the alcoholic censure of those above you until you're intoxicated and the resulting impairment of judgment reduces your strategic planning capabilities down to the zero mark ensuring you will never rise above your denigrated status in the hierarchy so that this vicious circle seems more medieval torture than game when you are on the receiving end of its harshest beverage-quaffing affronts.

'The Asshole is supposed to get screwed, but I'm not the asshole, Virginia is.'

'Don't lose your head, Matter. I'm supposed to embarrass you. There are rules . . .'

In Asshole, the ruling classes amend the game's simple but volatile constitution and thus Virginia and Matter run over and place synchronised kisses on the spitting lion's face every time that doubles fall. Although Rex is King the rule itself was dreamed up by Peter Diameter. That Rex stamped it with his seal of approval Matter finds odd in that Rex is ever so slightly psychotically possessive about the matter of his girlfriends, so it's strange for him to enforce a rule that places her in near-intimate contact with any male, even a friend like Matter.

Although extreme, Rex once rationalised his intense jealousy to Virginia: 'It's not my fault I can't trust my friends,' he had said. 'If you can't trust them, make them fear you.'

'Rex has a way with matters of the heart,' Virginia noted.

Still, Matter has the comfort of knowing that Virginia has it worse in a very certain and very visceral way. With every drink, she's got to clutch her chest and moan '*OH, FUCK ME!*' This second rule of Rex's reign was again created by Peter Diameter and the odd twinkle in his eye accompanying its execution suggests its prompting was more than mere misogyny.

The truly depressing thought Matter represses in some deeper cavern of his consciousness is that he knows he's experienced all of these events before, if in slight variations, during previous games of Asshole. All these events are returning in some horrible and heavy circle of retributive recurrence and he entertains the sickening conception that, as his life stretches across time reencountering the same events and the same people in summer reruns, they are compressed into one infinitely dark and dense singularity by sheer gravity alone.

'No one knows how to torture me quite like my friends,' Rex had once said.

'You didn't really enjoy kissing the lion that time. Take a drink.'

'Fuck you,' Matter snaps bitterly before Corona touches his lips.

'*YOU MUST CONFORM. RESISTENCE IS USELESS.*'

'Take a drink. Both of you assholes.'

'*OHHHHHHH, FUCK ME!*' Virginia clutches her impressive breasts per Peter's orders before the glass rim of the bottle meets her lips.

'Sorry,' Matter quietly offers watching her clutch herself.

'Second best rule I ever made.'

Earlier today she was heaping loads of suntan lotion onto those same heaving breasts while sitting by the pool, which was neither heaping nor heaving. Those same creamy white lumps of mozzarella; massive glowing headlights were attached to her when she was on Matter's shoulders during the chicken fighting in the pool. Peter, of course, was homoerotically astride Rex's. The two boys, obviously advantaged, were winning. Virginia, perched on Matter, was shoved back until it was too deep for Matter to stand. He was drowning, swallowing chlorinated water like those Coronas. Reaching up he grabbed the first thing he could; the buttock attached to the girl. He shoved the girl over by the buttock attached to her. The girl splashed in the water and, naturally, the buttock, attendant upon the usual rules of gravity, followed behind. Matter felt embarrassed afterward about grabbing her. Sure, he was drowning but he still felt uncomfortable touching, even aggressively or necessarily, her ass. Virginia now imploring all in earshot to fuck her didn't help his embarrassment much either.

Only Matter and Virginia remain, battling it out for last place. A left hand plucks one card from the right and slowly, slowly, Virginia turns it over where it lays resting on the table: the Queen of Hearts. Virginia is silent.

'Last card!!!!!' Matter yells as Virginia's face falls.

'You just got fucked,' says Rex.

You see, not saying last card is the cardinal sin. If someone should utter these two words before your final card falls, then you are automatically the asshole.

'I don't see how it matters since were out of beer.' Peter grins as Matter's victory collapses like the proverbial house of cards.

Matter slides back the balcony's glass door to adjudicate the veracity of Mr Diameter's alcohol-related truth claim. The fridge reveals four Coronas, which, divided by four people, equals one beer apiece. The harmony of said equation somehow reassures him as he returns.

'We're going to the ninth hole.' Peter commands, the rest obey.

7

Night air rushes them down the dark driveway in a dream of speed. The bright lights of phallic condo complex rip open the black sky.

'The city of Oz.' Peter points to the phallus.

They cross a bridge and cut through a swathe of trees that yields to the lush grass of the green, follow Rex's tyre tracks to the heavy inevitability of the ninth hole. The riders dismount, squat Indian-style. Matter opens his bag of magic tricks containing four Coronas and a further fact in the bottle of tequila that will sadly remain lime-less.

'Tequila . . . not so much a liquor as a bad idea,' Peter noted.

Matter greedily mosquito-sucks a swig of Sauza as those same bugs perforate the thin paper of his flesh. 'Drink me,' he says tossing the bottle and watching Peter and Virginia play hot potato with the passed-off potent potable. Peter lights another cigarette from the butt-end of his last like a pilot light lighting some internal inferno that burns and rages producing the exhaust he exhales. Rex is rolling the green leafy matter up in a soft supple paper. Nimble fingers dart back and forth to quick slips of the tongue, lashing out in viper-like licks and whetting the white paper. Matter chugs, feels the burn in the back of the throat that diffuses into the extremities of his chest, the dark pit of his belly. Rex twice flicks his lighter's revolving wheel, which sings until it bears a loving flame and when the flame and the cone kiss, it snaps and crackles with crisp pops as Rex inhales and exhales.

'Like the flesh of burning sinners.' Rex exhales.

'Gross . . . and don't bogart the . . .'

'This is my body. This is my blood.' The joint crosses from Rex to Virginia. Peter puffs and inhales. Puffs and inhales.

'Here Matter . . .'

'Damn it!' Matter winces in pain as he passes the roach.

'Damn it! My leg.' Virginia smacks the snow-white inner thigh marred by a mosquito's carcass and the shadow of blood.

'Fucking bloodsuckers!!! It's fucking vampiric!'

Peter Diameter sucks his cigarette and Rex coughs from the

smoke hanging like incense. The susurrus of burning cigarettes, the glug of swishing alcohol, these are the sounds of this rite on the green.

'We are all our own ram in the thicket,' Matter meditates as he feels his head expand suddenly. Subtly, slowly, the detached fiery head of his body begins leering at him and he's off occupying two points in space simultaneously without knowing where his body ends and where the world begins or whether he's sixty feet tall, a limbo that exists only as the space between two places, nothing signifying anything so that he wouldn't know a raised middle finger or the word 'death' or be able to distinguish an advertisement from a real TV program under the spell of these hazy drugs and fuzzier alcohol.

'This is tremendously exciting communication, fellahs,' Virginia drawls, 'but I think that I might have a quilt to finish sewing with some Amish people. You're so boring I can actually feel my life disintegrating into meaninglessness.' She moves a few stray hairs from her mouth to the soft crease behind her ear. Matter glances at her body and then the flagpole planted deeply in the cup of the ninth hole.

'Huh?'

'I'm high. I'm so fucking high that I'm practically floating on a cloud in heaven.'

'Alright, fellahs, that's it. Entertain me,' Virginia says. 'I need to be entertained.'

And she's right. We all need to be entertained. We all do.

6

Aaaaaannnnd Action!

'Come on, Matter! Snap out of it! We gotta go!' Rex rings out in the voice of salvation, recalling Matter from his pot-induced dimensional warp back to the mainstream conception of time and reality, and the headlights and the spots in his eyes provide all the necessary stimulus Matter needs to respond by hopping on his bike and pedalling, tequila-filled backpack slung across his shoulder. The dim apparitions of bicycles appear on the artificial horizon of his vision as a shadowy flash-lighted figure runs to the ninth hole filled with the emptiness left by the absent drinkers.

BMX tyres tear up the mown green, spitting turf behind. Matter moves without foresight, directionless, up a hill and descending into the Sarlac Pit of a sand trap, avoiding collapse by allowing his momentum to push him through like the voice of a speaker stumbling toward the sentence's inexorable period. He follows the two vague bike-figures in front of him and veers off the green toward an anfractuous golf cart path.

'Here, down here.'

Virginia points to a desolate-looking road materialising out of the wet fur of the sappy green. Minus an ET on his handlebars, this road less travelled is Matter's best means of escape and he pursues Peter and Virginia down into the depths of that unknown, dark, and unforgiving tunnel of night.

5

'Where's Peter?' Virginia's voice pierces the darkness of night.

'I don't know ... I ...' Matter pedals up alongside Virginia as they survey the land for their missing friend. Peter's gone. Two remain.

4

So Matter and Virginia set off down the road less travelled, two pale silhouettes embarking on the post-modern version of the long journey home, two figures alone in the dark corridor of primeval night, Adam and Eve at the end of history. True, the real nexus of their attractions lies in their sheer inability to communicate. He can't talk to her comfortably, nor she to him, and every awkward and pause-filled exchange is, for both, pure pornography. The path curves around the golf green, and the moon illuminates the whole scene, as it often does.

'Watch out! You're about to step in –' Matter's body reacts to the warm hands leading him around a dark, pungent pile on the ground.

'You should look where you're going,' she says.

Matter blushes, embarrassed by his near misstep and changes the topic.

'It looked like you were ready to crucify Rex back at the ninth hole there.'

'Rex can be an asshole. I accept that. But at moments he's unbelievably gentle. Most people haven't seen that side of him . . .'

I guess I haven't.

'Rex is real sensitive. You wouldn't know from all the shit he says, but underneath it all, he has the soul of a poet. He reads Whitman every morning, the *Song of Myself*, he's read it to me –'

' – In the voices of cartoon characters? Are we talking about the same Rex?'

'Maybe you just don't know your friends as well as you think you do.'

'Who knows anyone? Like that science experiment with cards.'

'Experiment?' Virginia drips with disinterest.

'These people were looking at cards, calling them out as the scientist held them up, but the scientist made trick cards.'

'Like what, a black Queen of Hearts?'

'Yeah,' Matters voice is wavering his left foot steps off the path and recovers itself damp from the dewy green . . .' At high speeds no one noticed, they'd just say "Queen of Spades" or "Queen of Hearts" as if nothing were wrong at all. But when, when they slowed it down, just a little, and asked again, people started hesitating . . . knew something was wrong, but didn't know what exactly, like they saw a red border around a black heart, or something . . .'

'Uh-huh . . .'

'. . . and, and when they slowed it down even more, most people just couldn't . . . they'd, they'd get so confused they'd say the card looked wrong, but they didn't . . . they . . . they didn't even know what was wrong . . . I . . .'

'Do you have a point, here, Matter?' Ahead the trees are thinning. There is a light and the dull outline of a phallus.

'Look, I don't know, you just . . . you can't be sure . . . what . . . what is that ahead? We're here? We're actually here? Isn't that the pool?'

'Wow ... I ... is it time for a celebratory swim?
'Why not?' Why not indeed.

3

In the pool with a beautiful woman, the weight of the past crashes into the future. But I want this to be clear: the pool is real, man.

This is Virginia and Matter in the pool.

This is Virginia asking, 'Do you want a cigarette?' This is a suggestion appearing ridiculously self-indulgent to Matter. This is Matter swimming over to the side of the pool where Virginia is. This is Virginia grabbing two cigarettes from the pack at the pool's edge. These are the waves in the pool made even by tiny imperceptible motions. This is Matter.

The room of a college campus somewhere, three years ago, where Matter's tongue slides down the throat of a college co-ed whose mouth yields in gaping embrace waiting to be filled by the emptiness of some drunken weekend passion. The two bodies converge at the tongue the legs the hips, as if they were using the old rule of sailing that one must always maintain three points of contact whilst going from boat to dock or back again, even as the dizziness causes them to fall back onto a desk with a loud thwack and the girl yells 'Fuck!' at the point where the desk hits her in the back and the woman that Matter loves and who loves him is sleeping somewhere as Matter giggles at the young woman holding her back in pain even as she laughs and says 'Ow' and laughs again.

These are two cigarettes being lit simultaneously. This is Matter inhaling. This is Matter exhaling. This is Matter watching his smoke puff out in broad circles like smoke puffing out in broad circles. This is Matter staring at the light glinting in Virginia's blue eyes. This is the light that's the light reflecting off the pool. This light is the light from the shining condo-phallus above. This is Virginia asking, 'What are you staring at?'

In a place called high school Matter visited a girlfriend whose rich parents took them to the Bahamas, and they went swimming in a blue hole. This blue hole was at least three hundred feet deep according to the best estimates, but no one had been able to ascertain exactly how far it went down. It was filled with fresh water that was perfectly blue and not a single living thing above microscopic size lived in this water. Matter looked down the hole with goggles and its depth was overwhelming. He felt the same awesome sense of the sublime that one feels while staring up close to a skyscraper but in reverse, downward, hell-ward, as if this were awe reaching straight down to the deep heart of things.

The co-ed laughs again and Matter says, 'Here, you want me to kiss it and make it feel better?' as he slips her shirt over her head like a peel off a banana and she laughs at both his insolence and the joke and they fall laughing under the desk, under the desk moaning, 'Oh yes, yes, kiss it.'

This is Matter exhaling. This is Matter watching his smoke puff out in broad circles like Matter watching smoke puff out in broad circles. This is Matter saying 'Nothing.' This is the weight of history snowballing. This is disloyalty.

The sides of the hole were smooth and oddly organic, like the way that volcanic rock resembles burnt flesh, only this stuff seemed closer to sections of smooth muscle tissue. He couldn't stay in the blue hole very long because he was convinced that this was the earth's bowels and some prehistoric creature believed to be extinct for sixty five million years would arise from the depths, devouring him in a burst of terror and anachronism. As if. As if there were something deep in the dark heart of the earth, which he could feel slowly rising, rising with its heat sensors locked on him.

This is Matter rotating his shoulders, confused. This is Virginia saying, 'What's wrong?' These are the waves in the pool made by even tiny imperceptible motions. This is Matter saying, 'My neck is sore from chicken fighting.' This is dialogue.

Matter is fucking the co-ed under the desk and he watches himself while he watches the girl that he loves and loves him sleeping somewhere and Matter knows even in this moment of ecstasy that there is something deep and dark within him, something that he can't excise or resolve as the girl moans beneath him, saying, 'Oh fuck me, oh fuck me, oh fuck me, oh fuck me, oh.'

This is Virginia saying, 'I can massage it for you. I used to be an athlete in high school. I do this stuff all the time.' This is Matter laughing. This is a raw chafing laugh that comes deep from the belly. This is a laugh that echoes across the pool. This is a laugh of total release and total confusion. This is what matters. This is laughing about the thought of being in a pool drunk, smoking cigarettes and getting a massage from a beautiful woman. This is a hearty laugh. This is your momma. This is how perfect the world could be if one moment were stretched to infinity.

Matter does the dead man's float in the hole peering down and awaiting something, anything, even horrible devouring, to take him from this stillness.

This is Matter floating in the pool, even though he feels so heavy inside that he should sink to the bottom, that gravity should pull him down through the cement and the ground and straight to the bottom of the earth, straight to the depths.

This is the pressure of the sin on his lips. 'Oh, yes, yes, kiss it. Kiss it and make it feel better.'

2
her body looks like this

and when your fingertips expand to touch the whiteness of the flesh you remember that eternity doesn't mean forever but existing outside of time as you stroke the curves surrounding her hips you know what it means to hear the chorus of heavenly angels singing in glorious unison as your hands move ever upward and onward you caress the curves of space itself these are the folds of the fabric of reality the fountains of life that give humanity its everlasting life the nectar and ambrosia of the mythological imagination the alchemy of the Taoists and you see the nipples that are a shade of pink so inviolable that they must be called a different colour may transgress the known boundaries of colour a sensory experience wholly new as the fleshy firmness gives seems to expand like stars hurtling away with that tell-tale Dopplerian red shift and beneath is the rumble of the heart beating that is the pulse of the universe the pull of the waves that gravity heaves ever inward and outward inward and outward in a sublunary tug of war and when you have entered the holiest of her altars descended to her depths you find that the entrance is an exit that the descent is ever swiftly upward out of the cave of Plato's allegory to where ideas become things in and of themselves and in the merging you remember that Milton said that when the angels fucked their entire bodies interpenetrated each other until they merged into one viscous and seething being a whole two emptinesses filling each other with substance and you are sucking at the tree of life where the roots have sunk deep in the soil where you find yourself still sinking until you feel the clap of thunder the Da the shuddering that shakes a body the amen the holy holy the wholly holy hole so be it so be it so be it till there lingers only the shadow of the valley of the shadow of death that follows upon the intensity of all experiences as you merge back into life shot from this womb you have ever so briefly cobbled together as after ascending and descending in DNA spirals you know that nothing ever ever will be as it was before even though it will be because it has to be and this too shall fade to dusty death you breathe the breath that is as it was in the beginning when the first shall be last

and this is what her body looks like

1

A plane descends in a cloud-muddled sky and Matter's copy of *Inferno* has ceased to hold his attention. The crumpled Money section of a *USA Today* lies next to Peter who is rapt in slumber. Rex's head tilts back, drool dropping from his dewy mouth and Virginia lies foetally curled on her seat like a napping cat. Matter is exhausted but unsleeping. His hung over conscience could benefit from an anaesthetic administered in one of those miniature liquor bottles that Rex's father keeps hidden away but he's drowsing too, and the key is somewhere deep in his pocket. Matter tries to hold himself in that nether-realm between waking and sleeping because he fears that, as he slides into sleep, he might feel something like his very self slipping away, that the dark things might possess his body, zombie-like. Maybe he feels just as desperately empty as all of the Corona bottles he stuffed into bow-tied plastic recycling bags this morning, or else's he's just recovering from a hell of a bender. Maybe that's why he feels like such an unbelievable asshole. He gazes out at the clouds, which now resemble some smoke-machined limbo from a dream sequence in a movie and silently wonders, *What kinds of clouds are these again? Cumulonimbus? What's the other kind? I keep wanting to say striated or Stradivarius.* Matter's squinting to peer through them and they yield nothing but a white theophanic density. Nothing but a promise caged off by twelve inches of glass. *It was just a weekend at the beach*, he tells himself. *It was all playing and games, there's no such thing as betrayal when you're just playing games* ... and his eyes peer upward and downward, while he hangs between, as he looks but doesn't see the one thing he missed during his weekend at the beach. He never saw the ocean. He never did see the ocean.

Lips

John De Laine

despite the blindfold, Angela, I know the taste:
your wine was bottled
in France.
and don't think
that pasta has got me fooled:
it's those San Remo spirals; the sauce you used
is hot red tomato and straight from
your parents' garden.
and you chewed on Doritos
behind my back.
you don't fool me: the serenade of a Mexican guitarist
glides on your breath,
his lyrics locked
between your teeth as you smile.
and I know you must be smiling.

the itch

Rachel Hennessy

she is thin and petite and not like anything he's ever seen before. a new thing, a creature made up of flesh and bone but only just pulsing. only just.

he watches her standing on the platform, scratching her nose. she looks up at the board with the lights showing the train stations. a man with a fluorescent orange vest walks past and she doesn't even blink.

a billboard asks 'In a rush to get to the top?' and someone shoves him in the back. hold on fuckwit. there's time. no need to shove.

the train's coming, that's the reason for the pushing, he knows that. there are some things he knows.

she takes a step forward. she's still behind the yellow line, obeying the rules like she should. she should be obeying the rules 'cause there's no reason to be doing the wrong thing.

the train pulls in.

his thin, petite girl steps into the carriage. she minds the gap between the train and the platform. he looks down at that gap, wondering what it'd be like to fall into it. squashed up against the warm steel of the train metal. squashed up and taken places.

'you gettin' on?' yeah alright. he's been standing there looking at the gap.

steps into the train, hopes she didn't see him standing there, thinking.

goes up the stairs to where the blue plastic seats are all fixed in one direction. she's in the third seat from the front of the carriage. she's scratching the back of her neck. she's a scratcher. he knows what that's like. itching. itching to get out of your skin, into

someone else's. not happy. not right. all the scratching and dissatis-
faction, dried cells under the fingernails, layers of dirt even though
you wash every morning. she's got shiny shampoo hair like in an
ad. bouncy.

the train starts moving through tunnels and city highlights.
she's staring out the window through the circles of a graffiti tag.
she's rubbing at her eyes with the back of her hand. she's thinking
about her night. what's she gonna do? sit on the couch watching
reality TV. eat toast. ring that guy from the pub whose number is
on the back of a beer-coaster in her purse. put on her flirty voice.
inflect up at the end of each sentence. 'you want to meet for a drink
sometime?' he knows her type.

on the loudspeaker they're rattling off the names of stations. she
must be going to the end of the line, going as far as you can go. he
can tell she's satisfied 'cause she's stopped scratching. it doesn't last
long. now she's biting at her fingernails. rubbing the edge of her
thumbnail in between her teeth. shaving it back.

someone opens a window and wind rushes in. the diesel wind of
a tunnel. it chokes him up. he starts coughing. can't stop now. he
coughs so much there's spit coming out of his mouth, flicking
onto the inside of his palm. she twists her head over her right
shoulder with contempt. he sees her pupils in the right corner of
her eyelids, her lashes lower.

it's that moment. he knows what he's gonna do.

a rush of tunnel air swoops in. some guy behind her starts
coughing and coughing. hacking. she turns her head to the right to
see who it is. twist of the neck, stretch of the muscle, drop of the
eyelids. he doesn't have a handkerchief. her mouth puckers. she's
sympathetic, hates the smell of the oil.

that's the moment. she sees his face.

'In a rush to get to the top?' the billboard asked him. couldn't
think of the answer. is he? not really. doesn't know what the top is.
top of what? top of the heap? top of the ladder? he'd been on top
before, watching their faces go crazy as he grinded. but that wasn't
what they meant. they wanted to know if he was eager to get ahead,
shoot into consumer heaven 'cause it was in their best interests to

get him to the top. more money to spend, more cash to cough up. he wasn't stupid. that's one thing he'd never been called. there were plenty of stupid people but he wasn't one of them. sometimes he was overwhelmed by the stupid people. what he said to stupid people in his head would've made their hair stand on end. he sniggers when he imagines that happening. hairs sticking up like pins.

the train stops at the place where all the Kooris hang out. he sees two of them sitting on the bench with the station name painted on it. they look like American basketball players: big sports shoes, caps, chewing mouths. the old woman behind him sniffs loudly. he can't tell if she's showing her racist disapproval or if she's got a cold. the train starts up again.

his petite woman has turned her head back to the window. she coughs into her hand, catching the tunnel wind later than him. now she knows how he felt. the thought of her feeling the way he did makes him feel even better. she knows what it's like to be me, he thinks, touching the inside of his leg with his right hand.

her handbag has fallen over and she reaches down to pick it up. she wants to hold her handbag, worried about snatchers. 'Where is your bag now?' the ads ask her. and sometimes she doesn't know. sometimes she can't even remember if she has put her purse in her handbag, or her filofax, or her sunglasses, or her keys. she's done it so many times there's no way to distinguish between having done it today or having done it three months ago. each one of her days blurs into the other like a mash of memories so sometimes she wonders if it's even worth bothering.

he scratches at the side of his cheek, at the pimple just beginning to form. he uses his fingernails until he draws blood. it's a relief, like the red stuff is leaching something out of him. draining. he likes to create release valves so that it doesn't get too much. otherwise his fingers start to drum together and people, mainly stupid people, glare at him like he's annoying. or else he starts to click his tongue against the roof of his mouth. he can see how that'd be irritating.

lamp posts go past like goal posts. goal posts look like cruci-fixes. speeding by a school oval, boys falling over at soccer practice.

boys who'd forget each other's names in ten years time, bump into one another on the street and look away, pretending they don't remember. the coach standing on the side silently yelling, forgetting how much he hated being screamed at when he was a school boy falling over at soccer practice.

station after station. he still knows, he thinks. this is so right, he thinks. no one says anything to dispute it. 'God has not said a word'. a line from a poem he read once. probably one he learnt at school, some ancient poet dead forever with no fucking idea of what it's like to get by now. to know what to do. to find a space to fit. he crosses his arms. hugs himself. tastes the blood on the end of his finger.

the train is slowing down. the petite girl stands up, shuffles along the edge of the seat, steps out into the corridor. stretches her neck to the left, then the right. getting rid of the journey. wants to get it out of her body, he thinks, loosen up, forget who she is at work. he can see the change. the way she's moving. different from what she was before. she's morphing. taking on the animal she is.

he stands up. the old woman sitting behind him goes past, sneezing into an embroidered handkerchief. he coughs. still got the remnants of the tunnel in his throat.

'gettin out?' some fuckwit behind him, stopped by him standing in the corridor of seats. yeah yeah. no rush. she isn't moving, just perched at the top of the stairs waiting for the jerk as the train pulls up. in one moment their bodies convulse forward with the momentum of the final brakes, then fall back. he sighs.

she knows where she's going. her feet, strapped into patent leather heels with an elaborate buckle, clip confidently down the stairs of the carriage.

'sorry mate'.

the fuckwit behind him actually bumps into his shoulder.

sure you're sorry you stupid fucker. can't even wait. can't even fucking wait your fucking turn.

'no problem,' he mutters, so faint it sounds like a whistle. clomps down the stairs and out the train door, over the gap. not so much of a gap anymore, the train seems to have got closer, more intimate with the platform. the petite girl is already halfway up the platform stairs, taking the railway bridge that crosses over the tracks.

he starts up the stairs. passing under the lights of the bridge he feels the pull of her. she is walking slowly. no doubt about it. there is no rush, no have-to-get-home to watch the greed spectacle. she doesn't need that tonight. and it is night now, not dusk. the darkness has stolen in, thieving the day away.

she drops something out of her jacket pocket, one of those jackets with a glowing look like they ought to be rainproof but they aren't. she's been rummaging round the bottom of her pocket finding bits of washing-machined tissues and an M&M she didn't eat.

when the thing falls out of her hand she lets it drop down the side of her leg, too embarrassed to be caught littering. he is far enough behind for her not to notice. close enough for him to see. she speeds up, getting away from the scene of the crime.

he bends down to pick up the token. stretches his fingers. feels the muscles expand and contract. watches his hand as if it isn't attached to his arm. hand opens. hand closes. ragged fingernails with the beginnings of a wart on the side of the thumb.

in his hand the token sits. a token of her affection.

it's a train ticket. creased along the middle. the paper marked. right hand corner folded then flattened out. thin black stripe of embossed ink, the coded message the machine reads. touch of the sound of gates opening, red jaws closing too quickly. tiny print of the cost of the ticket in the bottom left corner. dollar sign fading.

he puts the token in his own pocket. feels the edge of the cardboard on his own finger.

he walks on, through the patches of light up the suburban mall, spaces between the shops fitted with uneven hexagon paving and huge pots of drooping plants. his reflection a second behind him in the windows mixed up with the racks of unoccupied clothing hanging like dead men.

she has turned a corner. he can't see her for a second and it scares him. quickens up. gets round the corner. there she is. getting over the quiet street, one sedan slowing down to let her use the pedestrian crossing.

now she's walking through the park. a park that borders the beginnings of the beach. a park lined with imported palm trees, trunks like beer guts.

wait for me, his head screams. but he doesn't say anything. the petite girl is a shadow mixing with shadows. one minute part of the footpath, the next a tangle of branches and playground swings.

'On your way to the top?' another billboard asks. so many fucking questions. he feels like spitting. so much saliva in his mouth he feels kinda sick. too much juice. he is sure she knows he's there. her footsteps aren't rushing. there is definitely something between them. she coughs. there. that's it. she knows. a way to remember their past.

he follows the echo of the cough.

she walks into the laneway. dark in between two dark houses. no squares of light to reassure her the TVs are being kept company. she's walked down this laneway most of her life. sat here with her best friend trying her first fag. on the cement a love heart with initials. she can't remember who they stand for anymore. she's walked down this laneway dragging a schoolbag too heavy with romance paperbacks. now she has a round, sweet handbag, Prada imitation. there's her mother waiting at home still but no red welts on the back of her thighs for indiscretions 'unworthy of a lady'; the nuns willing to whip the sex right out of her. her mother will go to bed early and she'll ring his number, dropping her voice to a breathy whisper, planning an indiscretion: 'I'd love to go out. when do you finish work?'

a cat is scratching its bum on the timber fence, loving the splinters, purring like an engine. in the dark the cat's eyes glow. she doesn't touch it. they carry a disease that put her mother's sister's neighbour's cousin in the hospital for a year. disgusting animals, should be drowned in large vats of hot water. the scratching cat looks at her, feeling the hate. it stops purring, scrambles vertically up the fence, disappearing. she keeps walking down the lane, feeling the raised bump of cement, the overhanging branch which cuts at you if you don't duck. such familiar territory, the struggling rags of grass seem to wave hello. another day over. another journey from the train. another night with red wine and pasta.

behind her the sound of other feet. there's usually the man at the end of the street coming home from his job as a teacher, dragging his heels like he told the schoolboys not to all day. a mild flirt.

but these feet aren't dragging. soft and fast.

she turns her head like she did on the train. no sympathy this time. the swerve of fear, the need to see in the dark. too late.

he feels time stop. as if the particles in the air are hanging. in this non-time he sees it all. a severed bird's wing flying through the air, his mother's blood on the chopping board, a brown wooden stool. miniature bits of a mass he couldn't get to stop moving. it was too fucking much. when time stops, he thinks, it's gotta mean something. it's gotta mean this was meant to happen. this has to happen. this is what he has to do. without doubt. world without end.

her head swerves around. sees his eyes. for a moment she thinks it's the cat returned, full of hate. she knows she's wrong. so many times in her life she's been wrong. wrong about the married manager and his undying love, wrong about how much she'd like retail, wrong about her mother's nagging to catch a taxi home from the train station, a waste of hard-earned cash.

it's her laughing laneway full of secrets, whispered confessions, graffiti tags, the stain of dog's piss. she always wants to walk down this lane, always live in the memory of her childhood, sprinting home to hot chocolate. but as she is pierced by his eyes she wants to sprout wings, spiral off above the houses, leave the 'tsk tsk' at the stupidity of ads, the flicker of jumping channels, the screech at burnt forearms scarred by spitting spaghetti bolognaise, the howls of rage at wrong numbers dropping red-balled in Lotto, the bursts of canned laughter from American strangers, the grunts of hasty ejaculation slipped in between emergency room drama and late night comedy, the stink of wet washing waiting for the morning. up above it all. loving it and safe.

her body feels like lead. the heaviest thing. pinned down to earth. feet sprouting roots, going deep past the cement to the soil.

when he'd seen her on the platform, she seemed like something a world apart. like a creature from some other place he'd never visited. that place that would stop his feeling that somehow he'd missed the boat, or that the boat wasn't coming at all and he'd be standing on the pier watching, waiting for the trip that was never going to happen. the journey that was never going to get him there, starving for the sound of the train, that noise, that roar which said 'you are here' and 'you should be here' and 'you deserve to be here' and all the other noises which might make it seem that he wasn't an alien surrounded by the whispers of human beings.

it isn't going to happen. he knows it even when he's fantasising. even as he pulls himself off in the bathroom dreaming of the woman who could tell him. he doesn't wank to *Playboy*, that's not his style. he tries to wank with the world, that's his style. if he could've got into a rhythm, the same rhythm as everyone else. if he could've found that place.

there is no end, he thinks, it's all the same. a long ride, flashes of recognition, then darkness.

when he grabs her the heel of her shoe twists and snaps off. all four tacks get left behind in the sole. there is no scream. she's weighted down. the air is too thick to let her cry or call for help. her back slams into the cement.

the cat comes back and looks on. he hisses at it but it stands impassively watching. some kind of witness.

About the Authors

Patrick Allington

Born and raised in South Australia, Patrick Allington has published short stories as well as non-fiction. He has completed an MA in Politics at the University of Adelaide and is now enrolled in the university's Creative Writing PhD Program, where he is completing his novel, *Figurehead*.

Leanne Amodeo

Leanne Amodeo was born in 1971 in Adelaide, South Australia. She writes short stories and has also written for various visual arts journals and publications. She completed her Masters in Creative Writing at the University of Adelaide in 2004 with her manuscript of short stories, entitled *Fully Carbonated*.

Henry Ashley-Brown

After studying literature at the Australian National University, Henry reached writing via sculpture, discovering that like clay, words could be used to build up or take away from appearances. There are always so many others to thank too: the gift of Ignacio's 'Hupomnêmata' in the story *Finding Ignacio*, for example.

Chelsea Avard

Born in Melbourne in 1977 and raised in Auckland, Sydney and Seramban (Malaysia), Chelsea trained as a classical dancer. She now lives in Adelaide with her partner Tim and is in her first year of the Creative Writing PhD.

Dylan Coleman

Dylan Coleman is an Aboriginal (Kokatha) Greek woman from the far west coast of South Australia who believes we are products of our history. *Walbia Gu Burru* is based on one of many stories told to her by her mother Mercy Glastonbury, about her experiences growing up on Koonibba Aboriginal Mission.

John De Laine

John De Laine is an Adelaide born undergraduate in the English Department of the University of Adelaide, who first ventured into writing in 1995. His poetry and short stories have been appearing in magazines, journals and anthologies since 1997. His debut collection of poetry, *Rain Falling on the Garden*, was published by Wakefield Press in Friendly Street's New Poets Six in 2000.

Petra Fromm

Petra lived all over the world as a child, courtesy of the British army. She now has three inspiring, almost grown-up children of her own. With a BA in English and Classics, she is currently completing Honours in Creative Writing and in her spare time, co-writing a fantasy novel nothing like *The Lord of the Rings*.

Doug Green

Doug is a cook by trade and specialises in recipes for disaster.

Rachel Hennessy

Rachel Hennessy is currently completing a Masters of Creative Writing at the University of Adelaide. This year her short story 'Weight' will be published in *Spiny Babbler*, an online anthology of Australasian writing. Her play *S.S.W.L* was short-listed for the 2002 Patrick White Playwrights' Award while her most recent play *The Butcher Twins* received a Varuna Writers' Centre/Playworks Fellowship.

Sabina Hopfer

Sabina moved to Australia from Switzerland in 1999. She is currently completing a PhD in Creative Writing at the University of Adelaide. She enjoys cooking with words.

Glenda Inverarity

After completing her Masters degree Glenda taught English for seven years in Singapore. She has published a children's story, *Jack likes Jam*; is currently writing her first novel; writes regular book reviews for the UK journal *Modern English Teacher* and is presently working towards a PhD in English at the University of Adelaide.

Cath Kenneally

The editors are thrilled to include the celebrated Australian author Cath Kenneally.

Christopher Lappas

Christopher Lappas has been many things: student, musician, father, salesman, florist, labourer, painter, photographer, caterer, magazine editor. He would like to be writer when he grows up.

Stefan Laszczuk

Stefan Laszczuk is completing his MA in Creative Writing. He won the SA Writers' Centre short story competition in 2002, which resulted in the publication of a book of his short stories, *The New Cage*. He won the Festival Award for an Unpublished Manuscript in 2004. His novel, '*The goddamn bus of happiness*', will be published in October by Wakefield Press.

Amy T Matthews

Amy T Matthews would be perfectly happy to never wait on another table in her life.

Vanna Morosini

Vanna Morosini grew up in Adelaide, studied at the University of New South Wales in Sydney and then lived for a number of years in Rome and London. After working in various capacities in the film and video industry she began to concentrate on her writing and is currently developing a novel as part of her PhD in Creative Writing at the University of Adelaide.

James Roberts

James Roberts is a writer/director in the film industry. His broadcast work includes five documentaries and three ABC series. He co-edited the Penguin book *Writers on Writing*. His Honours project, *The Troubadour*, won the Driftwood Manuscripts Prize. He is working on his PhD in Creative Writing at the University of Adelaide.

Alice Sladdin

Alice Sladdin enjoys practising writing, silver-smithing, drawing and painting and has an especial interest in theatre.

Anna Solding

Anna is currently struggling to pen a novel of connected stories at the same time as she is wiping mashed avocado from her baby's face and trying to entertain said baby by sounding like a pig with a carrot up its snout. Sometimes it works – mainly thanks to her house keeping, dish washing, nappy changing, forever supportive partner.

Emmett Stinson

Emmett Stinson hails from the United States, mostly in and around Washington, D.C. The D.C. stands for 'District of Columbia' and not 'Da Capital', by the way. His work has previously appeared in *Canopic Jar, Close, Flashquake, Nuvein*, and *Pindeldyboz*. You can contact him at mylesnagopleen@yahoo.com.

Heather Taylor Johnson

Heather Taylor Johnson moved from America to Australia in 1999. She is very active in the poetry scene in South Australia as a member of the Kaleidoscopic Poetry Troupe (commonly known as KPT).

Stephanie Thomson

Stephanie Thomson has turned to writing after a thirteen year dalliance with English teaching. She is currently completing an MA in Creative Writing at the University of Adelaide.

Dena Thorne-Pezet

Dena Thorne-Pezet was born in the North East of England and is a lawyer. She worked in London before emigrating to New Zealand in 1997. Since 2000 she has lived in Australia. She is currently living in Adelaide with her husband Nick and two Jack Russells, Phoebe and Nipper.

Gwen Walton

Gwen Walton writes about the metamorphoses wrought on South Australian colonists by their new environment. Although not a new immigrant, she has had a few metamorphoses of her own: from career housewife and mother, to student, to librarian and back to student. She hopes, eventually, to call herself a writer.

Rikki Wilde

Rikki is currently completing his PhD at the University of Adelaide.

Lesley Williams

A long history of wandering, far, far in the mind and in unexpected places over land, has led to a deep desire to sing but while the spirit is willing, the voice is out of tune, so desire has turned to writing, and writing is becoming the song.

Dominique Wilson

Dominique Wilson migrated to Australia as a child from French Algeria. She has worked in a variety of jobs – everything from Charge Nurse in General and Psychiatric hospitals, to delivering pizzas, to tutoring dyslexic kids. She holds a Bachelor of Visual Communications: Illustration and Design and a BA: Professional and Technical Writing, from UniSA. She is currently studying for a Masters in Creative Writing at the University of Adelaide.

Acknowledgements

The editors would like to thank Professor Tom Shapcott and Dr Phillip Edmonds for their support and advice.

Thanks to Elizabeth, Luke, Sophie-Min, Tim and Oscar.

Thanks also to Gerald Matthews for the photography and cover layout, Ben Marton, for his hand and the idea, and Andi Butterworth, for a cold night spent getting the lighting just right.

Thank you to Rachel Hennessy for a tireless day spent copy-editing.

Many special thanks and lots of love to Stephanie Hester for all of her hard work; we couldn't have done it without you.

Thanks to Michael Bollen, Clinton Ellicott and Wakefield Press for their patronage. Their support has encouraged countless local artists and we are very grateful.

And last but not least, thank you to the staff and students of the Creative Writing Department at the University of Adelaide. Your talent and dedication is inspiring.

Room Temperature

Cath Kenneally

First-born, eldest daughter, Little Mother to her siblings, Irish-Australian, brainy schoolgirl at the time the Beaumont children vanish ... will the real Carmel please stand up?

When it comes time to venture into love and other alternatives, mutinous forces undermine her confidence, and malevolence turns to violence. Now she's starring in her own horror-home-movie.

Room Temperature, a mosaic of subtle allusion and canny observation, is a novel about memory, time and the struggle to break away from family pathology.

ISBN 1 86254 506 5

Around Here

Cath Kenneally

Cath Kenneally's poetry is unique: confident, discursive, witty writing driven by intuition and association and a doubting, quick intelligence. With a focus ever-shifting between local, global, present and past, familial and political, Cath draws you into her world with a compelling combination of emotional intensity and clearsightedness.

ISBN 1 86254 487 5

For more information visit www.wakefieldpress.com.au

Spirit Wrestlers

Thomas Shapcott

Spirit Wrestlers is a haunting, poetic novel by one of Australia's finest writers.

It tells of the arrival in rural Australia of a strange religious sect, an ancient Russian primitive group who believe in hard work, pacifism, vegetarianism – and the power of fire.

The group maintains a mysterious, closed existence that nevertheless begins to affect surrounding communities and individual lives. Two teenagers, Johann and Ivan, the local and the newcomer, discover similarities, and differences.

Spirit Wrestlers is a novel about faith, and competing faiths, acts of terror and acts of peace. In language of considerable beauty it speaks straight to the heart about our unsettled, dangerous world.

Follow Johann, Ivan and Olga in a saga of passion, surprise and discovery that you'll never forget.

ISBN 1 86254 645 2

For more information visit www.wakefieldpress.com.au

The Goddamn Bus of Happiness

Stefan Laszczuk

This novel is at once hilarious and deeply moving. It sets a cracking pace and pins you to the page with its outrageous episodes, intriguing characters and provocative observations. Yet there is tenderness in the writing. Deliberately humorous in the face of tragedy, it speaks honestly about the often ignored vulnerability of young men.

Laszczuk's novel will speak to anyone who ever wonders 'how to get back on that goddam bus that ... drives us through life to some sort of happiness.'

ISBN 1 86254 649 5

For more information visit www.wakefieldpress.com.au

Painted Words

Edited by
Brenda Glover, K*m Mann,
Scott Hopkins and Eva Sallis

Stories with a difference. The South Australian artist Dorrit Black, with five of her paintings as a catalyst, prompted this group of new writers to find a starting point, a window into themselves, but what they wrote as a result of this could never have been expected. This anthology brings together works of diversity and originality, and the liveliness of these individual new voices proclaims the enduring paradox of creativity.

ISBN 1 86254 503 0

For more information visit www.wakefieldpress.com.au

Forked Tongues

A delicious anthology of poetry and prose

Edited by
Rebekah Clarkson, Kerrie Harrison,
Gabrielle Hudson, Lisa Jedynak,
Eva Sallis and Samantha Schulz

'Using the menu of a seven-course feast (featuring recipes from Adelaide chef Cath Kerry) these writers have prepared for the reader something to savour and to remember. The common link in these stories, poems and memoirs is food, in various of its guises. For some of the recipes in this banquet, you need a strong stomach, but in others you can savour the most delicate flavours.'

Tom Shapcott

ISBN 1 86254 594 4

For more information visit www.wakefieldpress.com.au

Cracker!

A Christmas collection

Edited by
Heather Johnson, Mel Kinsman,
Stefan Laszczuk and Anna Solding

These writers have wrapped up the very essence of Christmas with words. Unwrap, and prepare to be surprised, for the essence of Christmas is a mixed bag: tears, joy, tragedy, memories, hope, horror, apathy, love and loneliness. And of course, the odd bit of ho ho ho . . .

ISBN 1 86254 627 4

For more information visit www.wakefieldpress.com.au

Wakefield Press is an independent publishing and
distribution company based in Adelaide, South Australia.
We love good stories and publish beautiful books.
To see our full range of titles, please visit our website at
www.wakefieldpress.com.au.

Wakefield Press thanks Fox Creek Wines
and Arts South Australia for their support.